I0735047

MARY CRAWFORD

ILLUSTRATED BY
LYSANDRA AGUIRRE

Jude's Song

HIDDEN BEAUTY BOOK 7

COPYRIGHT

Published on March 28, 2017, by Diversity Ink Press and Mary Crawford. Author may be reached at MaryCrawfordAuthor.com.

ISBN: 978-1-945637-44-5

Cover by Covers Unbound

HIDDEN BEAUTY SERIES

Until the Stars Fall from the Sky

So the Heart Can Dance

Joy and Tiers

Love Naturally

Love Seasoned

Love Claimed

If You Knew Me (and other silent musings) (novella)

Jude's Song

The Price of Freedom (novella)

Paths Not Taken

Dreams Change (novella)

Heart Wish

Tempting Fate

The Letter

The Power of Will

Hidden Hearts Series

Identity of the Heart

Sheltered Hearts

Hearts of Jade

Port in the Storm (novella)

Love is More Than Skin Deep

Tough

Rectify

Pieces (a crossover novel)

Hearts Set Free

Freedom (a crossover novel)

The Long Road to Love (novella)

Love and Injustice (Protection Unit)

Out of Thin Air (Protection Unit)

Soul Scars (Protection Unit)

OTHER WORKS:

The Power of Dictation

Use Your Voice

Vision of the Heart

#AmWriting: A Collection of Letters to Benefit The Wayne Foundation

Dedication

This book is dedicated to
anyone who has had their
dreams interrupted by life.

Keep going because you don't know
how the song will end.

This novel is also dedicated to the
phenomenal medical personnel at
St. Jude's Hospital.
Every day they make it possible for
the dreams of someone's child to continue
for yet another day.

CHAPTER ONE

TASHA

As I bring the last note to a close and draw in a deep breath, a low, slow clap breaks my concentration and brings me back to earth.

"Tasha, I swear you get stronger every time you sing. I thought you were good back in the days of 'the show which shall not be mentioned,' but you're even better now. Are you sure you don't want to extend this tour? We work well together. We could do a whole album, you know, something like Live from the Road," Aidan O'Brien offers.

Before I can answer him, my phone rings for about the seven billionth time. I look up at him apologetically. "I'm sorry, I have to leave it on because my grandma is in the hospital. Otherwise I'd just chuck the whole thing. It's driving me nuts."

"No worries. I've been there. If it gets too bad, I'll shut off my cochlear implants. I've got label business to do anyway."

"Okay, thanks." My face turns hot as I try not to

think about how unprofessional I look right now.

"Give me a shout when you're ready to start up again." Aidan gets off his stool and walks toward his office.

"Sometimes I wish I had the luxury to turn off my ears," I mutter under my breath as my phone rings again.

I take a deep breath and try to prepare myself for what's coming. Reluctantly, I answer the phone. "Hi, Ma."

"Princess, I've been calling for hours and hours. Do you know how long you took to answer the phone? Your grandmother could have died!"

"I'm trying to work here; I told you I had to rehearse today. Is Nana okay?"

"Of course she's okay. I was calling to tell you that *These Jagged Wounds* is falling back down the charts. It only made it up to one hundred and ten. I thought you said Mr. O'Brien told you he was sure it would break into the Top 100. I don't know if you should be hanging out with the likes of him. After all, he turned his back on Five-Star after all they did for him. I think being associated with him is bad for your career, but you never listen."

"Ma! Listen to yourself. If it weren't for Aidan, I wouldn't be on the charts at all. I'd still be singing in the lounge at the Hotel 6 and working weddings and bat mitzvahs on the weekends."

"Princess, that's not true. You were born to be on the stage. You've been competing in pageants since before you could walk. You've been singing and dancing your little heart out for decades," my mom argues. "If anything, he's lucky to have you to bolster his career. He's getting a little old and stale. He needs to freshen up his act. Who listens to piano players these days? It's a dying art — his demographic is people in nursing homes. I think you need to dump him and get someone more hip." My mom talks as if she's in charge of my career like some master puppeteer. The reality is, she's not. She wants to be, but my dad took care of that before he left.

"I hate to interrupt this philosophical discussion about Aidan's career, but our practice time is limited before we have to go out on tour. Does this phone call have a point, besides making me feel bad?"

"That's the other thing," my mom continues, clearly on a roll. "What man in his right mind goes out on tour with a girl who is barely out of a training bra? What does his wife think of all this?"

"Oh for Pete's sake! Mother, as you so aptly point out, I am a professional. Aidan is, too. He and his family have been around show business forever. As far as his wife being okay with me being here, you can ask her about it when we come into town on our tour stop. She'll be with us, along with Aidan's niece Mindy. I can't believe you don't trust me to do my job. Speaking of that, Ma, I gotta get back to work. Don't worry. You might not have to worry about it too much longer. I've got other irons in the fire."

"Princess, what do you mean?" my mom sputters.

"Ma, I haven't done a pageant in years. You don't

need to call me that. I told you years ago I wasn't interested in all that stuff." I roll my eyes. "I'll explain the rest of it later. Bye Ma, give Nana a kiss for me."

I hate it when my mom calls for no apparent reason. Well, she did have a reason — the same one as always. She called to let me know I'm never good enough. My dance moves are never crisp enough. I never hold the notes long enough. I never smile pretty enough. My hair is never teased enough. My skin is never smooth enough. The list is endless.

Stupid me. I thought if I was able to work with Aidan and he could show me the ropes, the criticism would stop. Yet somehow, it's more intense. Making Billboard's Top 200 isn't enough. Now I have to break into the Top 100 — or better yet hit the very top. It's stupid crazy. Is it wrong of me to want to have a normal life? I mean, I never even went to regular school. My mom was so busy trying to turn me into a star, she forgot to let me live.

Okay, there were those three years when I was little. I was fighting for my life, but I barely remember that time. I had leukemia as a kid, and I guess I almost died. My parents took me to St. Jude's Hospital. Ma says God saved me for a purpose and my destiny is to be on stage. She's been pushing me to be a professional singer ever since I could utter a word. She even has an old VHS tape of me in the hospital singing for the doctors and nurses all hooked up to my IV poles and everything — can I tell you I looked pathetic with a bald little head? I looked like a Q-tip … a really sad, skinny cotton swab. I'm fine now, and my mom needs to get over it. I'm fine and I'm not a baby. I'm nineteen. I want to have my life back.

I go back to a dark corner backstage and find a heavy-duty chair. Sticking my headphones in, I do what I always do when I'm stressed. I place my leg on the back of the chair and perform some basic stretches. I locate an open area on the floor, find a focal spot, and start to spin.

I'm startled when I catch Aidan's wife Tara mirroring me from the corner of my eye. When I wind down my pirouette, Tara lets out a laugh of pure joy. "Wow, I haven't done that in a while. It's fun to just let loose and spin. Let's not mention that to Aidan, okay?"

"Why not?" I ask, feeling a little lost.

"Oh, we're still doing the fertility meds and my ovaries are about the size of watermelons. I'm supposed to be taking it easy, but that was too much fun to resist." Tara shrugs.

"I suppose so," I concede. "It's my stress release."

"Is my husband treating you okay? He's not picking on you, is he?"

"Oh, Gosh no!" I exclaim, horrified she'd believe that. "He's been nothing but patient with all the craziness in my life."

Tara walks over to her backpack and hands me some Skittles and Starbursts. "What's going on?"

I cringe when she asks me a direct question because I don't know if I'm ready to have this conversation. On the other hand, I don't want to lie to her.

I sigh. "Let's just say it's difficult to meet all my

mother's expectations. We have very different ideas about what makes me happy."

Tara looks thoughtful. She sits quietly and studies me for a moment before she replies. "The path you forge for yourself will make you feel the strongest."

"That's what I think! How do I choose without crushing everyone else's dreams around me? My mom has me committed to engagements until I'm, like, thirty-five. She's living her dreams through me. It seems almost cruel for me to change the plan."

"You know, you should really talk to Aidan's brother, Rory, about this. His life was a lot like yours for many years until Mother Nature threw him a curve ball. In fact, in some ways, it's been Aidan's story too. You know how he sometimes plays classical music on the piano? That was supposed to be his destiny as a child. When meningitis struck, he was thrown off one life path and onto another. I toured with Mr. and Mrs. O'Brien for a long time, and from what I've overheard of your conversations with your mother, she sounds an awful lot like the O'Briens were back in the day."

"Really? Mrs. O. brought us cookies the other day. She wasn't anything like my mom. My mom resembles those bizarre stage moms you see on TV. If those reality shows would've been on TV when I was young, my mom would've signed me up for every single one of them. Aidan seems totally chill around his mom. I'm a nervous wreck every time my mom is around. She makes me forget my name."

Tara laughs softly as she recalls, "You know, it wasn't always this laid-back between them. Mrs. O. used to be a fire-breathing dragon when it came to her kids. Especially Rory — he was the golden child she expected to be the shining star of the family. He was supposed to take the dance world by storm. Aidan was an afterthought who happened to play the piano, and I was merely along for the ride."

"So what changed her attitude?" I ask as curiosity gets the best of me. I doubt anything will change my mother, but maybe there's hope out there somewhere.

Tara looks lost in thought for a moment before she answers. "Mostly, I think it was time. Time and some unfortunate life circumstances." She chuckles softly before continuing, "I don't think grandkids hurt anything, either. They have a way of softening hard edges and putting things in perspective."

I know she didn't mean to, but Tara's words are like an arrow to my heart. Sadly, babies are not in my future.

Tara reaches out and grabs my hand. "Tasha, I'm sorry, that was thoughtless of me. I'm tired and I wasn't paying any attention to what I was saying."

"How did you even know? I didn't even say anything to you," I whisper.

Tara shrugs. "I'm weird that way. Before you draw any conclusions, get some more current information. The science of fertility has changed a lot since the doctors gave your mom the news when you were treated for your leukemia."

I have to pick my jaw up off the ground. I have no idea how she would even know any of that stuff. I've never told a single soul. I mean, who would I tell? I don't even have a boyfriend — I haven't had time for relationships. Heck, I don't have time for a life.

"You're a little scary," I blurt. Immediately, I regret my words when I realize how disrespectful they sound. This is my boss's wife, after all.

I am completely blown away when Tara throws her head back and laughs. When she sees my look of abject horror, she pats me on my shoulder. "Relax, you aren't the first person or even the hundredth person to tell me that. Sometimes I freak myself out. I don't know how I know the stuff I know. I just do."

I look at her with skepticism. "You can tell everybody's future and all that crap — like those people at the fair with a crystal ball?"

Tara smiles, but her eyes are full of pain. "It's funny you should mention that — because at one point, I used to do that schtick. When I worked at the carnivals, I never used my true gift. We followed scripts when giving readings." Tara pauses for a moment and then amends her answer. "Honestly, I added the truth every once in a while — but only if I thought it was a matter of life and death."

I tumble that idea around in my brain for a couple of moments as I remember all of my follow-up visits at St. Jude's Hospital over the years and all the sick kids I met at summer camp. Any way I look at the picture, the result is the same. No wonder it sometimes looks as if Tara has the weight of the world on her shoulders; it must feel as if she does. "Wow! That is an epic amount of responsibility." I don't know whether she's performing some sort of parlor trick or she really can tell the future. Truth be told, I'm a little afraid to find out. "Do you get tired of knowing what's going to happen to people?"

Tara sighs softly. "Sometimes. There are times I wish my gift had an off switch."

I can see the distress on her face, so I quietly reply, "I'll do my best not to put you on the spot or in the middle as I make my decisions."

"Tasha, as much as I appreciate that, in this case, it sounds like you've already made your decision. I have to be honest with you, I know it will break my husband's heart a little when he finds out what you need to do. I think in the end he'll be supportive. He's been in your shoes."

"Do you think he'll hate me?" I ask with more emotion than I'm comfortable revealing.

"No, Tasha … I don't. I think he will miss you though. He genuinely likes you. You were supportive of him when many people were not. To him, that means the world."

CHAPTER TWO

JUDE

SOME PEOPLE HAVE ALL the luck in the world and throw it all away. I can't believe what I'm hearing. What is she thinking? I know I'm just the equipment monkey, but I've been doing this a few years and I've heard lots of people. I've heard some greats like Aidan and I've heard some people who should never, I mean *never* sing — not even in the shower.

I'm not even sure how some of these folks make it to the big stage. I don't know if it's money, influence, sheer determination or stupidity — but a lot of them don't have enough talent to bleed through a Band-Aid, let alone bring folks into an auditorium. That's not the case with Tasha. Her voice makes you stop and take notice. Tasha's voice is sexy without trying. Lord knows, I think about it far too much.

Right now, her voice is driving me *loco*. I heard Aidan offer her a shot at a live album today. If I understood the conversation I just overheard, she plans to turn him down. Who in their right mind does that?

Did she forget she was talking to Aidan O'Brien? A live album with Aidan O'Brien — the man is at the top of the charts. He's prepared to hand her a golden ticket to fame. What the frick? It must be nice to have your life in such order you can stand to pass up the opportunity of a lifetime to go chase another. It's total craziness. I've been busting my butt since I was fifteen years old. I've been chasing garage bands around moving equipment here and there and freakin' everywhere trying to get a small crack at a break.

I don't want much — I just want someone to listen to me play and sing a little and maybe take a look at a couple songs I've written. I want to know if maybe — just maybe — I've got a shot at my dreams. I know I'm bucking the stereotype. I could go home to Texas, sing in a mariachi band, and perform at weddings and *quinceaneras* — but that's not really what I want to do. Even though it's traditional given my heritage, that music is not what I like. My *abuela* likes to claim it's because there's gringo blood on my dad's side. Since he took off before I was old enough to remember, I have no idea whether she's right.

As I rearrange the speakers under the stage, I look up to watch Tasha dance in crazy circles on the stage. She seems totally lost in whatever music is playing through her headphones. Tasha is simply mesmerizing.

Oddly, even though she's dancing quickly, she isn't paying any attention to the world around her. As soon as that thought registers in my brain, my body goes into full alert. *¡Mierda!* She isn't paying any attention. I sprint to the other side of the stage where Aidan has moved the orchestra because there are better acoustics from that side of the stage. I don't think Tasha knows about the changes in the layout to the stage because she and Mindy took off early with the wardrobe people.

I reach the side of the stage just in time to catch her as she falls backward off the stage. It isn't the most graceful of landings — her lower back strikes my kneecap as I drop to one knee to support her body weight.

"Ouch! That hurts," she complains.

"Well, Princess," I reply dryly, "it would hurt a lot more if your head would've smacked the cement floor. You know, most people would say something like, 'Gee, thank you so much for saving me.'"

I think I must have said the wrong thing because Tasha's jaw sets firmly as she replies, "Oh, I'm sorry. My brain was probably short-circuited by your profound body odor. Somehow, I always expected my Prince Charming to smell better when he rescued me. You're positively overwhelming — and I don't mean that in a good way."

Her statements should've been offensive, but she's absolutely right. I've been moving so much stuff today that I am beyond ripe — but most people are so anxious to get near Aidan they'll tell me anything they think would get them closer to such a big star. To have somebody completely call me out on the fact that I smell like overripe produce is awesome. I throw my head back and laugh. "Point taken. I clean up nicely, but do you? Would you like to put your money where your mouth is? I could meet you in an hour and a half for dinner."

"Did you just take it upon your stinky self to ask me out?" Tasha asks with an incredulous expression on her face.

I look around as if I'm searching for someone. "I don't see anyone else here, so I guess it must've been me," I answer with more bravado than I actually have.

"You're crazy! Why should I go out with you? You smell rank!"

"I smell funky at this very moment, but I don't always. Besides, I saved you from a gruesome fall. It's the least you could do."

Tasha barely disguises her eye roll. "I'm very grateful you saved me from a skull fracture, but I don't want this to turn into some weird casting couch like they have in Hollywood. So, are you sure this is just dinner?"

"I promise, this is simply dinner. Well, dinner and maybe some dancing in a slightly safer environment — if you're up to it."

"Well, I suppose that would depend on how you smell," Tasha replies with a smirk.

***

It seems I'm not the only person who cleans up nicely. Tasha looks killer in stage costuming, but it's nothing compared to how she looks all dolled up for a simple date. Her dark brown sweater slouches off her shoulders, her jeans are just the right amount of tight and she's wearing the sexiest shoes I've ever seen. Leopard-skin and sky-high — they make Tasha nearly as tall as me. As always, her long inky curtain of hair distracts me to the point where I almost forget my name.

Much to my embarrassment, Tasha walks around me like I'm a store mannequin and gives me a slow assessment. Finally, she announces curtly, "You'll do."

The breath I've been holding escapes all at once. "What?"

Tasha looks up at me with a mischievous look in her eyes. "I'm just yanking your chain. How does it feel to be on the other end of things?"

"U-umm —" I stutter

"Never mind, that was mean of me … I shouldn't have done that. I'm sorry. You look handsome, and you smell yummy too."

"Well, it's not a huge accomplishment, since I smelled like the city dump this afternoon. It doesn't take too much to make progress." I roll my eyes for emphasis as I open my truck door and help her in. It would be nice if I had a cool sports car or something to wow her with, but I don't.

Tasha laughs at me. "You'd be surprised at the rank things I've smelled when guys try to impress me. Some of the things which pass for cologne should be labeled as toxic waste — but you smell nice."

I'll admit I'm not great at small talk, but this is out-of-bounds-awkward even for me. I'm not even sure what to say to her comment. Do I say "thank you"? That seems dumb. I just slapped on some stuff my sister had lying around. She considers herself to be some sort of fashion stylist. If Fernanda's ideas aren't too crazy, I usually end up wearing whatever she tells me to. I don't think I get to take too much credit. Rather than try to figure out how to follow up appropriately, I change the subject. "I hope you're not one of those girls who plans to order salad. We're not going to one of those kind of places."

Tasha raises an eyebrow at me. "How long have we been hanging out together? You should know better than to say something like that. I'm starving to death. My mom decided to talk my ear off during the last meal break, so I didn't get a chance to eat much."

Without thinking, I reply, "Yeah, I heard. It sounded pretty intense."

Tasha's eyebrows raise in surprise. "Eavesdrop much?"

I wince. "Sorry, I don't make a habit of it, but it's an occupational hazard. People forget guys like me are in the room. Your mom was pretty loud on the phone. It was hard not to hear her. What's up with that anyway?"

Tasha stares straight out the window as we drive down the highway. For a moment, I think she isn't going to answer me, but finally she takes a deep breath and let it out. Traffic is a little heavy, so I can't take the time to look over at her, but it sounds as if she is on the verge of tears.

She sighs deeply before she answers. "I don't even know how to answer your question. I guess it boils down to the fact that she has different dreams for me than I have for myself."

"What? She doesn't want you to tour with Aidan

O'Brien? Is she crazy? Your first single is just outside the Top 100 on the Billboard chart. That's not even going mainstream — that's on his new indie label, Silent Beats. It's a huge deal!" My mouth is agape, my eyes open wide.

Tasha shakes her head in resignation. "Oh, make no mistake — Ma wants me on those charts, but she wants me to be at the very top of them and she's not sure Aidan is the person to get me there. The only problem is I'm not sure I want to be on the charts at all."

From the conversations I overheard today, I had a feeling she would say something like this, but to hear it said so bluntly and matter-of-factly was like getting a knee to the groin.

"What? Don't even make that face. You don't know what it's like to live my life."

"All I know is that I would trade places with you in a heartbeat. I'd give anything to have Aidan's ear for five minutes. I can't imagine having a shot at a whole album and not just any album, but an album with him. Do you realize what he's offered you?" I ask, still incredulous. "I can't believe Aidan O' Brien is giving you the world on a platter and you're just going to shove it back in his face. It's not every day you get offered your dream job —"

As we stop at a stop sign, Tasha whirls on me, her eyes bright with anger. "Put a sock in it. If I wanted to hear that kind of garbage, I'd call my mom. You aren't listening to me. This is not my dream. It's never been my dream. It's always been my mother's dream for me. There is a difference. Ever since I was a little girl, I've always wanted to be a nurse — an oncology nurse, to be precise. I want to help little kids with cancer like the nurses who helped me at St. Jude's."

My response is so resentful, it borders on rude. "It's nice to have good intentions and all, but what about your talent?"

Tasha buries her face in her hands for a moment before she turns back around and faces forward. I notice she wipes away some tears. "As much as I love singing, I wish I would've never started. Maybe the whole world would shut up about my stupid so-called talent and I'd have some control over my own life. Why is it so wrong of me to want to decide what's right for me? Why do I have to live up to everyone else's expectations? Why can't I be like a normal person? Why can't I just be nineteen and stupid?"

"I don't know — I've heard you have to be pretty smart to get into nursing school," I tease. "Seriously, you got major skills. Little girls all over the world dream of having pipes like yours and you can shred a guitar like guys twice your age. It seems tragic to let all that go. My *abuela* says ignoring a God-given talent is like kicking him in the teeth."

Tasha gives me a watery smile. "That doesn't sound like a very good idea — but what if I'm just as good at nursing as I am at singing? How will I ever know if I don't try?"

"I don't know. I suppose there aren't any easy answers."

"Speaking of easy answers — why don't you have Aidan's ear? You know he's looking for talent to add to his label. He's not exactly a hard guy to track down — he has jam sessions with us all the time. I haven't seen you sit in on them."

My shoulders sag as I grip the steering wheel tighter. "It's not that easy. It's not like I'm one of the musicians or anything. I'm just the guy who moves the equipment around. Most of the musicians barely even know who I am. It's like I'm invisible. Plus, what I do is weird."

"What are you talking about?" Tasha asks with a puzzled look. "Aidan says you're one of the best equipment guys he's ever had. He never has to worry about whether he's got the right stuff or if you're going to be late setting up. He loves the fact that he can count on you. I don't think it's so weird."

"No, my music is weird. Most people who look like me don't sing country music. My family expects me to sing in Spanish and perform traditional music. In fact, they're not happy I'm here helping Aidan at all. When my sister Fernanda followed me here to break into the fashion business, it was the last straw. My family doesn't want to talk to me until I make something happen. My *abuelo* put it in crasser terms — but that's basically the gist of things."

"So … basically you and I are in the same boat."

"Come again?" My voice drips with disbelief. "I don't think I heard you right. I clean up women's panties from the stage and wipe sweat off of the instruments before I put them away. You're one signature away from a record deal of a lifetime and a worldwide tour with Aidan O'Brien — I don't think our situations have anything in common at all."

She shrugs. "The way I see it, we're both a little too afraid to stand up for ourselves because we're afraid we're going to fail."

"Hernandez, why do you always have to fall for the lethally smart ones —" I mutter to myself.

"I'm sorry, I don't think I caught that." Tasha's eyes twinkle.

"It's probably better for me if you didn't."

CHAPTER THREE

TASHA

WHEN JUDE ASKED ME out on a date, I didn't know what to expect. I had no idea he would pull out all the stops and drive us all the way to Portland. I don't really know much about Jude Hernandez, other than that he's cute and quiet.

I've noticed he seems to be a study in contrasts. He's almost painfully shy, yet he was bold enough to ask me out on a date after I told him he reeked. Jude doesn't hold a high-powered position within Silent Beats with a corner office and a title, but Aidan trusts him with every aspect of his business. He claims to be invisible, but he knows every person who comes in and out of the building and can direct them to the correct location. Even his appearance is a big contradiction. He dresses like a rodeo cowboy, but he carries himself with the confidence and bearing of a military officer. His easy laid-back smile is in direct contrast to his intense, arresting eyes. When I first met him, I thought perhaps he was wearing contact lenses, but he assured me his heterochromia is not only one hundred percent natural — but the bane of his existence. It soon became clear Jude is not the type of guy who would manufacture something like having one brown eye and one blue eye to draw attention to himself.

As I think back, I don't think I ever knew Jude was a musician, even though he could easily pass as a member of our band. Sure, I've seen him carrying around a worn guitar case, but I always assumed it was one of Aidan's. It isn't hard to envision Jude as a country music star though. He usually wears a beat-up cowboy hat, jeans and cowboy boots. His unusual eyes, thick, curly hair and engaging smile have star power written all over them.

I reach out and turn up the radio in his truck. It's full of pops and skips, but there's no mistaking one of my favorite songs by Brooks & Dunn. "There you go, Cowboy. There's a song right up your alley. Knock my socks off and I'll be the first official member of your fan club —"

Jude clears his throat. "I can't really do that."

"What do you mean, you can't? Don't you know the words? I thought everybody knew the words to this song. This is classic country."

"Oh, I know the words. I know them by heart. I've even made up a special arrangement for the bridge."

"So … what's the problem?" Most guys I know go out of their way to show off in front of me.

"When I try singing in front of other people, it's like I become paralyzed."

"I understand. I have to meditate and psych myself up every time I get on stage. Stage fright is no laughing matter."

"No, it's more than that. Stage fright is what I used to get when I had to give a report in front of the class. This is so far beyond stage fright I can't even explain. It's like my vocal cords don't even work." Defeat cascades from Jude.

I study him with confusion before I finally blurt the question my curiosity won't allow me to keep contained. "If you can't sing in front of anybody, how do you know if you're any good?"

He grins at me sarcastically. "Give the lady a gold star."

I involuntarily recoil at the bitter tone in his voice. "Sorry, I was just asking a logical question."

Jude groans in frustration as he tries to gather his thoughts. He takes a deep breath and sighs. "Look, you're right. I'm being an jerk. Honestly, I don't really know whether I have your level of talent — or any talent at all. I used to make videos of myself on my iPad while I was learning to play guitar. It helped me with chord transitions and technique. I thought they were private, just for me, but my pesky little sister found them and showed my mom. Apparently, someone in my family knows somebody in the music business and showed the videos to them. This dude was going to sign me with some big talent agent. I don't know what I think about the offer because the guy wanted some money from my mom for publicity shots and some other junk. It all seemed like some big scam. It's hard to know what to believe."

"Yeah, I hear you." I shake my head. "People like that are a dime a dozen in the pageant world. I don't even want to know the amount of money my mom spent trying to make me a star."

"Maybe so," he answers darkly, "but there's a real difference between us. You're a star now and I'm just a guy who hauls around gear — who happens to like to write songs I can't sing."

I can tell from Jude's flippant, angry words that he wants to be the guy who doesn't give a crap about this — but what he's trying to project and what I see are two very different things. As Jude pulls his truck to a stop in front of the restaurant, I try to figure out what to say. I don't know what it is about Jude, but just looking at him seems to make the wrong words fly out of my mouth.

Jude's not the kind of guy to draw attention to himself. Even so, he's been on my radar for a really long time. He totally earned my respect a couple years ago when Aidan's friend, Trevor, was getting married and asked me to sing at the wedding. The news media and paparazzi were sniffing around and looking for a good story, but Jude not only ignored the cash bribes, he sent the photogs in a completely different direction. A lot of people I know would've sold us out in a heartbeat. So I know he's not the shallow, uncaring jerk he pretends to be.

The hostess walks us back to our table, and Jude takes the time to pull out my chair. He even stands by to help me out of my jacket. It's such a quaint, old-fashioned gesture that it makes me blush. I'm not used to being treated like such a lady. Nearly everyone on Aidan's crew has been nothing but nice to me, but they tend to treat me like a little kid and sometimes forget I'm even a woman. To them, I'm just one of the guys. After the rigors and the uber-competitive environment of the pageant scene, it's been a refreshing and strange change of pace.

Jude sits across from me and places his napkin across his knee. "I hope you're feeling adventurous tonight. I know this isn't a typical place to eat, but it's a great way to get to know someone."

There's something about the weird subtext in his statement which causes me to look around the restaurant a little more closely. It's only then I realize everyone has little pots in the center of their tables. A gust of surprised laughter erupts from me. "Fondue? We drove all this way for melted cheese?"

Jude nods slightly. "Yep. Have you ever had it before?"

"I can't say I have. I've tried lots of stuff, but fondue is not on my list."

Jude's face lights up. "Tell me … how adventurous are you feeling tonight? This could be fun. I guess the only questions to be answered are: are you open to new experiences and how much do you trust me?"

I smile shrewdly at Jude. "I'm game if you are."

At first, he smiles broadly, but his grin starts to fade as he studies me. "Why do I get the feeling we're talking about more than just bread cubes and *queso* here?"

"Probably because we are," I answer, dodging the question. "I guess I can be just as mysterious. How adventurous are you feeling and how much do you trust me?"

"I don't know, *Sirena*. I'm always of two minds whenever you are near. Part of me wants to run and escape and pretend we've never met and the other part wants to stay and learn everything there is to know about you so we never have to part ways."

Instinctively, I react. "Serena? Did you forget my name? I'm Tasha. I thought you knew me better than that."

"I know who you are, Tasha. I cannot forget. I did not say Serena. I said *Sirena*, as in the one who lures me with your songs."

Jude's simple explanation takes my breath away. I am silent for a moment as I struggle to find the right words. "Honestly, I'm not really sure how to respond. It's a little insulting, yet strangely poetic at the same time.

Jude looks chagrined as he replies, "I apologize. I meant it as no insult. It's honestly how I feel. Do I trust you?" he asks with a shrug. "I suppose I do — as much as I trust anyone. Aidan trusts you and as nearly as I can tell, he's got good instincts. I don't understand why you are throwing this chance of a lifetime back in his face. Then again, I suppose I don't have to understand that to trust you."

I sigh deeply and shake my hair out around my shoulders in frustration, barely resisting the urge to resort to my childhood habit of chewing on the ends of it when I'm frustrated or nervous. "I don't know what to tell you. We may never see eye to eye on this because you don't walk in my shoes." I can't keep the anger and disappointment out of my voice.

Jude reaches across the table and puts his hand over my wrist as he looks into my eyes with an earnest, somber expression and says, "*Sí*, that is true — but remember you are not walking in my shoes either."

I take a moment to gulp the strawberry lemonade the waitress surreptitiously placed in front of us a few moments after she took our order. I was so caught up in figuring out the ramifications of the conversation between us, I didn't even hear what he told her we'd be having. It was all mixed in with the whole "trust me" discussion. I'm about to ask Jude how he knew how much I loved strawberries, but then I remember he doesn't miss much. I pick up my glass and hold it up in salute as I comment, "You know what? It's kind of a pain, but I like guys who are cute and have brains."

Jude flushes a dusky shade of red. "I don't know if you should call me the brainy type. I just haul equipment for a living."

"Right … but you're a man with a plan, and there's a lot to be said for that." I set my glass back down on the table and stare at him intently as I ask again, "How adventurous are you?"

Chapter Four

Jude

IT WAS A SIMPLE question. Even as I answer it, I can't shake my feelings of regret — especially after Tasha's lips slide up into a smirking smile.

"Are you sure about that? I have to warn you; I can be pretty tough. Some people say I'm a little like a drill sergeant. I guess it comes from all the time I spent on the pageant circuit. In some ways, I'm more like my mom than I'd like to admit — but I'll try to take it easy on you."

"Wait a second! You didn't say what I agreed to — you only asked me how adventurous I was feeling. You're not entering me into a beauty contest or anything, are you?"

She seems to be turning the idea over in her head, but eventually she appears to dismiss it. "No, I don't think it would be a good idea. It would be counterproductive because you're so shy. If you were younger, I think it might've been a good idea to help you overcome your stage fright; but pageants are one of those things you have to start early. As my mom always tells people, it's a lifestyle. It's a weird life, but she's right. If you haven't been involved in them since you were a kid, it's hard to break into them." Tasha stops for a moment and chuckles softly. "Who am I kidding? They're weird — no matter what age you are."

"I thought pageants came with all sorts of perks like scholarships, cars, makeup, and other magical stuff?" When Tasha looks at me with a quizzical look of surprise, I hastily clarify, "At least that's what my little sister always told my mom when she used to beg to be part of them."

"Your sister was in pageants? I wonder if I competed against her."

"No, my mom was never able to get the money together — but Fernanda used to watch them on television all the time. That's how she fell in love with fashion design and makeup."

"Yeah, I can see how it could happen. There's lots of sparkle and glamour involved." Her expression turns glum.

"So, if you're not planning to enter me into a beauty contest, what exactly did I agree to? What are you going to make me do?" I try not to sound like a high school freshman facing his first day of weightlifting class.

"I'm going to help you," she announces simply, as if that explains all.

"Help me do what?"

Tasha blows her hair out of her face in frustration.

"I'm beginning to wonder if I jumped the gun on the conclusion about you being a smart hottie."

"Don't say I didn't try to warn you." I take a drink of my Coke.

"Think about it, Jude. What do I do every day?"

"You sing like a goddess, *Sirena*. I told you that already.

Tasha looks incredibly embarrassed. "I don't know about the goddess part, but I do okay. Anyway, you want to be able to sing your songs for Aidan, right?"

I sigh. "Yes, that's my dream."

"Good, because I need some adventure this summer. I have a feeling the rest of it won't be so great." She sighs wistfully. "So let me pay it forward for once and be the expert."

***

I adjust the oversized headset on my ears, then struggle not to curse in front of Tasha as the string pops when I pick up my guitar.

Tasha sees my grimace as the broken string snaps back to bite me in the hand. "Oh, let me grab you some new strings. Aidan got a bunch of new ones in. They might be my favorite brand yet."

"I'd really rather you didn't do that. Those strings aren't mine to take. It's not like I'm one of the musicians or anything."

She looks a little taken aback by my protest. "No, it's *totally* okay. You should see how many manufacturers send Aidan free stuff all the time. He puts it in a big box for everyone to share. He even told the part-time guys who have other gigs to use the stuff on their other jobs. He doesn't have time to try out all the random things people send him. If we all like something a lot, he'll look into the company and see if it's something he can endorse. He's talked a lot of companies into giving instruments and equipment to schools and hospitals and stuff that way, so it works out for everybody. He would totally be okay with it."

"Okay, I guess if you're sure. It's not like I have a bunch of other options. I don't have any guitar strings with me." I frown.

"Seriously, it's cool with Aidan. Don't sweat it." She shrugs off her backpack and places it next to the table beside the soundboard. "I'll be right back."

As soon as she leaves, I take a moment to soak in my surroundings. I can't believe I'm standing in this room contemplating setting down some tracks using the same microphone Aidan O'Brien and Tasha Keeley routinely use. This is surreal. *Am I insane?* I don't know any more. No one has ever been able to talk me into so much, so quickly. I feel like I'm like a helpless marionette in her presence. I have no idea whether I'll even be able to repeat my lyrics in public, and now she has me in the middle of a flippin' recording studio — not just any recording studio either, but *Aidan O'Brien's* recording studio.

It's not as if she's been rude, or condescending. It's actually been totally the opposite. For the first time in a long time, I'm enjoying music again. It's a little like being at home. For several weeks, we never said a word to each other during our "helping sessions." She would come and sit next to me as I played my guitar. Then she started riffing beside me. For a few days, we played covers of other people's music. Eventually, I got brave and started playing a few chords of my own and improvising. She accepted my challenge with glee — matching me chord for chord — and soon without meaning to, we'd composed a song.

A couple of weeks ago, she was humming along as we were playing the song. She turned to me as she remarked, "Jude, this song is amazing, but it needs some lyrics and a title. I feel a little silly calling it 'Jude's Song'. Don't you think we should go with something a little catchier?"

I shrugged as nonchalantly as I could. "I don't know, it kinda has a nice ring to it." What I didn't want to tell her was the fact that she liked my random improvising enough to consider it a real song means the world to me and made me even more motivated to compose worthwhile lyrics to match.

Tasha opens the door to the recording studio and I'm so lost in my thoughts, I come close to hitting her with the guitar as I swing around in surprise.

"Are you okay?" she asks as she ducks.

"Yeah, I just got caught up in the craziness of this moment. How will I know you can't hear me?"

Tasha smiles smugly. "You won't. That's the beauty of this. I've covered all the indicator lights so you won't be able to tell whether I'm listening or not. I'm working on scholarship applications for college, so my mind will be on other things. I may or may not take a few moments to listen in on your progress depending on how things are going for me."

She lays out all her paperwork on the table in front of her and cringes and continues her pep talk. "You're a talented musician. I know you can do this. I don't have to listen to you to know you have music coming from the depths of your soul. I can see it in every movement you make and hear it in every note you play. You have the heart of a musician. I don't need to hear you to confirm that. However, if you want to share your gifts with the world, other people do. This is just one hurdle. Singing in front of people will get easier every time you do it — I promise." Tasha takes the guitar from my suddenly stiff hands and starts to string it faster than anyone I've ever seen.

"I could've done it. I am the equipment manager after all. This is what I do," I remind her.

"Not today. Today, you have a new dream," she proclaims. After a few minutes, she finishes stringing my guitar and shoves me through the doorway to the sound booth. "Now go on … stop procrastinating. Tell me if the static level in your left ear creeps up and I'll adjust it. Those are my favorite cans, but they have a weird glitch."

"That's it? You're going to push me out of the nest without even a kiss for good luck? Don't you have any sympathy for the fact that I'm completely petrified?"

Tasha raises an eyebrow at me. "Are you telling me all that's standing between you and your turn in front of the microphone is a kiss?"

I suck in a deep breath to fill my suddenly starving lungs. I'm quickly starting to understand the meaning of a no-win situation — talk about backing myself into a corner.

I look around — although I'm not exactly sure why, since it's clear we're completely alone. "Well, I don't know if it'll solve everything, but it certainly wouldn't hurt."

Tasha rolls up on the balls of her feet to stand on her tiptoes as she plants a brief kiss on my lips. "There. Now you can consider yourself fully armed and dangerous. Go conquer your demons. I'm right here if you need me."

With that advice, she gently pushes me into the recording booth and shuts the door. I'm left standing alone in the room with a microphone and two stools. A brief vision comes to me of the two of us recording songs together, and my heart beats faster. Almost as quickly as the thought crosses my mind, I laugh at myself because the idea of being in the same singing league as Tasha Keeley is just ludicrous. Still, it was a fun thought while it lasted.

I dig my lucky pick from my pocket and sit down on one of the stools as I try to focus on breathing and collecting my thoughts. As I'm tuning my guitar, Tasha's husky, smooth voice comes over my headphones. "Can you hear this okay?"

I lean into the microphone. "Loud and clear."

"You can cozy up to the mic if you want to, but Aidan has the settings tweaked so you can just sing naturally in this room and the mic will pick it up just fine. You can try to forget the mic is there if it makes you feel more comfortable."

"Sweet. Thanks." I try to swallow the lump in my throat.

"Jude, you can't sing if you don't breathe. If you can't lay down a song during this session, there'll be dozens of other chances this summer. Just try to have fun."

Instinctively, I take a deep breath and let it out. I know she's right. On the other hand, she's worked so hard with me that I'd like to blow her mind with my progress. I don't want to look like a complete loser. When I stop to take a drink of water, I notice my hands are visibly shaking.

Tasha interrupts my mini-panic attack. "Hey, Jude, am I finally going to get to hear you sing Jude's Song?"

I laugh. "Umm … That would be a no. I'm nowhere close to finished writing, let alone being ready to show anybody. What do you think I am, a miracle worker? Some of us have day jobs, you know."

She chokes back a snort of laughter. "Who exactly do you think sings at these concerts you set up? My throat is still sore from last night. I thought Aidan was never going to stop with the encores."

I nod. "Yeah, he was a little over-the-top. I think it's because his niece Mindy was in the audience, and he wanted to show her and her friends a great time."

Tasha smiles. "It was so awesome he gave her a chance to come up on the big stage and sing with us. Her friends were totally impressed. I don't think any of them knew she sings so well. I suspect she's being bullied at school. I hope this stops some of that."

"She did a phenomenal job, you'd never know she doesn't do this professionally."

"We could be singing your songs up there one day, but you gotta get through this first. The hardest step is always the first one."

"Okay, I can take a hint. I don't know if I can make any promises here, but I'll give it my best shot."

"That's all any of us do every day. I know it seems like there's some special secret to it all, but it boils down to trying your best every day and hoping tomorrow is better than today."

"I don't think there'll be any doubt tomorrow will be better than today," I joke quietly.

"I'll leave you to it then, because if I don't get these scholarship applications filled out, I'm never going to be able to go to school." Tasha turns her back and picks up a pen.

Feeling lost for a moment, I decide to go back to an old favorite. First, I pick my way through *He Stopped Loving Her Today* by George Jones. I move on to *Amarillo by Morning* by George Strait and then begin to play *Wichita Lineman*. I love this song. When I was younger, I used to pretend my father was one of the linemen and his job explained why he wasn't around for us.

Before I start a second run through of the song, I change my position on the stool so my back is facing the window to the room where Tasha is sitting. I know this is futile and silly because all she has to do is turn on her acoustic feed to hear me, but for now it's the best I can do to set up a barrier between us. I want so much to be able to do this, and it seems like the more I want this dream, the harder it is to achieve.

It wasn't always this way. I'm not sure exactly when it all started. I don't remember, to be honest. As a little kid, I was outgoing — but then I hit school and something happened to my confidence. It was gradual at first. Nobody seemed to know what to do with me. I didn't really fit anywhere. My Hispanic friends noticed I was white and my white friends started noticing I wasn't like them. When I spoke Spanish, my white friends made fun of me. When I spoke English, my Latino friends got upset and called me a gringo. I started to get self-conscious about who I was.

To make things worse, one of my friends — or someone I thought was a friend — discovered I liked instruments and singing. After that, Juan José became my tormentor-in-chief. In order to fit in, I started playing soccer and baseball. I pretended I didn't even know how to sing. There was no way I could know my choice might have permanent repercussions.

In an effort to calm my nerves, I take another huge gulp of my drink and carefully set my bottle of water down. *Come on, Hernandez, you can do this.* I repeat in my head as if it's a mantra. I sneak a glance through the window over my shoulder. As she promised, Tasha is fully engrossed in her paperwork and appears to be completely oblivious to me.

I begin to play *Wichita Lineman* again. At first, I softly hum the melody as I play. I play the bridge and start over again. Although Tasha's been infinitely patient with me, I'm afraid of what will happen to us when she loses patience with my stupidity.

Us — now that's a loaded word if I've ever heard one. If I'm honest with myself, I don't even know if there is an official 'us' to worry about. Tasha's been so singularly focused on helping me work through my fears I haven't had an opportunity to ask her out again. Still, I feel the need to go outside of my comfort zone and stretch my personal boundaries so I can impress her. The thought is so overwhelming I miss a chord. I haven't done that since I learned how to play the guitar. Of course, I would make a stupid bonehead mistake like that while we're in a recording studio. I have no way of knowing whether Tasha is listening or recording.

Straightening my shoulders, I decide as far as huge milestones in my career goes, today is about as monumental as they come. This is probably how Tasha felt when Aidan asked her to join the group. Trying to forget my nerves, I take a deep, shuddering breath and start to sing softly. This classic country music song always takes me to a different mind space. I concentrate on the words and try to lose myself in the song. It's simultaneously the easiest and the hardest thing I've ever had to do. I didn't come here for easy — I came to make a career for myself which doesn't involve dragging other people's equipment around. With that in mind, I sing a little louder.

These head games are so dumb. I love to sing. It's probably not the most macho or the coolest thing to admit. As I start to gain confidence and sing louder, I'm again reminded how much I miss the ability to belt out a ballad as if not a soul in the world cares about who you are or what you're doing.

Shaking off the rest of my nerves, I settle into my own little play list of songs. Some songs are old, and a few of them are current songs on the radio. This is something I had forgotten in all the years I didn't sing out loud to anyone — I really enjoy this stuff. There's a weird sense of freedom about singing songs. You can take the traditional route, sing it precisely note by note, or you can play with the melody and make it into something else entirely. I've struggled for so long, I forgot how much fun this can be.

After I finish a small set of songs, I turn around and study Tasha for clues. However, she's in almost exactly the same position she was in when I chanced a glance before. I don't know whether she even heard my accomplishment. If she did, she's not giving me any indication whether it was complete garbage or halfway decent.

All the mellow feelings and confidence I gathered evaporate in that millisecond of self-doubt. Initially I was so adamant that I didn't want her to hear me, I never stopped to consider how much I was counting on her feedback. What if I accomplished this massive milestone and she never even noticed?

CHAPTER FIVE

TASHA

MAYBE I SHOULD'VE SET up this "operation sing in public" scenario a little differently. When I thought of this idea, I didn't think about all the ramifications of the blind audition. Jude seems to be taking my lack of an enthusiastic response to his singing as some sort of implicit criticism. Nothing could be further from the truth.

I guess my acting skills are better than I imagine, because Jude thinks my nonchalant, casual, and fully understated response means I either didn't listen or hated what I heard. In truth, I'm basically struggling to keep a lid on it. I know good when I hear it. Jude is beyond good, he just doesn't know it yet. Even though it's been a few weeks since our first recording session, Jude is still skittish about his talent.

I've heard so many demo tapes in my life, I can sort them in my sleep. Even before I joined Aidan's tour, he ran demo tapes by me to see what I thought before he interviewed a potential new act. Jude is every bit as good as those people — better even, because he has a knack for arranging music and writing songs. Somehow he can play songs all the way through in his mind before he ever approaches an instrument. I thought I was a pretty talented songwriter before I met Jude. He makes my skills seem as if they came from a Cracker Jack box.

I tap on the glass to get his attention and motion for him to put his headphones on. After he does, I announce, "Aidan made some upgrades to the recording equipment. He wants us to experiment with it to see how it works. Are you game?"

For a moment, Jude turns a little green. He grips his guitar fret and looks me straight in the eye. "You know, I trust you, but this is scary for me. Promise me you won't use this against me at some point."

"You know me better than that," I respond with an exasperated sigh. "We're doing this to help Aidan. It's not a big deal. You've been singing in this booth for a month now. In case I haven't told you this clearly enough before, you are a great vocalist."

"Thanks." Jude blushes and ducks his head. "Still, it's not like I don't have a point. You can be very sneaky. I just want to make sure you won't do something underhanded with these tapes."

I roll my eyes and give a small huff. "When have I ever done anything which wasn't in your best interest?"

Jude shrugs. "Up until this point, nothing ... but you never know."

"Oh, quit your bellyaching and make some beautiful music for me. I've had a terrible day."

Jude straps on his guitar. "What's wrong, *Sirena?*" he asks with a concerned expression.

I slump in my chair. "It's the same old family stuff — but it's getting really old. I don't know how many different ways I can tell my mother to butt out of my life. She thinks I'm still a toddler. She wants to make me up like a perfect little doll and parade me on stage in a pageant somewhere. It's so stupid. Aidan doesn't have a problem with how I dress or do my hair, but every time my mom sees a picture taken by the paparazzi, she calls me and berates me. I don't know how to handle this anymore."

Jude takes his headphones off and sets his guitar down. Before I can even blink, he's opened the door to the recording studio and is striding across the room toward me. He takes my headphones off and sets them on the counter before giving me a gentle, but thorough kiss.

He pulls away from the embrace and runs his thumb down the side of my face. "So don't."

"So don't what?" I ask, distracted by his closeness and the ever-changing emotions rolling through his eyes. His brown eye is the color of whisky and his blue eye is cool like flint.

"Don't deal with your mom's craziness. Let me and Aidan handle it so you can focus on your work."

"It's not your job to deal with her. Trust me, no one should have to deal with this junk. I won't put that on Aidan. It's not his job. I'm not a kid anymore, I need to be professional and handle my own drama."

"Fair enough. That approach might work with

Aidan, but I want to be involved in this. I don't like to see you hurting. No one should treat you like that. I might not understand your decision to leave, but it doesn't mean you should have to put up with your mom's garbage."

I bury my face into his shoulder for a moment as I gather my thoughts. It's almost impossible to explain my pain to someone who hasn't been through what I've been going through my whole entire life. I shrug as I try to shake off my negativity. "You're right. I shouldn't have to, but I'm nearly all my mom has left and I don't know how else to deal with all of this."

"You have to be in the studio tomorrow to cut Aidan's new song, right?"

I smile a watery smile. "Yeah, it's a little weird because it's a romantic ballad. I have no romantic feelings for Aidan at all. He's kind of like my big brother. We've been friends for years."

Jude looks at me skeptically. "So, you're telling me you never, ever had a crush on Aidan O'Brien? I clean up the mess after shows, so I know firsthand how obsessed fans can be about him. He's the definition of a heartthrob."

"Hero worship, yes — crush, no. That might be because I met Tara at the same time as I met Aidan. It was clear there was more going on between them than simply sign language interpreting. I might've been young when we met, but I wasn't totally clueless."

"Does that mean I'm still in the running?" Jude responds with a teasing grin.

"It most definitely means you're in the running.

Not only that, you're the only one in the contest. I don't make a practice of kissing my coworkers — especially on the job. It's safe to say I've never done it before you. No matter how you slice it, you're a one-of-a-kind."

Jude's expression grows intense. "There was a time in my life when I would've given anything to blend into the crowd and not stand out — but I have to tell you I'm more than happy to be your one-of-a-kind."

"Are you telling me there is an official 'us' now?" I ask, trying not to sound too hopeful.

Jude looks puzzled. "I thought we've been a couple for a while."

I placed my hand in the middle of his chest over his heart. "I don't know how it happened or when the official start of us began. Still, this is the first time we've ever really talked about it."

"I feel stupid now because I didn't know we had to. I suppose I should have told you how I feel."

I swallow hard as I study his face for clues. "Jude, I didn't mean to corner you."

Jude places a finger on my chin and tilts my face up so I'm looking at him. "No. Stop. I need to tell you this. You haven't cornered me in a place I don't want to be. I understand I'm probably just a summer fling until you go away to college, but I'd like it to be more."

I shake my head vehemently. "You are so not a summer fling. I don't do that kind of thing. This might be news to you, but I'm dating you because you're funny and smart. You make me smile even when I don't feel like it."

Jude looks stunned by my outburst. "I'm glad you feel that way. I don't know if I deserve all this praise. I'm just me. I like you a lot too. Please let me help you. I'll take your phone tomorrow so you can concentrate on working with Aidan."

I look away as embarrassment colors my face. "You have a job too. It isn't fair to ask you to babysit my phone. My mother can be obnoxious — especially if she can't reach me."

"I'm just checking rigging before we pack the bus. I'm totally capable of fielding a few phone calls for you. That is, if you trust me."

I laugh out loud. "I trust *you* fine. My mother, not so much. She might shred a nice guy like you."

Jude squeezes my shoulder gently. "I've held my own against tougher than your mom. I'm not worried and I don't want you to be either. This isn't a huge deal. I'm just trying to help make things go more smoothly for you. I like that part of being an 'us.'"

I duck my head in shame. "I still don't think you know what you're getting into, but if you want to handle my phone tomorrow, more power to you. You need to know I'm not like my mom."

Jude pulls me into an embrace and whispers into my ear. "No, you're not like her. You've been amazing when I whine and complain about trying to reach my own dreams. You never criticize me for that."

I have to wipe my eyes as I pull away and try to steer the conversation to less emotional topics. "Speaking of the recording session tomorrow, we need to lay down some tracks to see how the new system works."

"You're right. I have an idea — I don't even know if this is possible. Can you preset the recording equipment so you can come in and sing with me?"

"I don't know. I guess we can try. It might take a few more run-throughs to adjust the settings."

"Let me do a solo first so you can set things up. After you're finished, I think I'm ready to sing with you."

Inside my head, I'm doing cartwheels and backflips. I try not to let it show as I answer casually, "That sounds doable."

Jude's made so much progress from where he started. When we first started this adventure, he was hesitant to even play his guitar in front of me, and now we're going to sing together.

"Just 'doable'?" Jude asks with a pained expression.

"Yes, 'doable.' Actually, it's more than that — but I didn't want to stress you out."

"I appreciate that, but I was hoping for a little more excitement."

"Okay, if you want me to be honest … I've been looking forward to singing with you for months. This is like Christmas, New Year's, and my birthday all rolled into one."

Jude looks a little gray. "Umm… Okay. Nothing like a little pressure. I can't guarantee I'll be able to hold up my end of things, but I'll give it my best shot."

I lean forward to give Jude a quick kiss before I sit

down in front of the soundboard. "See? That's why I didn't say anything about how excited I really am. I figured you'd be uncomfortable if you knew."

"Well, I guess I'm going to have to get over being weirded-out. We've got to get this done for you, so everything is figured out by tomorrow." Jude goes back into the recording booth.

I watch as he settles onto the stool. His quiet confidence makes me smile. He's still jittery about singing in front me, but those nerves are disappearing quickly. As I adjust my headphones, I'm surprised to hear him singing a Keith Urban song. His range is incredible. He knows songs from Porter Wagoner to Hunter Hayes, and seems equally comfortable with both.

I'm so lost in the sweet lyrics; I almost forget why we're here today. As he comes to the chorus again, I adjust the gain in the microphone and hit the record button. Jude stumbles over a word when he sees the red light come on. He shoots me an embarrassed smile, but continues to sing. By the time he's finished, I feel like one of the screaming fans at Aidan's concerts. There is something to be said for a sexy, humble guy singing a romantic song directly to you. Over my headset, I say, "That's the best I've heard you sing so far. I love that song."

I swear I see him blush before I change some settings on the soundboard. I grab my favorite guitar from the corner of the room and strap it on as I walk into the recording booth.

After I settle into the stool next to him and start

tuning my guitar, I ask him, "What are we going to sing?"

"I don't know. A lot depends on how familiar you are with country music," he responds with a mischievous smile.

"I think I'll be okay. New York isn't Tennessee, but I'm a fan of many kinds of music. Go ahead, hit me with your choice and I'll see if I know it."

Jude adjusts his customary cowboy hat and winks at me as he plays the Willie Nelson classic, *Mamas Don't Let Your Babies Grow Up to Be Cowboys.*

A hoot of laughter escapes me. "Here's a little-known fact about me: Nana's a huge Willie Nelson fan. We used to sing this song on the way to pageants just to annoy my mother. Ma thinks Willie Nelson is an uncouth criminal and hates his music."

Jude starts the intro again as I join in. He smiles slyly as he remarks, "Well, it's too bad your mom isn't here. After all the garbage she's put you through, it'd be fun to annoy her some more. Maybe you should send her the tape."

"I appreciate your gallantry on my behalf — but are we going to sing, or what?"

"You're on." Jude keeps time with his boot against the rung of the stool.

I can't wipe the smile off my face as we make our way through the campy classic.

We're having so much fun Jude transitions into another classic duet, *Islands in the Stream.* He glances over at me as if he's expecting me to be unfamiliar with the song. However, what he doesn't know is I adore Dolly Parton and spent many years trying to be just like her. Again, my nana played a big role in my music choices as I was growing up. She lived with us for a while after she broke her leg and we spent a lot of time looking up all the old standbys on YouTube. Nana was completely flummoxed by the idea that you could look up old concert footage and music videos and we've spent many hours attending virtual concerts together.

As Jude and I hit the last verse, I'm startled when I hear a voice over my headphones. I'm was engaged with harmonizing I didn't even notice Aidan come into the control room. Jude looks equally startled. He flushes a dark shade of red as he says, "Aidan… we were just messing around. I hope you don't mind."

"I don't care. After all, it's what I asked you guys to do. I think Tasha's been holding out on me. She never breathed a word to me about your singing chops."

"D-don't blame it on Tasha, sir," Jude stammers. "I swore her to secrecy." Panic fills Jude's expressive eyes. I want to reach out and reassure him but I don't want to embarrass him by holding his hand at work in front of Aidan.

I hold my breath as Aidan takes a long drink of his coffee. I know Jude deeply respects his opinion. Aidan's verdict will shape everything to come. As I wait for my boss to say something, I regret my decision not to tell him what we've been up to.

Aidan sighs deeply before he looks at Jude and asks, "What have you been waiting for? Had I known I already had you on my team, I wouldn't have spent the last three months listening to demo tapes — some of which are horrible at best."

Jude looks like someone punched him in the gut. He seems to be fighting tears as he tries to explain. "You'll never know how much I wanted to join your jam sessions, but it's complicated."

Aidan raises an eyebrow. "So … uncomplicate it for me. You're really talented. Most people I know in your shoes would've been banging down my door for a shot."

Jude looks like he's struggling to find the right words, so I jump in. "Aidan, do you remember the background singer we hired when we went to Florida?"

"Margo?" he asks with a puzzled look. "What about her? As I recall, she was an incredible singer."

"I agree she was, but remember her paralyzing stage fright?"

Aidan chuckles softly to himself. "Oh yeah. I forgot about that. In the beginning, she could barely sing at the audition — but by the third night, she was belting out songs like Adele."

"Jude is a little shy like Margo. We're working on it."

Aidan glances over at Jude. "The next two months are going to be crazy with our bus tour. Come see me when we're done, though. I want to talk to you."

I can't keep the excited grin off my face, but when I glance over at Jude, he looks as if he's swallowed battery acid.

I hope I haven't made a huge mistake that could

cost us everything.

CHAPTER SIX

JUDE

I TRIED TO PLAY it cool, but I pretty much had a stroke when Tasha told Aidan about my stage fright. I don't know what she was thinking, but confessing my weakness was about the last thing I ever wanted to do.

At first, I was furious with Tasha. I left the studios at Silent Beats without even talking to her. I was so embarrassed, and I wasn't sure how to cope. I don't know why she felt she had to tell Aidan my business. If I wanted him to know, I would've told him. Now he'll think of me as some strange, defective singer he has to keep an eye on. I never wanted that to happen. This totally sucks.

When I got home and told Fernanda what happened, she basically told me to get over myself. She hasn't even met Tasha yet, but she firmly believes Tasha has my back. My sister's reaction surprised me because Fernanda doesn't usually trust anyone.

I've been hiding in the bus because I don't know what to say when I finally come face to face with Tasha.

It's obvious I'm trying to avoid her, but it's awkward with a crew this small. I really need to get my crap together and decide what I'm going to do.

I'm busy arranging Delilah's drum set in the luggage compartment of the bus when Aidan taps me on the shoulder. "That's a real nice thing you're doing for Tash. It takes a huge weight off her shoulders. I need her to be able to concentrate today. We've got a limited time to lay down these tracks before we have to leave."

I'm confused for a moment until Aidan hands me Tasha's phone. In all the drama surrounding her unexpected disclosure, I forgot that I agreed to babysit her cell phone today. I shrug. "It's a temporary solution to a much bigger problem. I wish I knew how to help her with the rest of it."

"You're not the only one. I don't know the best way to get her out of the situation with her mom. I guess we'll do what she allows us to do. There isn't any other way to approach it. I can't ban telephones on set because we use them so much in our jobs — but her mom has no sense of boundaries."

I take her phone and set it on the seat of the bus. "Well, you can count on me. She won't have to deal with it today unless the world implodes."

"You're a good guy. I've never had any doubts," Aidan says with a smile. "Just watch out for Tasha's mom. Nadine has some wicked claws once you get to know her."

I raise my eyebrows in surprise. It's not like Aidan to talk about other performers. It's even more rare for him to talk about our families.

"Word to the wise, don't tell Tasha I said that. She has enough to worry about without stressing over her mother's behavior."

"I think I can handle everything on my own. Ms. Keeley won't be the first disagreeable person I've ever dealt with in my life."

"True enough," Aidan says as he tilts his head to examine me. "I guess I better get to it. I'll see you on the other side. If you have time, you could come check Tash out. We're singing a pretty heavy-duty love ballad. Something tells me you'd be more of an inspiration to her in that realm than I am."

I can't help but be a little embarrassed. "I don't know about that. I'm a huge fan of Tasha, both as a performer and as a person, but sometimes our relationship is confusing. Still, doesn't it get weird for you to have your wife watch you sing a love song with someone else? I don't want to make it awkward for Tasha."

"If it was just a voyeuristic fan, that would be one thing. I love having Gracie visit the studio when I'm recording. It reminds me of all the reasons I do what I do. I think Tasha would feel much the same about you. She doesn't feel anything mushy for me, that's for sure. It would probably be great for her to have a muse around."

I try to ignore the heat of embarrassment creeping up my neck. "Okay, when I finish up here I'll see if I've got time to stop by and visit. I'd love to see you working together. Usually when you two perform on the road,

I'm backstage or under the stage dealing with stuff and I don't actually get a chance to watch the two of you."

"Good plan. Speaking of plans, pack yourself a couple of guitars and anything else you play. This is a long road trip, you'll probably want to jam with us."

As I stand up straight, I almost hit my head on the door to the luggage compartment on the bus. I'm shocked by Aidan's offer and I'm not exactly sure how to respond. I have two choices here: I can figuratively throw Tasha under the bus and deny I have any issues singing in public or I can be honest and tell him exactly what's going on.

As Aidan stands there calmly waiting for my answer, I decide I don't have much to lose by being honest. Tasha was right. Of all the people on the planet, Aidan needs to know what's going on if I want to stay on with Aidan and take a different path. Taking a deep breath, I confess, "I've wanted to be part of those jam sessions ever since my first week here — but I don't know if I'm ready to handle it."

Aidan narrows his eyes and nods slowly. "Jude, relax. I know exactly where you're coming from. You might not know my whole story, but I used to have normal hearing. After I lost it, it took me years to regain my confidence to stand on stage — especially as a singer. Many times, I was afraid I'd never find the courage to be who I needed to be to be happy."

"Really? You've had so much fear about singing that you feel like you're going to pass out?" I ask, dumbfounded by his candid admission.

'Sometimes I still have that kind of fear. I don't

know if it ever truly goes away completely. I like to think it keeps me on my toes."

"Wow, I guess I thought I was the only one who dealt with this." I'm barely able to keep my voice from cracking.

"No, we all live with it. It's what makes what we do so edgy and unpredictable." Aidan points at me. "You are planning to be part of the jam sessions, right? My crew will treat you right."

I finally summon up the courage to stammer, "Yes sir. I appreciate the opportunity."

<hr>

Aidan isn't gone long before Tasha's phone begins to ring. I run into the bus to grab it. "Hello?"

"You're not Tasha! Why do you have her phone? Who are you? Have you done something to my daughter?"

She's yelling so loud I have to pull the phone away from my ear. "Mrs. Keeley, Tasha is fine. She's in the middle of a recording session with Mr. O'Brien. I agreed to watch her phone in case something happened to her grandmother."

"It's Ms. Keeley. There is no Mr. Keeley. Oh for Pete's sake! Dottie is fine. The way my child worries about her Nana is sickening. She doesn't worry that much about me. If she did, she would answer her own darn phone."

"Mrs. — *Ms.* Keeley," I correct myself. "I'm sorry. It's not possible for Tasha to have her phone right now.

She's in the middle of recording."

"Well, can't she just stop the song for me? I am her mother after all. I heard that musicians don't really sing on those CDs anyway. It's all electronic gibberish. A computer could probably sing better than Tasha. I don't think Mr. O'Brien is doing any favors for my daughter's career. She'd do much better in pageants where people could see her true personality and talent without all the distortion."

The longer I listen to Ms. Keeley, the more I understand Tasha's anxiety over answering the phone. No wonder Aidan said she has claws. It seems as if she has a few teeth as well as a couple of chips on her shoulder.

"Ms. Keeley, I don't know if you've heard Tasha perform recently, but I have the privilege of hearing her every day. There's nothing manufactured or artificial about her voice. She is simply magnificent."

"Are you dense?" She spits the words at me as if they're bullets. "I don't know who you are, but you don't have to tell me my daughter is talented. That's what I've been trying to tell you. She's too talented to be following around a washed up piano player like some over-grown groupie. She should be front and center, on her own with her name in lights."

I sigh as I respond, "No, ma'am I'm not dense. I'm not as smart as Tasha, but I can hold my own. Was there a message you wanted me to give to your daughter?"

"Yes, you can tell my daughter there's a reunion of Miss Fantabulous pageant girls in New York City next month. I expect her to be there and show these women how it's done."

"I can let her know, ma'am, but next month is going to be incredibly busy. We have several concert dates."

"I don't know who you think you are, young man. You don't speak for my daughter. She's not busy until she tells me she's busy."

"With all due respect ma'am, my name is Jude Hernandez. I'm the equipment manager. I know the schedule better than anyone because I arrange for everything to be transported. I happen to know we barely have any breathing room between gigs next month. I thought it might be helpful for you to know that."

"Jude! Did you say your name is Jude? Don't mention that name in my presence. I hate the name Jude and anything related to cancer."

"I understand. It must've been terribly difficult when Tasha had leukemia. If it makes you feel any better, you can call me Judas." I emphasize my Spanish accent. "Or Vincente — that's my middle name."

"I should've known you'd be named after a traitor," she responds snidely. "I'd rather speak to my daughter directly. Have her call me as soon as she's free."

"I'll be sure to tell her you called."

"You do that. Don't be playing any games. If I don't hear from her, I'll be calling her back." The phone suddenly goes dead.

Not even a half an hour later, the phone rings again and I roll my eyes. I fully expect it to be Ms. Keeley and I'm all wound up to let her have it for calling so quickly. As soon as I answer the phone, it's clear I've made a grave mistake.

I hear a distorted voice say, "Bitch, check your messages."

As soon as the line goes dead, I search her phone for her message app. I immediately click on it and then regret my decision as a full-color picture of Tasha's face unfolds before me. It's Tasha's face but not her body being mutilated by a garrote. Someone has Photoshopped Tasha's face onto a body which is obviously not hers. The message attached says, "I gave you a chance to talk to me, but you chose to ignore me. This is what will happen if you ignore me again."

My hands are shaking so violently I almost drop her phone.

Who in the world would send such garbage? Why hasn't Tasha told me there's some sort of threat against her? Apparently, this isn't the first time she's communicated with this freak.

I spend several moments frozen in the bus seat staring at the gruesome picture, paralyzed with indecision. My first instinct is to go find Logan, who's been providing security for us. Yet, I know Tasha is really private about her personal life and I don't know if this is related to her life as a performer or some personal drama I don't know about. Even though it seems like a violation of her privacy, I try to look back at the history on her phone to see if I can find any clues. Unfortunately, there's nothing there. Not even messages from her mom.

Tasha's phone looks completely different from Fernanda's. My sister has every conversation she's ever had with everyone since the time she first got her phone when she turned sixteen. I think she keeps every selfie she's ever taken too. The absence of any personal information on Tasha's phone seems very strange.

As I am considering my options, another text message arrives. I open it with a great deal of trepidation. "Bitch, I warned you. You have twenty-four hours to decide what to do. Make the wrong decision and you will pay."

Attached to the text message is a .GIF file of a pig carcass exploding. I recognize the shot from an episode of *Myth Busters*. Even so, it's chilling. My stomach lurches and a shiver goes up my spine.

Just then, someone taps on the bus window and I about jump out of the seat. I look up and see Tasha smiling at me.

She peeks her head in the bus door and cheerfully asks, "Hi, what are you doing?"

I set her phone down on the seat next to me as I respond, "Oh, a little of everything. Getting ready for a bus tour is crazy."

"So, you can be honest with me … How many times did my mom call?"

"Only once — but it's safe to say she's not my biggest fan."

Tasha sits next to me and slumps down in the seat.

"I was afraid of that. What did she want this time?"

"Apparently, there's a reunion of one of your pageant events next month in New York and she'd like you to attend."

"Next month? Is she delusional? I have a *job*. Next month is absolutely packed from start to finish," Tasha exclaims.

"I know, I tried to explain — which is why she is not my biggest fan. She thinks I don't know what I'm doing and that I couldn't possibly know about your schedule. She would like you to call her back at your earliest convenience."

Tasha laughs dryly. "Oh, I bet she does."

She reaches down to the bus seat and tries to grab her phone. I place my hand over hers. "*Sirena*, that's not the only thing which happened while you were gone. I don't know how to tell you this without upsetting you — but you got a couple of really disturbing messages too."

Tasha rakes her hands through her hair in an aggravated fashion. "Oh Gosh! Don't tell me Creepy Stalker Dude is back."

"What? This has happened to you before?" Shock makes my jaw slack.

A frightened look crosses Tasha's face. "Yeah, I know all about him." She pauses a beat or two before she shrugs. "Actually, that's not true. I don't even know if it's a him, I just assume it is because who else would send me naked pictures of someone who isn't even me, but whatever —"

"Have you told anybody? Does Aidan know? What about Logan? Have you called the police? I'm assuming you haven't told your mom because she would go high and to the right."

Tasha appears frustrated. "No. I haven't done any of that. I changed my cell phone number, I took my contact information off my fan page, and I don't go anywhere by myself. I figured they didn't need to know all about what was going on with me. Aidan doesn't need one more thing to worry about. If I'm going to be somebody in this business, I need to learn how to watch out for myself."

It's all I can do not to grind my teeth as I hold back what I want to say. Finally, I compose myself. "Tasha, fans can be absolutely crazy and obsessed. You need to use the tools that are there to protect you. There's a reason Aidan pays big bucks to employ people like Logan. He doesn't just hire college kids looking for a summer job, he hires ex-military and ex-law enforcement folks. He takes safety seriously. You need to let them know what's going on. It doesn't seem like this guy is messing around."

"The police probably can't do anything. I don't even know who this person is and I've already taken all the safety steps they recommend on the Internet. I mean, after all, they're just a few text messages. For all I know, it's some thirteen-year-old kid trying to show off for his buddies."

I take a deep breath before I plead, "Tasha, please trust me on this. I have a feeling it's bigger than something like that. Just promise me you'll tell Aidan what's going on so he can have somebody deal with this. If you've already changed your phone number and contact information and this person tracked you down, it's over-the-top-freaky. This person is more persistent than your average, everyday prankster. You need to pay attention. I'm worried about your safety."

She bites her bottom lip before she concedes, "I promise I will tell him — but I can't do it right now. We're in the middle of recording. We just had to take a break because we had to change a fuse. I should get back. They're probably waiting for me."

"Okay, I'll be there in a few minutes. I have to put some mic stands in the bus."

———●———

It's really different being on this side of the glass. The sound engineer, Jimmy, invited me to sit next to him and watch Aidan and Tasha record. Tasha's completely lost in the lyrics of the romantic ballad. She doesn't even realize I'm in the recording booth. I feel a little like a voyeur. For people who don't know Aidan and Tasha, it would be easy to believe they're very much a couple in love. Their performance is that convincing. At least it is until Aidan messes up a lyric and lets a cuss word slip.

Tasha lets out a surprised chortle of laughter. "You are so busted. You can't even deny it because it's on tape," she snickers. "At the rate you're going, there'll be enough money in the swear jar for you and Tara to go to London sooner than you planned."

Aidan looks a little like a kid whose been caught with his hand in the cookie jar. "Yeah, you'd think I

would know the lyrics to the song better than that —
since I wrote it and all. Maybe it's my subconscious
letting me know I need to take my lovely wife on
vacation. Things have been tough lately. Maybe a trip to
London is exactly what we need."

"Does Tara like to watch the famous ballet
companies perform, or does it make her sad?" Tasha
asks.

Aidan looks befuddled for a second before he
answers, "I can't believe I've never asked her that
question before. When she performed with my brother,
she was at the top of her game, but that was years ago. I
don't know how she feels about watching other
principal dancers."

"Maybe I'm a closet romantic, but I can see you
taking her on a whirlwind tour around the world seeing
the top ballet companies."

Aidan kisses Tasha on the forehead. "For such a
young squirt, you are incredibly brilliant. I've been
racking my brain for months trying to come up with the
perfect anniversary gift. I wasn't planning to tour in
February anyway, so the timing would be perfect."

Tasha blushes clear to the roots of her hair. "I'm
glad I could help, but I still think you should take her on
vacation before February."

"I will. We have a few days off after the Fourth of
July. I'm going to take her on a mini-vacation."

Tasha looks through the window directly at me
and says, "I think we could all use a vacation from the
crazy schedule we've been keeping."

Mary Crawford

I'm not sure how to read all the messages in that look, but my pulse is racing and my brain just went into overdrive.

CHAPTER SEVEN

TASHA

TO BE HONEST, I thought Jude was overreacting to the messages from Creepy Stalker Dude — until I actually saw them.

I'm glad I waited until after I was done with the recording session to look at my phone. If I'd seen those messages before I finished, I'm not sure I would've been able to.

All I can say is I'm grateful for Jude's quiet, steady presence beside me as I read the vitriolic words. "Who could hate me that much?"

Jude moves his hand in a slow, concentric circle along my shoulder blades. "Do you want me to go with you when you go talk to Logan and Aidan?"

I wipe tears of frustration from my lashes. "I don't know if this has to involve Aidan at this point. He's got so much to worry about. We leave tomorrow. When I walked by his office, he had a stack of messages about four inches high."

Jude shrugs. "Okay, we'll play it your way, but I'll be willing to bet as soon as Logan hears what's going on, he'll call in Aidan anyway."

I nod tightly before I stand up and hold my hand out to him. "Come on, let's do this before I lose my nerve. I hope this doesn't get me kicked off the tour."

Jade puts his arm around my waist as we walk toward Logan's office. "Won't happen. That's not the way things work around here. Aidan's one of your biggest supporters. He'd never kick you off the tour. If anything, he'll just get you some more security."

I tentatively knock on Logan's door frame, and he motions for us to come in as he hangs up the phone.

"What can I do for you, T?"

"Honestly, I don't know if you can do anything for me, but Jude thought I should talk to you."

"Is that so?" he asks, looking at Jude.

"I think it's important," Jude explains as he takes a seat. He gently pulls me down onto the hard plastic chair beside him when I seem paralyzed by indecision. Part of me still wants to flee this whole conversation.

"Why?" Logan grabs a pad of paper to take notes as he glances at both of us.

"This is so stupid, I can't believe that I can't handle this on my own," I mutter angrily.

"Teamwork is what makes this act work, remember? Aidan would have a pseudo-big-brother-meltdown if he knew you were trying to handle something on your own that you felt was too big."

I sigh. "You're right. I suppose I should've said

something sooner. I thought this goes along with being famous. I wasn't too worried about it until the Creepy Stalker Dude started getting violent. Then I started having nightmares about it and watching over my shoulder."

Logan perks up and scoots forward in his chair. "Tasha, is someone threatening you?"

"Graphically and specifically," Jude answers for me. "Whoever this is has taken 'sick and deranged' up a notch."

"Tasha, take me back to the beginning — when did this start?" Logan asks with an intense expression on his face.

"I don't know exactly. I get lots of fan mail since my song is doing so well on the charts. Usually, I send a canned response thanking them for their support — but this one person seems to want more personal details. I can't tell whether this person wants me to sing or wants me to stop. Sometimes their comments are flattering and sometimes they're disparaging. Sometimes they give me flowery compliments and other times they tell me to burn in hell for what I do."

"Always from the same email address?" Logan asks, writing down information on a legal pad.

"No, this person doesn't seem to use the same email address more than once."

"How do you know they're from the same person?"

The bottom drops out of my stomach as I consider what he's saying. It's true, I could have multiple stalkers. I guess I never thought it through. "You're right. I don't know if all the messages are from the same person, I assumed it was because he always addresses me as 'Bitch.'"

Logan rolls his eyes. "Obviously whoever this is doesn't know you very well."

"Like I told Jude today, I'm not even sure if it's a man. I figured it's a somewhat weirded-out guy in his basement wearing threadbare pajamas and smoking weed. I don't know if that's true — it's just how I pictured him."

"What's different about today?" Logan asks. "You've been getting these for a while, but something prompted you to tell me about them today. Why?"

I squirm in the sticky plastic chair. "Honestly, I probably wouldn't be here today if Jude hadn't insisted I tell someone."

Logan turns to Jude. "Why did you urge her to tell me, today specifically?"

"If I'd known she was dealing with this before today, you would've been informed. Today was the first day I've seen any of these messages. From what she's told me, today's messages are more specific and violent than any of the messages before."

"How violent are we talking?" Logan presses.

"Whoever is sending these messages is cropping Tasha's head onto a different body and blowing it up. I recognize part of the footage from a *Myth Busters* episode where they blew up half of a pig analog for the human body."

Logan swings his eyes around to me in surprise as he demands, "Is this true?"

I nod meekly. "Yes, it's true. I didn't want to bother any of you. I thought if I ignored him he'd go away, but it's gotten worse as I've gotten more popular."

"Tasha, I hope you know that Aidan hires me to deal with threats like this. Obsessed fans and stalkers are not something to mess around with. It's serious stuff. Please tell me you kept the threats from today. Better yet, tell me you've kept every single threat." Logan presses his lips together in a grim line.

"If she didn't, I did," Jude responds. "I don't have the threats from before, but I sent a copy of today's messages to my own phone."

I whirl around on Jude as I hiss, "You didn't have any right to do that. Those were my private messages."

Jude looks uncomfortable and a bit ill. "Under normal circumstances, I would never violate your privacy, but this pervert isn't normal and these are not ordinary circumstances. I'm trying to keep you safe. I figured we needed another record of what you were sent in case something happened to those messages. This is a direct threat on your life due to be carried out within twenty-four hours. It doesn't get any more serious than that."

I tremble as I look at the bodyguard. "Logan, do you really think they are serious about hurting me. I thought the creep was probably showing off for his friends. I never thought it would come to this. I didn't even keep the other messages because they were all sorts of creepy and weird. I thought if I deleted them from my phone and computer, they wouldn't exist in my world. I know it was stupid, but I just didn't want to deal with it."

Logan is doing his best to disguise the fact he thinks I'm the world's biggest idiot as he holds his hand out to take my cell phone. "We'll start with what we have here, and I've got some contacts within law enforcement. Maybe they can work with the phone company to unearth something else."

"Is there anything I can do to help?" Jude grips my hand tightly.

"Do you have any special skills in self-defense or martial arts?" Logan studies Jude's lithe build.

"Unfortunately, my athletic prowess is limited to soccer and baseball," Jude replies with a sad shake of his head.

Logan studies Jude for a moment. "Soccer and baseball are good. It shows you're quick on your feet and have good instincts." He turns to me. "I've seen you dance, I know you are agile and flexible. I want the two of you to be part of Tara's martial arts workout during the tour."

"Tara's coming with us?" I ask. "I didn't know that. She'll be great for Aidan. I know how much he misses her when we're on the road."

"Yeah, he's a lucky guy. I wish I had somebody like her in my life." Logan turns to Jude. "Until the police and I can get a better handle on what's going on, I want you guys to be like the Double Mint twins."

"The police? Do you think we have to go that

far?" I ask, my voice squeaking as panic starts to set in.

Logan walks over, puts his hands on my shoulders, and looks me square in the face. "Tasha, I won't lie to you. You know me better. The reality is you're not playing at coffee shops and birthday parties anymore. We fill huge football stadiums now. The risk is exponentially higher when we scale up. The fact that someone is specifically targeting you is concerning. We're there. You need to act like you're a big talent now. You don't want to know what the next step is. It's my job to protect you from what comes next. So, let me do it before it's too late."

The intense expression on Logan's face is the scariest thing I've seen in a long time. It's even more unsettling than the GIF file I received today. If Logan is frightened, this has gone way too far.

I attempt to smile. "This isn't just a guy thing where you guys are being super-overprotective, is it?"

Logan shakes his head. "I'm afraid not, T. Your guy here has great instincts. Unfortunately, whoever is after you has a lead on us, but hopefully we'll outsmart them."

"What if we can't?" I ask hollowly.

"Let's not have that conversation yet. We're a pretty bright team, and we just got the case. We're on it, T. Give us a chance to do our jobs."

CHAPTER EIGHT

JUDE

USUALLY, I PREFER IT when we stay in one spot for a while. It makes my job much easier. However, in this case, I'm relieved that we're in a different venue almost every other night. We're spending most of our time traveling on the bus. After Logan informed Aidan about Tasha's stalker, he added another security guard, Nick, who is retired military, and upgraded all of our hotel arrangements to more secure locations. This means an upgrade for me. I don't typically stay with the rest of the musicians. To save money, I usually sleep in the back of one of the buses, but because of the threats Aidan has specifically asked me to stay with Tasha in her room.

I'm not sure what Tasha thinks of these arrangements. We haven't talked about it much. Aidan booked a business suite for Tasha so there are two rooms. I'm in a very weird place right now. I've never been in a position where I'm dating a coworker. We haven't been obvious about our relationship, but we haven't hidden it either. I'm sure Aidan is well aware I am head over heels gone for Tasha, but he hasn't said anything.

I'm trying not to be obvious as I search for Tasha while I check the cords on the lighting system to make sure we don't have any surprises tonight. Aidan and Tasha should be finished with their sound check soon if everything is working properly — but these things can be tricky. No matter how many times we set up and take down, every venue is a little different and there's always a slim chance something can pop up at the last minute.

The first leg of the tour has been pretty low key. Aidan had already planned to do an obscure circuit. It fits with his plan to scale back media appearances and social media exposure. He is dubbing this the "Forgotten City Tour." We're traveling to a lot of college campuses which don't usually get a lot of big-name stars. In some ways it's cool because we've been treated really well. In other ways, it makes my job more complicated because they sometimes don't have all the equipment we usually find in the bigger venues.

As I go backstage to put my stepladder away, Tasha's sitting on the floor singing quietly to herself with her guitar. That in itself isn't unusual — but the tears streaming down her face are. I prop the ladder against the wall, walk over, and sit down beside her. "Sirena, what's wrong?"

Tasha looks up at me as if she's surprised by my presence. She wipes away her tears with her sleeve. "Oh, I'm being stupid. It turned out to be nothing, but for a while it was scary." She lays her guitar down in her case and starts to nervously rub her hands on the side of her jeans.

"Did you get another note? I thought Logan was screening your incoming messages and mail." I kneel beside her. Adrenaline courses through my body and sweat trickles down my back. The last images she got still haunt me. Despite Logan's assurances that he would involve law enforcement, nobody seems particularly interested in a few creepy text messages. Apparently, Tasha Keeley isn't enough of a household name for them to sit up and take notice.

Tasha puts her hand over my wildly beating heart. "Geez, Jude, take a chill pill. This doesn't have anything to do with the stalker drama. This is all about my other drama."

"What do you mean?" I stand up and hold my hand out so she can get up off the cold cement floor.

Tasha gracefully stands up and with one hand unfolds the stepladder and sits down on it. "It doesn't take a rocket scientist to guess my mom and I got into it again. I swear she's got some sort of hidden camera to figure out when I'm smack in the middle of working with Aidan." She rolls her eyes.

"What did she want this time?" I try not to roll my own. It's odd for me to have such a profound dislike for a woman I've never met, but I hate the way she can destroy Tasha with a simple phone call.

"Nana was putting dishes in the dishwasher and tripped over her kitchen rug. She hit her cheekbone on the counter and my mom had to take her to have an x-ray. Somehow this is all my fault because I should've been there to stop it all from happening."

"I'm sorry your *abuela* got hurt, but what difference would it have made if you'd been there?"

"My mom just spent twenty-five minutes arguing with me. She insists if I'd been home, I would've been the one doing the dishes and my nana wouldn't have been hurt."

"That's dumb. My mom sprained her ankle this year by stepping off a curb. There was no way I could have prevented that, and you couldn't have stopped your grandma from falling even if you had been at home. What did your *madre* expect you to do — hold your Nana's hand while she was doing the dishes?"

For the first time since we started this conversation, Tasha's eyes light up. "I don't know about your grandma, but Nana would have chased me out of the kitchen with a broom and tell me to go do something fun. Dottie hates all the stuff Ma makes me do. She's always wanted me to be a normal kid. Whenever I went over to Nana's house when I was young, she'd go out of her way to get me as dirty as possible. We would do all sorts of stuff which drove my mom completely batty. Nana would let me do crazy, messy things like finger paint and roll down big grassy hills while I played in the mud. She encouraged me to sit around and read books and watch cartoons on television instead of practicing my singing lessons or dance moves."

"Go Grandma!" I chuckle, imagining Nadine's face.

Tasha smiles as she reminisces. "Nana would take me to Sears and get regular play clothes from the boys' section instead of my usual over-the-top frilly girl stuff. One time, my mom came to get me earlier than my grandmother expected and we thought she would pass out on the spot when she saw me in my muddy overalls and a backward baseball cap. After that, my mom didn't let me go to Nana's house quite as often. It's too bad though because the one thing I've learned from Dottie Abalone is that it's okay to be one hundred percent who you are regardless of what other people think."

"In my family, that person is always my little sister Fernanda. Even if I'm the first person to try something, she always comes in behind me and does it bigger, better and bolder. It's weird to say my little sister gives me permission to be more 'me' in my family, but she does. She is so absolutely fearless I look at myself and wonder what I'm always so worried about."

"It's funny how our families influence us. My grandma used to tell me my great-grandma was a pinup model for one of the biggest modeling companies back in the day. Nana always said if her mom was brave enough to take her clothes off for a bunch of strangers and have near life-size posters made, everything else was as easy as an apple pie at a church potluck."

"Do you need to go see your *abuela*? It would be tight, but we could probably do it before the next round of shows start."

"No! That's just the thing." Tasha wildly punctuates each word with a hand gesture. "My mom called me at work and argued with me for what seemed like forever and my grandma only has a bruise on her face. It's not even a bad bruise. I talked to Nana on the phone and she told me she'll probably get a shiner from it, but the doctor told her not to worry. She doesn't have to go back into the hospital or anything. My mom was being overdramatic is usual."

"I don't know," I mumble, unable to hide my distaste. "Your mom seems like a piece of work. She wants you to make it all the way to the top of the pop charts, but she doesn't want you to put any work into making it happen."

"I've never been able to figure that out either. She's fine with letting me work my butt off, as long as she gets all the credit and the sympathy for all the sacrifices she's making."

"Don't forget — it can't interfere with her schedule."

"Yeah, I think that's a big part of what this is about. She's mad because I went behind her back and contacted the pageant organization and told them I wouldn't be able to be at the event in New York City. She still considers herself to be my manager."

"Do you even have a manager?" It occurs to me I haven't seen Tasha traveling with a huge entourage like some acts Aidan works with.

Tasha shrugs. "Not really. After the debacle with Five Star, I backed away from the whole being famous bit for a while. When I was on TV with Aidan, they made us all sorts of promises about how their company would launch our careers into the stratosphere, but nothing happened from winning the show. I had a lawyer helping me then, but sadly, Mr. Potter died and I haven't thought about having anyone replace him."

I gesture around to the stage and all the surrounding lights. "How did you get caught up in all of this?"

"Before Aidan left America's Next Star, he and I were friends. He was like a big brother crossed with a father figure. He did all he could do to protect me. A few years ago, he came to my hometown to perform and I went to see him. When he saw me in the audience, he approached me during the intermission and asked me if I would sing a song we'd performed on television back in the day. He pulled me on stage and we picked up as if nothing had changed."

"I bet that felt odd."

"It did, because I was a kid when I last sang with him. On the other hand, it felt a bit like a great big family reunion. After that, I sang background vocals on his studio albums and performed at his family events. As soon as I turned eighteen, he began hiring me for real gigs in public. I owe a lot to Aidan and Tara. Without them, my teenage years would've been much more difficult. Aidan's quiet faith in me — even when my career was virtually nonexistent — made all the difference in the world."

"It sounds like Aidan has done nothing but good things for your career. Why does your mom have such a beef with him?"

Tasha sighs. "Because Aidan allows me to be who I am and helps me be successful almost in spite of my mom — in ways I never was when my mom was 'in charge' of my career. I think it is just that simple. I'm happy and popular and she hasn't chosen every step of my path."

I walk behind the ladder and hug her from behind as I kiss the top of her head. "I'm sorry she can't just be happy that you're doing well and leave you alone to do your job. How can I help?"

Tasha tilts her head back to kiss me on the chin, then stands up to grab her guitar. "Well, it's Jerome's birthday today, so Aidan ordered in some lunch. We should be starting our usual jam session any time now. I'd like you to sing with me."

I thought maybe she wanted me to talk to her mom, Aidan, or maybe even Logan. I didn't expect her to ask me to join the jam session. I know I've been promising to do it eventually, but I didn't think today would be the day.

I swallow hard. "Sure, let me grab my guitar. What should we sing?"

Tasha's eyes light up with fire. "I know this isn't usually your thing, but how do you feel about John Lennon? I feel like being a bit rebellious today. I need to sing a protest song or two today just to keep my sanity."

I place my arm around her waist and grab her guitar. "I love John Lennon, but are you sure it wouldn't be better to write one given the mood you're in?"

Tasha laughs. "You're right. I do my best song writing when I'm ticked off at my mom. Unfortunately, today I have a duty to be a real live, social human being, so let's go jam and sing one of the greatest songs ever written."

I've been playing guitar with some guys on the bus to pass the time — but this is the first time I've ever done a full-on performance with Tasha in front of anybody except Aidan. My hands are shaky and more than a little sweaty as Tasha and I take our places in the makeshift band.

When Aidan sees me join them, he grins from ear to ear and gives me a thumbs up. "It's great to see you, Jude. We always give our new guests their choice of place in the lineup. Where would you like to sing?"

If I was nervous before, now my heart rate is through the roof. Even after all the time that I've been working for Aidan O'Brien, it still feels odd that he considers me as another musician. Tasha squeezes my thigh as she whispers, "You're doing okay. We all felt this way our first time up."

I clear my throat. "Lucky for me, I brought a partner who sings like an angel. So, I'd like to go first. We'd like to be able to enjoy the rest of the jam." Turning toward Tasha, I ask, "Ready?"

"Let's do this, Secret Music Man. They deserve to know what Aidan and I know," Tasha answers with a smile as we begin to play the introduction to John Lennon's *Imagine*.

When Aidan hears this, his eyebrows raise. "Not what I expected from you — but great song choice." He makes himself more comfortable at the piano bench and starts to play along.

Jerome, the bass player grins widely as he strums

and taps his foot. "I agree. We tend to get stuck in our own style of music, but this stuff rocks."

As more musicians join the song, it becomes less about me and more about the love of the music and I relax. By the time we reach the chorus, I find it's easier to take a full breath and focus on harmonizing with Tasha. She smiles over at me as we dig into a guitar riff like we do when we're writing together.

This. This is what music is supposed to be like — fun, spontaneous and joyful. If this is what Aidan and Tasha feel like every time they are on stage, I understand why it's so addictive.

We end the song and silence breaks out in the room. My heart drops. Did I misread everything? Was it as awful as I built it up to be in my head?

Jerome walks over to a box and pulls out a custom-made Aidan O'Brien guitar pick. He stands in front of me for a moment just watching me before he says, "Brother, I don't know where in the world you've been hiding or why you haven't shown up before — but welcome to the club. That's some of the best pickin' and croonin' I've heard in a while." He looks over his shoulder at Aidan. "Why are you wasting your time auditioning those spoiled brats the record labels keep sending over when you got this sittin' under your nose?"

"Jerome, take it easy. I know it's your birthday and everything, but this is Jude's first time in the jam session. Can we let him hang around a while before you start signing him to multi-year contracts?"

"Sorry Boss, I'm pointin' out the obvious here. This kid is going places, and I don't want him to get away."

It's totally surreal to have two talented musicians talk about me and dissect my talent right in front of me. I know Tasha has been telling me all along that something like this could happen. Still, I was afraid to believe it might be possible.

Stella, one of the background singers gives me a slow once over like my *abuela* does before mass. "Honey, I've been around this business for a long time — more years than I care to admit. Let me tell you, you're good. Real good. You and your girl — that's something special too. You guys would make a great duet team."

Stella is one of the most respected people on our tour. She's spent a career singing backup with some of the best acts in the business from country music to rock-'n'-roll and everything in between. I fight back my emotions as I struggle to process her words. As often happens when I am emotional or nervous, I fall back on to the language I grew up with as I respond, *"Muchas gracias por tus lindas palabras. Es muy amable de tu parte."* I blush as I realize what I've just said and I start to translate, "Sorry, this is all a little overwhelming. I meant to say, 'Thank you for your kind words. They mean a lot to me'."

Stella chuckles. "Don't you worry about a thing. Politeness in any language is a good thing." Stella picks up a microphone and glances down at my guitar. "I'm about to sing some Dolly Parton, I would love it if you would accompany me."

"I'd be honored," I respond with a smile. With sudden clarity, I realize I mean it. This experience has been all I ever dreamed it could be and more.

Tasha leans over and whispers in my ear, "I told you that you'd kill it — but it went better than even I could've hoped."

CHAPTER NINE

TASHA

THE CROWD IN NEBRASKA is absolutely electrifying. As we've gotten into the swing of the tour, the scary cloud hanging over my head seems to have dissipated. The warm-up band is kicking it and the whole crowd is alive with excitement.

I'm putting some last-minute touches on my makeup and hair while Jude is replacing a broken tuning peg on my favorite guitar when Aidan knocks on the door frame.

I put my mascara wand down when I glimpse Aidan's expression in the mirror. He clears his throat softly. "Can I talk to you guys for a minute?"

I take a seat on the edge of the counter. "Sure. It looks like it's going to be a great show tonight."

Aidan grimaces. "That's what I came to talk to you about. Izzy had an unfortunate encounter with a door and some fans. Tara's taking her to the hospital to have her hand checked out, but it means I'm down a guitar player. Would you guys mind filling in tonight?"

"You're kidding, right?" Jude jaw goes slack.

"I wish I was. You know our play list, right?" Aidan asks, looking directly at Jude.

"Like the back of my hand — but that doesn't mean you want me on stage."

"Actually, it means I need you. I don't even have to put a spotlight on you, you can play in your own corner."

I walk over to Jude and give him a hug as I assure him, "I know this isn't what we planned, but you're totally ready for this."

"How do you know I'm ready?" Jude asks, searching my face. "I've only been playing with you guys for a few weeks."

"True, but you've been singing with me for much longer than that, and on your own for years. I know you're ready. Aidan and I will be right there; we won't let you crash and burn." I look over at Aidan. "I know a lot of our staging calls for me not to have my instrument, but can I keep my guitar on me and play with Jude?"

Aidan nods as he responds, "Absolutely. This tour is all about breaking the rules and doing things our way. If tonight calls for some spontaneity, so be it. Do whatever works for you guys."

I grip Jude's forearms and look directly in his face. "I believe in you. Aidan believes in you. Do you believe enough in yourself to do this?"

Jude sighs. "Fine. I'm in — but don't let me think about this for too long or I'll completely freak myself out."

I'm so excited I can barely contain myself. This is the kind of break Jude has needed for a long time. He just doesn't know it. Sometimes, fate hands you the kick in the pants you need whether or not you want it.

After Aidan leaves, Jude slumps in my arms and laments, "I don't know what I'm thinking. I don't even have anything to wear on stage. What the hell possessed me to say yes?"

I can almost read the battle brewing inside him through his expressive eyes. In his brown eye, I can see his budding excitement. It practically glows with anticipation. In contrast, his blue eye is clouded with worry and angst.

I study my handsome boyfriend with appreciative eyes. "I don't know. You look fine to me. The girls will go wild when they see you. I'm glad I have dibs on you."

Jude turns around and looks in the mirror. "Although I appreciate the compliment, I think you're full of crap. There's nothing special about me. I'm wearing a flannel shirt and a beat-up straw hat. Nobody's going to put me on the cover of *Country Music Daily* looking like this."

I hand him a soft blue chambray shirt from the costume rack and remove his cowboy hat. "It'd be a shame to cover up your gorgeous dark hair. I love your new haircut. With this little wardrobe change, you fit right in with the rest of the band. Now, make sure you have a bottle of water with you out on stage. It's hot work."

Jude gives me a pained look. "Are you sure? I can't remember the last time I was without my hat."

I point to my blinged-out denim jacket and high heels. "We all make sacrifices for our art. You'll survive, I promise. I've got your back.

<hr>

It's unfolding a lot like I thought it would go. At first, Jude is playing mostly in the background. As he becomes more comfortable on stage, he gravitates toward me — which means he's in the spotlight. Of course, the crowd takes notice because he's an incredibly gifted guitar player, and they respond accordingly.

During a set change, Aidan comes over and announces, "I'm having some trouble with my cochlear implant. Can you guys cover for me while I see if changing the batteries solves the problem?"

Jude looks like a deer paralyzed by oncoming headlights, but finally he blinks slowly as if he is coming out of a trance. "Sure. Anything in particular you want us to sing?"

Aidan's concentrating on reading Jude's lips and eventually gives up in the darkened backstage environment. "Do whatever keeps the show going. I trust you," he says after Logan comes over to sign Jude's question.

Finally, I shoo Aidan out the door. "Go take care of whatever's going on, we'll sort out the rest."

I look over at Jude. "Isn't it fun living life on the edge and being adventurous?"

<hr>

As Stella takes a moment to sing a Tanya Tucker song to

give us a break, it's hard not to be a little spooked by how far Jude and I have come in just a few months. If I didn't know this was his first time on stage, there's no way I'd be able to tell. We had only a few moments to put together a quick play list, so we're sticking to songs we've been doing for a while. Jude is absolutely slaying *Wichita Lineman* and the crowd's going wild for him. When I first introduced him, the crowd was largely silent because they weren't sure what to make of the newcomer. Now they're actually chanting his name and asking for an encore. I'm not sure if this is making it easier or harder for Jude to continue, but at least he doesn't look like he's facing a guillotine anymore — like he did when we first started working together all those months ago.

Jude shocks me and starts playing a new Hunter Hayes song we've recently added to our repertoire. At my look of surprise, he winks and shrugs. No one in the audience will ever know what a huge milestone this is. To me, it means the world. For the first time, Jude is moving forward toward his dream without a huge shove from me. During a guitar riff, he notices I'm fighting back tears. He takes special care to catch my eye before he mouths the words, "Thank you for this."

Reaching the chorus of the bluesy, country duet, I realize how much his quiet fight against his own fears has impacted my life too. Jude Hernandez is quiet, unassuming and shy, but he's also one of the most talented, driven people I've ever met. I'm so happy his dreams are coming true. I wish I could sort out my own life, too.

As we step off stage, Aidan makes a point to come over and speak to us. "For a last-minute, substitution act, you guys absolutely killed it. Heck, forget what I said. You guys were flat-out amazing. *Period.* I don't suppose there's any chance I could hire you guys to do that again. You're chemistry goes clear to the back row."

Jude regards Aidan with skepticism. "Did you really have a problem with your implants or did you make it up to have an excuse to push me out on stage?"

Rather than be offended, Aidan laughs out loud. "I think you've been listening to too many urban legends about me. I'm resourceful, but I wouldn't go quite that far. It turns out I had a loose wire in the charger. Fortunately, my wife had the foresight to order me a backup pair of implants after the last time I won an award from Billboard and my music went crazy on the charts."

"How's Izzy's hand?" I ask.

"It looks like there's some soft tissue damage but nothing broken. She'll have to wear a splint for a couple weeks. If it doesn't get better, they want her to go in for follow-up x-rays because sometimes these injuries don't show up."

"It's good that it's nothing terribly serious," Jude replies.

"Yeah, now, are you ready to go meet your new adoring fans?" Aidan asks Jude. "A word to the wise, don't sign anything you don't want your grandma to see on Twitter. Logan and his men will collect any phone numbers for you and dispose of them properly."

"Do I have to take phone numbers?" Jude asks with a grimace. "I guess I never thought about what would happen after I made it on stage."

I slide my hand down Jude's jaw. "No, you don't have to take the phone numbers, but trust me, it makes it go a lot faster. I don't mind if you do because I know it's part of the game."

"Do the fans know it's part of the game?" Jude asks sharply as he turns to Logan. "Do you keep a record of these phone numbers and notes she gets directly from the fans? Could they be a clue to the text messages?"

"Initially, we weren't keeping them, but since the security issues have arisen around T, we have started keeping records of all the fan contact with her, no matter how small." Logan's expression is somber.

Aidan regards us all. "Since the connection between Jude and Tasha is about as obvious as the one between Tara and me, maybe you should keep records of anything that comes in for Jude too."

Logan nods at Aidan. "Understood."

"Jude, I'll assign Yasmin to you. I think it will be less obtrusive than one of my guys. Just let her know what your boundaries are."

Jude looks at me with a blank expression on his face. "Boundaries?"

I clutch Jude's hands as I clarify, "Relax and breathe. This is easy. Logan and the guys know I'm okay with fans shaking my hands and taking selfies, but if a fan tries to reach anything below my waist or grab my breasts, that's off limits. I sign CDs, T-shirts and that kind of stuff, but I won't sign skin."

Jude pales a little. "*¡Cielos!*, this just got a lot more real." He addresses Logan as he pulls me closer to him. "Tasha's boundaries sound reasonable. I'd like the same. If you don't mind, I'm going to stick close to Tasha. I don't think I'm ready to go out on my own yet."

Disregarding all the other people in the room, I give him a quick kiss. "Don't worry about it, I've got your back. I wouldn't let anything happen to you."

"That's what I'm counting on. I thought getting on stage was the scary part. Now I'm beginning to reconsider," Jude replies. He breaks away from the kiss and takes a large gulp of water.

Jerome rolls his eyes. "If you two are done playing kissy-face, we've got fans to meet."

Jude and I are working our way through the VIP room when I see someone I'd hoped never to lay eyes on again. Jude practically trips over me when I stop dead in my tracks. "Logan, you need to go get Aidan," I say under my breath, trying to keep my panic at bay.

"Tasha, are you calling a code red?" Logan asks urgently.

"No, not yet. I don't know if this is related to the text messages — but Aidan needs to know she's here. I don't think you need to evacuate us quite yet unless Aidan decides she poses that much danger."

"She who?" Jude asks with a scowl.

"Clover Branch," I mutter with a sinking feeling in

my stomach. "The last time I saw her, I was about fourteen and she almost completely destroyed both Aidan's career and mine."

A look of comprehension crosses Logan's face. "You're kidding. The boss will want to know about this one for sure. I wonder what she wants. The last I heard, there was talk of restraining orders between the two of them."

"It was about that ugly. I have no idea why she's here — but I know it can't be a good thing."

Before I can say anything more, Aidan comes over with his new bodyguard, Nick. "What's up?"

I tilt my head over to the cluster of people and Aidan's face immediately grows tense. He turns to Nick. "Go get Tara for me. She's grabbing Izzy a bite to eat at the snack table."

Nick looks to Logan for permission to leave Aidan's side. "Against protocol."

"It's all right Nick. There are two of us here already."

Looking pained, Nick responds, "Affirmative. I'll be right back."

Jude looks puzzled. "I don't understand. What does Tara have to do with this Clover Branch woman?"

Aidan rubs his hand down his face with a wry grin. "Everything and nothing. You'll see." He fishes a scrunchie from the pocket of his jeans and places it on his wrist as we wait.

"Does this kind of stuff happen often?" Jude looks around the crowd with renewed scrutiny. "I'm usually putting away equipment when you all are doing this, so all of this is new."

Aidan chuckles as he concedes, "It can get a little crazy ... but this is crazier than average."

Tara rushes up behind Aidan with Nick following close behind her. "What kind of trouble have you gotten yourself into now, husband-of-mine?"

Aidan quickly signs something to Tara.

Her expression darkens like a thundercloud. "I wish those people would get a clue. They're worse than hot pink glitter — no matter how hard you try to get them to go away, they never truly disappear."

Jude watches with wide-eyes as Tara sheds her brightly colored jacket and bangle bracelet. Aidan presents his wrist to his wife where she retrieves the scrunchie he put there earlier. She quickly tames her wild black hair into a smooth ponytail and anchors it with the scrunchie. Right before our very eyes, she transforms into a quiet, subdued interpreter.

"Let's go face this. The monsters we don't know are always worse than the ones we do." Tara signs as she speaks.

As Aidan and Tara leave the room ahead of us, Jude turns to me. "Did you know she could become a totally different person?"

"Yeah, I watched her do it every day when we first met," I recollect with a small smile. "I was one of the privileged few to have a front row seat as those two fell in love."

CHAPTER TEN

JUDE

THE ABRUPT CHANGE FROM a party-like, celebratory mood to whatever's going on here is crazy. There's a sense of danger and foreboding. Everyone seems to be steeling themselves against the unknown. I appear to be the only person who doesn't fully understand what's going on.

Aidan, Tara, Tasha and I, complete with our three bodyguards, move over to the crowd of people in the corner of the room as if we're a swarm of ants. The serious expressions on Logan and Nick's faces are probably enough to scare most fans away with one glance, although this particular group of fans is curiously overdressed for this laid-back venue in a college-town.

A tall woman with her hair in a severe ponytail is texting on her cell phone as Aidan and Tara come up behind her. One of the people in her entourage catches her attention, and she spins around to face Aidan. As the woman begins speaking, Tara does something I've never seen her do much in the whole time I've known them — she begins to quietly interpret everything the woman says. Everyone knows Aidan O'Brien is deaf, but he functions so well with his cochlear implants, it's easy to forget he has any form of hearing deficit. Although Aidan and Tara often use sign language around the office, seeing him formally use Tara as an interpreter is an odd sight.

The woman with the ponytail moves in to give Aidan an air kiss as he instinctively backs away. "Clover Branch. I have to admit, this is probably the last place I ever thought I would see you. Last I checked, you are not my biggest fan," Aidan says pointedly. "The middle of Nebraska hardly seems like your kind of scene."

"That's true — although, I must admit you still put on a heckuva show. However, in this case, you left me no other recourse. My office has tried repeatedly to contact you and Ms. Keeley to no avail. More direct methods were necessary."

"There is no need for you to contact me at all. You have my lawyer's phone number. Since Tasha is employed by Silent Beats Studios, she's covered as well. If you have business to do with us, you can do it through them."

"There seems to be some miscommunication because your lawyer's office isn't returning my phone calls." She almost stamps her foot in frustration.

Aidan waits for Tara to interpret the woman's statement before he answers. "Well, I don't know if my lawyer is handling any matters with Five-Star. I guess the reason they're not responding is because any business

Tasha or I had with Five-Star has been concluded for nearly a decade."

A severe frown forms on the woman's face. "I wish for once, you would listen to what I have to say before you decide everything about me is bad."

"Clover, I have a whole room of people waiting to meet me. They paid good money for their tickets, I can't let them down. For the sake of all of us, just state your business," he says, his signs underscoring his displeasure.

"If you insist," Clover says with a self-satisfied smirk. "Recent events in the news have caused us to go back through our old agreements. In particular, our agreement with Tasha is in question."

Tasha's eyes widen as she looks at Aidan with shock. "What is she talking about?"

Clover pins her gaze on Tasha. "You co-wrote your latest hit with Aidan, correct?

"Well… Yeah. Why?" she answers cautiously, seemingly taken off guard by the question.

"Remember, we had you write a song as part of the competition on *America's Next Star*? Well, our music analysts have determined the song you wrote for our competition is substantially similar to the one currently on the Billboard Top 200 list. This violates your contract with us. We believe we have damages against you."

My hand is on Tasha's waist and I can feel her start to tremble as she asks Aidan, "We came up with that song from scratch. Can they do this?"

"I don't know if I would turn to him for your legal

advice. He may be sitting in the same kettle of hot water as you," the woman snaps at Tasha. "There are some parts of the melody which are remarkably similar to the songs he submitted to our producers."

Aidan steps between them. "Tasha, I'm not sure what's going on. This is not the place to deal with this. We have places to go and people to see — if you'll pardon the cliché. Just remember, this is not the first time Ms. Branch and Five-Star Entertainment have bluffed over a hand they simply overplayed," he adds with a lethal warning in his voice.

Clover steps closer to Tasha. "You're an adult now. Since you are presumably handling your own career, I would urge you to reconsider an offer from Five-Star Entertainment. We can give you better exposure and more radio airplay than a new, untested startup record label. I know you feel some loyalty to Aidan because you're friends, but friendship shouldn't get in the way of a smart business decision. If you were to sign on again with Five-Star Entertainment, I could make all of this legal mess go away and we can start over again with a clean slate."

I don't know who this woman is or anything about the agency she represents. I vaguely remember the drama involving Aidan leaving a television show at the top of his game, but I don't know the details of it all. Being on Aidan's team has been a spectacular move for both Tasha and me. For her to suggest otherwise is a flat-out lie. You don't get much more social media reach than with Aidan O'Brien and Tara Imasu. They have a broad spectrum of fans who are insanely loyal.

Tasha stiffens her spine as she answers in a frosty tone, "You can provide your number to my bodyguard. I'll forward it on to my attorney. If there's something to all the mumbo-jumbo you're spewing, someone will return your call. Otherwise, we're done."

"How can you dismiss an opportunity like this so easily without even talking to me? You don't even know how much our company has grown since *America's Next Star*. We could launch your career into the stratosphere. You're good, and you are even better with Justin over here. You could be like Kelly Clarkson and Justin what's-his-face. You know, like the next hot couple of the pop/country music hybrid."

"My name is Jude," I answer. "I believe Ms. Keeley was clear —"

"I do have one more thing to say," Tasha interjects. "When I was a lonely teenage girl with nothing but hopes and dreams and a little talent, you did nothing to 'help' me. Why are you so interested in me now? If it's because I'm suddenly hot, I've got some news you might find interesting. This tour, right now where the fans are waiting on us all, may be my very last one."

"What do you mean?" Clover asks with shock in her voice. "You sound amazing."

"Sometimes, you have to pursue the dream that's right for you and not the one that's right for everyone else — even when there's a price to pay."

"*Excuse me?* A lot of people have worked really hard to get you where you are right now. Why would you throw it all away? There are thousands, if not hundreds of thousands of girls who would love to be in your shoes. Are you sure you are ready to give that up for … whatever?" The woman gives me a pointed look as if I have something to do with Tasha's decision. "You know … boys — even as cute as he is — are a dime a dozen. Don't give up what you have to chase a relationship."

Tasha raises herself up to her full height — which in her stage boots is quite tall — and goes nose-to-nose with Clover Branch. "I used to look up to you. I thought you had it all together as a professional woman — but now I see I was wrong. You missed a train or two along the way on your journey to become a decent human being."

Clover chokes on a cough and dramatically covers her mouth with her hand, but Tasha pays her theatrics no mind. "Yes, I like Jude. I like him a lot and the reason I like him is because he is the kind of man who, although he disagrees with my decision to give up my career, supports my right to do it. He understands singing has never been my dream. I know you never bothered to ask me what my dream was, but if you had taken the time to listen to my answers way back when I was on your television show, you'd know I've always wanted to be a pediatric nurse. That hasn't changed."

It's all I can do not to puff up my chest and give my woman a standing ovation for her strength as Clover just stands there and silently blinks as she listens to Tasha speak.

Tasha's not about to give up any ground. "I want to go to college like a regular person. I'm sorry if that disappoints you, Aidan, my mother or anyone else. I have the right to make the decision for myself. In answer to your question, if everything goes right in my world, I won't even need your representation. As for the rest of it, I'll let the lawyers sort it all out. All I know is that Aidan and I had a good idea for a song. One day, his family and I went out rock climbing with a bunch of kids and during some downtime we wrote a song. That's about as complicated as the story gets. If you want to make more of it, I can't stop you. This is a big night for us. Let us celebrate it, please."

Suddenly Tasha seems to lose her fire as she turns toward me and wilts into my chest. I give her a brief hug and glare at Clover Branch as I practically growl, "If you'll excuse me, we have other fans to meet. You know, those people who appreciate what we do?"

Tara stops signing and lets her hair down as she tucks the scrunchie back into Aidan's pocket. "Clover, you and I have had a complicated relationship for a long time, but let me spell this out for you. I'm not speaking as Aidan's interpreter right now. I'm speaking as his wife. I watched you suck the joy out of music for my husband. He almost lost everything because of the power games you played. You failed to recognize Aidan has faced bigger, scarier obstacles than you and came out on top. If he could do that back then, when he was waiting tables, imagine what he can do now. So help me, if you try to destroy the career of another musician I love and admire, you can kiss any respectability you have in this field goodbye. Do you have any questions?"

Clover looks taken aback by the anger in Tara's voice as she croaks, "No, thank you. I will be in touch with your lawyers."

Stella, who's been observing our conversation from a distance, walks over and taps Clover on the shoulder. "I know you don't know me and probably don't care who I am in this business. For argument's sake, let's say my contact list reads like an invitation to an after party at the Grammys. I want to give you a few words of friendly advice. You may think you know what's up in the music business. Trust me when I tell you that you don't. You're just a guppy swimming around in a mud puddle. Before you choose to fight a battle you read about in the tabloids while you were buying your rotisserie chicken and tater-tots at the supermarket, you should know it won't give you the notoriety and the credibility with the boss-man and the big-wigs you hope it will. It's gonna buy you a lot of bad karma in this business — karma you can't afford. Before you go to bed tonight, you might want to consider whether you actually want to pick a fight with one of the most popular musicians to ever climb the charts and his new protégé. If you take on Aidan O'Brien and Silent Beats, you will have a bigger fight on your hands than you could imagine."

Clover studies the older redhead as if she's trying to decide if her opinion is worth considering. "My research tells me I'm on solid ground here, but thanks for sharing."

Stella rolls her eyes and shrugs. "Well, honey, when this all comes back to bite you in the butt, don't say nobody never warned you about what would happen when you try to claim rights you don't have to someone else's work."

Stella walks over to Tasha and puts her arm around her shoulder as she escorts us away from the tense situation. "Come on guys, I want you to meet some of your fans. You should see the collage they made for you, Tasha."

<hr>

After the most adrenaline-filled hour of my life, we all end up back in Aidan's suite. Ironically, we are doing what most people do on a Friday night — munching down on pepperoni pizza and watching awful horror movies on Netflix. None of us are truly watching television but it gives us something to focus on while we decompress from the intense meet and greet with fans.

In typical Tasha fashion, she pulls the throw cushions off the couch and tosses them on the floor. I'm propped up behind her and she's cuddled in my lap. Even though she's trying to give the appearance that everything is fine, she's trembling.

Tara hands her a soda. "How are you?"

"I guess I'll survive." Tasha shrugs.

"That's not exactly what I asked. How are you feeling?" Tara asks more pointedly.

"Honestly, I'm more than a little freaked out and quite a lot pissed off. I'm wondering what I ever did to these people to make them want to destroy all my hopes and dreams ... again. I thought they were gone from my life for good. That's why I hired an attorney to take care of all that for me. Why are they back and what could they possibly want from me? I'm not even sure I'm going to do this whole music thing anymore. I'm trying to get into college. Why do they have to mess with me? I can't go to school and fight a lawsuit at the same time."

Tara collapses onto the floor in the most graceful way I've ever seen as she leans over to give Tasha a hug. "Oh Tasha, you have to understand this has never been about you. In reality, it probably wasn't even about Aidan — even though they want to make it seem as if it's all about him. You guys were pawns in a game of chess bigger than you. But guess what? You guys rule the board now. You have all the power."

Tasha shakes her head. "Aidan has the power. I don't have any power. I'm just a half-a-hit nobody. If it weren't for Aidan, I wouldn't even be on the charts. He's the one with the star power, I'm just a coffee shop singer who has a really generous friend."

Before I can voice my own protest, Tara rolls her eyes and openly scoffs. "Oh come on. I was there, remember? There was only one contestant who gave my husband a run for his money and you were only thirteen years old when you pulled it off. You're even better now."

Tasha blushes. "I was almost fourteen, but my mom thought it was better if the producers packaged me as a thirteen-year-old."

"It doesn't matter — fourteen or forty — you have a solid fan base who loves you. Did you forget who won?"

"Yeah, I came in first place because Aidan wasn't in the competition. If I would've had fair competition, there would've been no way I would've won. It didn't do me any good to win. My career still died, so I obviously wasn't all that great."

"Tasha, I don't think it's fair of you to make that kind of judgment. After Aidan left the competition, it all kind of fell apart because it wasn't legitimate. But it's not on you. Your talent was one hundred percent real. Their promotion was sketchy. That's a completely different issue. You had, and continue to have, loyal fans. All you have to do is look at your Twitter account and Facebook feed. It's amazing. You built your fan base up all by yourself.

Tasha slumps back against my chest. "Even if all that's true, what difference does it make if she has the power to take it all away with the stroke of a pen?" All of Tasha's carefully held composure shatters and she sobs. "If it's not my dream anymore, why does it hurt so much to give it up?"

Stella puts her glass of white wine down and clears her throat. "Honey, this world would be a very sad place if you could only have one dream in your whole lifetime. I don't think that's how all this works."

I lean down and kiss the top of Tasha's head. "I hope Stella's right, because I know my dreams have gotten a lot bigger since I met you."

She leans her head back to look at me. "I hate that all of this drama has ruined your first night up on stage. Was it all you wanted it to be?"

"Are you kidding me? It was everything I've dreamed about on steroids. No wonder you guys are always completely jazzed afterward. Although I have a new appreciation for the exhaustion part too. I didn't count on it being so difficult to talk to a few people."

Tasha grins. "Yeah, it's a completely different skill set to talk to people one-on-one. Even so, you did great in both arenas. I thought the girl in the pink denim jacket was going to faint dead away when you started talking to her in Spanish. That was so adorable. I hope someone caught it on video."

"How in the world did she have a sign with my name on it?" I ask, still befuddled by the development. "I didn't even know I was going to sing tonight. How did the fans know?"

Aidan shakes his head. "I have a loyal group of fans who've been with me since the very beginning when I used to sing in hotel lobbies and hole-in-the-wall-beer-joints. They sometimes come on the road with me and follow the bus. It's possible they heard from the crew that you were going to sing and helped recruit other fans."

Tara touches Aidan's shoulder. "Speaking of that, have you been able to coordinate anything with Ruth's family?"

Aidan nods sadly. "Yes, they're postponing the memorial ceremony for a day so we'll be able to attend."

I look over at Tara with a questioning glance, but Tasha is quick to pick up my tension, so she answers my unspoken question. "Ruth was Aidan's number one super fan. She was also one of his oldest. She used to like to send the tabloid tongues a-wagging by planting bright red kisses all over Aidan's face in indelible lipstick. She would simply cackle with delight every time one of those pictures was published in a rag magazine.

More often than not she and Tara would be reading about their 'mad feud' in the paper over tea and cookies the next morning."

Tara looks profoundly sad as she picks up the explanation. "Ruth died this morning and we're trying to find a way to pay tribute to her."

"I knew Ruth, but I never knew her name. She told me to call her Red," I respond with a nostalgic grin. "She would always ask me at every venue to put her in the best spot to take pictures even if it wasn't in the front row. Honestly, I always thought she was related to you."

"Only in my heart," Aidan responds with a soft smile.

"This would cut into your break a little, but you could juggle your media junkets and squeeze something in before your visit to St. Jude's."

Aidan looks at Tara with pleading eyes. "Does this give me a legitimate excuse to skip the media junkets altogether?"

Tara shakes her head with mild disapproval. "Sadly, I don't think so. There are some people counting on you to make a high-profile stop to encourage donations."

Aidan walks over to Jerome and taps him on the shoulder. Jerome practically drops his pizza as he jumps in surprise. "Hey! I was communing with the food here," he protests as he takes his headphones off.

"No problem. I'll let you get back to that in a second — but I need to know if you still have your commercial driver's license."

"Sure do. I help my uncle on his farm when I'm not working with you. Why?"

"After you get a few hours of sleep, I want you to relieve Randall and drive a shift so we can make up some time on the road."

Jerome perks up. "For real? You're going to let me drive the mansion on wheels? This might be the most fun I'd had since my best friend rented a Ferrari for senior prom."

Aidan laughs. "Easy, tiger. I want the whole band to arrive in one piece in Tennessee."

Jerome rubs his hands together with glee as he says, "No sweat. What is that? Three days away? I can probably do it in eighteen hours, tops."

Aidan comically looks around the room as he clutches his chest in mock fear. "I don't suppose anyone else has a CDL?"

"The leg to St. Jude actually takes about 24 hours — give or take," I interject.

"I'd like you and Randall to take the full three days. We were originally scheduled to make the trip in four. I don't want you guys to do anything stupid because you're tired. Ruth's family can't make it until Tuesday anyway."

Jerome sighs as he sets down his pizza. "I'm telling you, Boss, I've got mad skills. It's like I can bend time or something."

Aidan smirks as he replies, "I'm sure you do. I'm just not sure I can afford the traffic tickets required to prove it."

Everyone in the room is laughing at the interplay between Aidan and Jerome. Everyone except Tasha.

CHAPTER ELEVEN

TASHA

I DON'T KNOW WHY the news hit me so hard. I've known all along we were going to go visit St. Jude's Children's Hospital. It's one reason I signed up to go on this tour with Aidan. His commitment to charitable causes is one of the things I like the most about him. He doesn't just throw money at a problem. Aidan becomes personally involved — very personally involved. He knows all about my history with leukemia. It's not like I've kept it a secret or anything, but most of the time I don't even think about it.

Cancer Survivor. Those two words are playing an increasingly large role in my life. Maybe it's all those college essays I've been filling out or the fact that I'm having to repeatedly justify why I want to leave show business to become a nurse. My status as a cancer survivor with capital letters seems to be taking over my life these days. I'm not sure how I feel about that. It's an accomplishment, but it's not really *my* accomplishment.

The doctors and nurses did all the hard work. I

was young enough that I don't remember a whole lot of what happened. I remember a big hospital bed with railings and eating far too much ice cream and pudding. To this day, I become queasy when I look at either. My mom likes to play up how heroic I was throughout my cancer journey, but is it fair to categorize me as a hero if I don't even recall all the details about how horribly sick I was? I don't know. It feels as false as the flippers my mom used to make me wear as a kid to make me look like I had perfect teeth when I had anything but.

Jude walks by my bed on the way out of the bathroom. I try to hide my stress, but I'm not fast enough. He comes and sits on the bed beside me and pulls me close to his side as he says, "So, are you going to tell me what's wrong or do I need to play twenty questions?"

I smile as he repeats what I often ask him. "No wonder you always get annoyed when I say that to you. This will probably sound dumb — but I'm a little nervous about going back to the hospital. I haven't been to St. Jude's in several years. They gave me the all clear when I was about twelve and I haven't had to see an oncologist since then."

"Are you afraid it will be bad luck or something?" Jude asks.

"No, that's not it so much. I guess I'm afraid they'll see me as some sort of role model for their recovery. I barely remember my recovery I don't know what to say to them. Did Aidan tell you this girl specifically requested me for her 'Dreaming While Awake' experience? Can you believe it? That's crazy to me. I'm just a little nobody singer who got chosen for a bogus television show. Of all the famous people on the planet, she wants to meet me? What if she's really sick and doesn't make it? Does this family want to waste their wish on me?"

Jude hugs me close to him. "Why wouldn't she? You're beautiful and kind. You sing better than most pop stars out there, and you're phenomenal to all your fans. Why wouldn't she want to meet you?"

I shrug. "Well, here's an obvious thing — Aidan O'Brien is going to be at the hospital too, and he's a much bigger deal than me — not to mention that Tara's a phenomenal dancer and a beautiful person inside and out. She's been famous for many more years than me."

"*Sirena*, have Aidan or Tara ever had leukemia? Have they ever been a patient at St. Jude's Hospital?"

I shake my head. "No, not that I know of."

"You've made no secret of the fact that St. Jude's helped save your life. It's possible this patient knows that about you and feels some special kinship surrounding your shared past. Or she could like your music or your beautiful long hair. Maybe it's because you're from New York and she is too. You don't know."

"What if she meets me and is disappointed?"

Jude kisses me. "What if you're everything she ever dreamed you'd be? I think that's probably more likely. I know that's what happened when I got to know you."

Jude isn't a guy who speaks in flowery speech. He doesn't write long, intricate poetry. In fact, he doesn't usually say much. When he comes out and says something so incredibly sweet, it means a ton.

I wind my arms around his neck and pull him closer as I kiss him deeply. Pulling away, I whisper, "You've exceeded my every expectation too. I didn't get a chance to tell you earlier today because of all the craziness, but I am so proud of you. You took on your fears like a beast and put the needs of the band in front of your own. In my book, that makes you a hero."

Color rushes into Jude's face. "If you'd known how close I was to throwing up every second I was up on the stage, you probably wouldn't think I was so heroic."

"No, that's what makes it so heroic. You stayed up there even though every instinct told you to run — that made your performance even more epic. Did I mention your performance was amazing? Not just amazing for your first time. Amazing. Period. End of sentence. Drop the mic, you can go home now. I felt like a proud mama."

Jude snorts at me. "I so do not want you to feel that way about me."

I grab the bottom of his T-shirt and pull it over his head as I say, "Okay, how about if I tell you I felt like a very possessive fan? Let's say I was glad I'd already called dibs on your gorgeous self."

Jude gives me a crooked grin. "Oh, I think nearly everyone could tell that. Logan said you just about threw down a cartwheel when you saw him file away the phone numbers he collected instead of giving them to me."

"Do you blame me? Some of those girls were hot!" I exclaim with a pout.

"Were they? I never noticed. The only woman I have eyes for is you."

I chuckle as I respond, "Did I mention you might be the most perfect boyfriend ever?"

"Not recently, but you can spend some time convincing me," Jude suggests.

"That won't be a problem," I promise as I pull the blankets over us.

⚬

I'd met Ruth's daughter, Myrtle on tour once or twice before, but this was my first time meeting her other daughter, Agnes. When I try to formally introduce myself, she skips the handshake altogether and hugs me as she quickly corrects me. "Only the government calls me Agnes. Everyone else calls me Aggie. I'm just so sorry Mama isn't alive to see this. She would've busted her buttons if she would've known her Aidan was going to give her a private concert."

I smile. "Something tells me she probably already knows. She's likely bragging to all of her friends in the world beyond that she has better than front-row seats now."

"You can say that again. Mama was always a little annoyed because most of her friends had already passed on a few years ago and she didn't have anybody left to brag to. She tried to make friends on the Internet, but she always said it wasn't as good as playing a good hand of bunko."

Myrtle looks around the room and whispers, "You know, it's too bad y'all don't have a few of those paparazzi following you around. Mama would have loved it. There was nothing she liked better than a big ole juicy tabloid story. She didn't even care if it was true. She just liked the huge, splashy pictures."

An idea hits me and I hold my finger up. "If you'll excuse me, I need to speak to Aidan and Tara for a moment. Just so I'm clear, you guys both want copious amounts of trashy news coverage of your mom's funeral?"

Aggie's brows furrow for a moment. "Well, I don't necessarily want Jerry Springer and his whole crew here, but a tad trashy would be fun because it's what Mama would've wanted."

"I want to make this everything you need it to be, so let me see what I can do," I promise as I dig through the contact list on my phone.

I track Aidan and Tara down on the bus. Aidan's thumbing through his song library trying to come up with an appropriate play list for the memorial service.

When he sees me approach, he asks, "Can I help you?"

"Honestly, I don't know. I have an off-the-wall request. I'm trying to make Ruth's family happy. Does Madison still have all of her contacts in the newspaper industry?"

Aidan looks a little confused by my question. "I really don't know. You'll have to ask her. Why?"

"Okay… Keep in mind this wasn't my idea. Ruth's

daughters thought it would be a great idea to have the paparazzi cover the memorial service."

Aidan does a double take and reaches up to check his cochlear implant. "I'm sorry, I thought you said they *want* the paparazzi to attend."

"That is what I said," I respond. "That's why I thought it would be a good idea to involve Madison. At least she'd know who was ethical and would treat the story with the appropriate amount of respect. I don't want it to be twisted into something sick and morbid."

Aidan cringes. "And you've got how long to pull off this miracle?"

"Until tomorrow afternoon." The enormity of the task starts to hit me. "Darn me and my mouth. Perhaps I should've thought ahead before I promised the whole world."

Tara shakes her head at me. "Tasha, girlfriend, you'll need to invoke the powers of the Girlfriend Posse for this."

Of course, I've heard about the legendary powers of the Girlfriend Posse. I just never thought I'd actually be included in it. "Really? Do you think it's possible?"

"Oh, absolutely. We've married two couples in a single day and planned whole weddings in a couple days, we can rustle you up some paparazzi. That's not a big deal."

"Thank goodness. I thought for a moment I had promised the impossible."

———•———

"Ma! Stop screaming at me. I was supposed to look terrible. We were at a funeral for God's sake. Yes, I know the media was there. That's what happens when I perform on a public stage. People are interested in what happens in my life. Ruth Ackerman was my friend, and I was honored to perform at her memorial service. I'm sorry I didn't measure up to your standards."

I set my phone down in my lap as I pull my hair back in a ponytail and put in new earrings. I can still hear my mother ranting and raving. Much to my embarrassment, she starts to go on about the alleged relationship between Ruth and Aidan. I look up at Aidan in horror as he scowls at the phone. I know it's bad when he can hear it from across the bus and over the road noise, even through the distortion of his cochlear implants.

He motions for me to hand him the phone. I reluctantly hand it down the line of people until it reaches Aidan.

"Ms. Keeley? How are you today?" he asks, pleasantly at first. My mom must be doing some industrial-strength backpedaling because Aidan looks amused. Then he looks annoyed as he says, "Ms. Keeley, I know we've had this discussion before, but I feel the need to remind you that you're calling your daughter's workplace. Repeatedly, inappropriately, and without her permission. We have both asked you to stop. Do I need to make things clearer?"

Aidan's lips thin out to a grim line and his voice hardens. "No ma'am. You misunderstand the situation. I

116

am not in charge of your daughter's life and neither are you. She's a fully grown adult who makes her own decisions. I am her employer, her friend and her mentor. If she chooses to follow my advice, I am honored. However, she doesn't need to follow my suggestions ... or yours. If my mother or anyone I knew spoke to me the way you speak to your daughter, I would run the other direction as quickly as I possibly could. Perhaps you should keep that in mind. For the rest of the day, none of us will be available by telephone because we have a prior engagement. Tasha will contact you when she's ready. Please don't bother her until she's ready to speak to you."

Aidan hits the end button on my phone and hands it to the person next to him. It quickly passes back to me.

Logan, who's sitting beside me, digs through his backpack and hands me a phone.

"What's this?" I ask as he tries to hand me a box.

"It's what it looks like — a new phone." Logan crosses his arms. "You shouldn't have to deal with crap from your mom. It's like an emotional water-boarding every time she calls you. This phone has a new number. I've set it up with a masking number for texting so she won't be able to tell where you're texting from or call you directly. That way you can check on your grandma anytime you need to."

I don't know if it's the recent verbal attack from my mom, the fact that we are on the way to St. Jude's, or the stress of the tour, but I feel like I am about to snap like a frayed guitar string.

"Do you guys even understand how ridiculous it is that you have to protect me from my own mother? It's crazy! She should be on my side. You shouldn't have to bend over backward and do special favors for me because my mom is being a bully."

Logan shrugs. "We've dealt with weirder stuff. It's no big deal. This helps protect you from your other issue too, so we're killing two birds with one stone. Don't sweat it." He winks at me. "Besides, you're a girl, right? I thought all girls went googly eyed over the latest phones and snazzy cases."

I stick my tongue out and blow a raspberry at him. "Obviously, you haven't checked out my bell-bottoms and Birkenstocks recently. I'm not exactly your traditional high-tech girl."

Jude nods. "She has a point. She writes most of her music in a spiral notebook. I haven't converted her to the computer yet."

"Okay, I take it back. You don't have to take this because you're a girl. But I want you to take it to be safe. Please?"

I pluck it from his fingers and take the phone out. Much to my surprise, it's already customized. I raise an eyebrow and ask, "Pretty sure I would take it, were you?"

"Eventually," Logan says. "Between your mom and Creepy Stalker Dude, things are getting dicey."

"Have we heard more from him?" Goosebumps chill my skin.

"No, not specifically, but with those new pictures

hitting the Internet, I expect we'll be hearing something any day," Logan says grimly.

Aidan draws my attention. "Tasha, are you ready for this? You'll be meeting with a girl by the name of Hayden Riley Rose. She's thirteen years old. She developed bone cancer and they've had to amputate part of her arm. She has been a fan of yours since you were on TV with me. According to her mom, she would like to talk to you because you know what it's like to go through cancer."

My heart skips a beat and my throat goes dry as I admit to Aidan, "I don't know if I remember what it was like. I was pretty little. I remember being tired and sick, but she's older than I was when I went through chemotherapy so she'll remember things in a lot more detail than I can."

"Tasha, all I can tell you is that you don't have to do the talking. Sometimes all you have to do is listen," Aidan replies softly with a sympathetic smile.

Right. I can listen. That's what I'll do. I'll simply listen.

Jude reaches out and grabs my hand. "*Sirena*, you listen better than anyone I know. You seem to know what I'm going to say before I say it. You'll know what to say. I don't have any doubt you'll do fine."

━━━●━━━

I lean against Jude and I realize how quickly I've become more than a little accustomed to his steadying arm around my waist. I wasn't this nervous when I competed at nationals in the Miss Fantabulous Pageant or when I was on *America's Next Star*. Yet there's something about meeting this particular fan which has my stomach tied in knots.

I clutch the special CD Aidan and I made for her in one hand and a bouquet of brightly colored balloons in the other as Jude subtly guides me forward through the doorway.

"Oh my gosh!" an enthusiastic voice calls from inside the room. "My cousin Juliann won't believe this!"

"Hayden, you might want to introduce yourself first before you burst their eardrums," an older woman chastises gently.

"Sorry, Mom — but it's true. Juliann would have kittens if she knew Jude is here!"

Jude stops dead in his tracks and his jaw drops open. "I'm sorry… Did you say my name? You know who I am? I'm just the equipment manager."

Hayden's mom takes the gifts from me and sets them on a bedside table as she watches her daughter with amusement.

Hayden shakes her head and grins. "Nuh-uh. That's what you *used* to do. Now you're a singer like Tasha. My cousin saw you in Nebraska. She sent me clips on Snapchat. She said it was totally awesome. She was adopted when she was little and she doesn't have any people in her neighborhood who speak Spanish and you talked to her like a regular person. She told me she about passed out. She said she was super embarrassed, but she thought it was the coolest thing ever."

I elbow Jude in the ribs. "There you go. You've got a third fan member in your official fan club. You're on a roll now."

"I'm sure he's got way more. You two were wicked good together. You should put out an album. It would probably be better than Alex and Sierra. I like their stuff — I just wish it was more country."

"I appreciate your feedback. I'm brand-new at this singing thing. I'm grateful you like it, though. Tasha is the real star here. I wouldn't be here without her."

I blush at his compliment and try to deflect it. "Don't let him sell you short. Jude has phenomenal talent. You can't teach what he has."

Hayden shrugs. "I used to be musical." She holds up the stump of her arm. What's left is still angry, red and swollen. "All the plans I had for my life, including being part of the Boston Pops Orchestra, are gone now. I can't play the piano like this."

I feel like a third-rate jerk. I try to tamp down my growing anxiety by taking a deep breath. This is exactly what I was afraid would happen. I try to remember Aidan's advice as I sit down in the chair next to Hayden's bed. "I remember these rooms so well. Did they ever fix the noisy heaters?"

Hayden smiles. "This room isn't so bad, but the last room I was in had a weird rattle. You had leukemia when you were little, right?"

I nod. "Yeah, I got sick when I was around two years old. I kept falling down and getting bruises which never got better — at least that's what my mom tells me. I don't remember much. I was pretty sick and very young."

Hayden winces as her IV pulls when she adjusts herself in bed. "Lucky you. I remember too much. But you're all better now —"

I answer carefully, not sure how much to disclose — but I feel like I should be honest. "Mostly. They say I've been in remission long enough I probably won't have a relapse. Unfortunately, there are some lasting effects of the leukemia. It's not likely I'll have children in the future. They weren't able to do anything with my ovaries because I was too little."

Hayden looks sympathetic. "I'm sorry. That sucks. I have Ewing's sarcoma. They were able to get mine by removing my arm, so they don't think I have to do the heavy-duty stuff that's going to kill everything in my body. At least not yet."

"I guess that's a little good news among a bunch of bad news."

"Yeah, I'm trying to think of it that way but it's hard. I used to be really good at the piano, and now I don't know what I'm going to do."

"I totally get it. Sometimes you have to change your plans even when your heart doesn't want to. Do you know much about my boss, Aidan?"

Hayden shrugs. "He's kinda old — but he plays the piano good. I didn't start watching *America's Next Star* until after he left, though."

"There was a time in Aidan's life when he planned to play the piano professionally. Like hardcore, on the classical music circuit. He was that good."

"What happened? Did he stop practicing?"

I nod. "For a while, he had to because he completely lost his hearing. He got meningitis when he was a little younger than you. He completely lost his ability to play music. He had to totally reteach himself to play."

"How does he play music if he can't hear?"

"Aidan uses cochlear implants, but he'll never hear music the same way as he did when he could hear. He tells me it's like hearing music through really muffled, staticky speakers that are tuned between two radio stations."

"Wow. I wonder why he didn't just give up," Hayden says with awe in her voice.

"I don't know. I'm sure he was discouraged lots of times. He's heard people tell him he can't do things a lot more times than he can count. Aidan is one of those people who has to live, eat and sleep music. I don't think his soul would be happy without it, so he had to find a way to make it work."

Hayden holds up her amputated arm. "What if I'm not like Aidan? What if I can't reinvent myself to be better than I was before?"

"There isn't just one path to be successful. Besides, Aidan's recovery took years and he had a lot of stumbles along the way. He wasn't a rock star right from the beginning. It took him more than a decade. This hasn't even been a year, right?" I gesture toward her bandaged arm.

Hayden giggles. "No! Like not even a month. I'm

still learning to do things with my left hand. I'll get a prosthetic arm as soon as my stump heals completely."

Hayden's mom, Pennie walks over to the bed and hands her a large iPad. "I think you should show them."

An embarrassed expression crosses Hayden's face as she glances at her mom. "It's not as good as I used to do. I don't think they'll like it."

"Like what?" I ask.

Hayden blushes. "Oh, you'll probably think this is stupid, but I like to draw — or I used to. So, the occupational therapists hooked me up with this drawing app on the computer. I made some drawings of you and Jude. I wasn't even going to show you, but somebody here opened her big mouth —"

"Hey, if you can draw anything better than stick figures, you're way better than me."

Jude snorts as he says in a conspiratorial tone, "She's not kidding, you know. She barely knows how to turn one of those on. I had to show her where the home button was. She's very old-school. She likes pencils with erasers."

Hayden turns to me. "True?"

I nod. "Unfortunately. I draw like a toddler."

"Really?" Hayden hides her giggle behind her hand. "I kinda thought all the artistic stuff was interchangeable."

I chuckle softly. "I guess I got all my coordination in my toes and ankles. I can plié and pirouette with the best of them. Ask me to draw a puppy dog or horse and I'm lost."

"You're funny! You remind me of my big sister, Jayne. She's at college now. She's going to a fancy fashion design school in Chicago. It's a long way from where we live so I don't get to see her very often. She told me not to die because she would be really sad. If you couldn't sing for a living, what would you do?"

It takes my brain a second to catch up with all the things Hayden just told me and to sort through her non sequitur.

It hasn't been that long since I was her age, but I feel so much older. It amazes me that I was on national television at thirteen. It felt like life and death at the time, but it was nothing compared to what Hayden is facing now. I haven't told anyone outside my inner circle about my plans, but I think now is as good a time as any so I walk over to the table and hand Hayden my CD I made with Aidan and Jude.

I lower my voice to a whisper. "I'm about to tell you something I need to stay between us for now. Can you keep a secret?"

Hayden nods eagerly.

"You know how I talked before about dreams and how they change?"

She looks at me wide-eyed and nods very slowly.

"Well, a very long time ago while I sat in a bed very similar to the one you're sitting in I decided I wanted to be a pediatric oncology nurse."

"But ... That's not what you do —"

"It's not what I do now, but it's what I *want* to do. So, I've applied to several colleges and I'm trying to get scholarships to go to school."

"*Oh my Gosh!* You're just going to *stop* being Tasha Keeley?" Hayden asks with a look of befuddlement. "But you have *two* songs on the charts right now. You worked really hard to get them there. Why would you change your life now?"

"I know. I never planned to be a singer at all; it was my mom's plan for me. I've always wanted to be a nurse. It was other people who wanted me to be a star. Don't get me wrong, I love being a singer. I'm like Aidan. A part of me will always be a musician, but it's not all of who I am."

"How do you know you won't miss it?" Hayden asks.

"I don't," I reply with brutal honesty. "That's what makes all of this so scary. I could try something new and be epically bad at it. All those people who tell me that it's a bad bet and that I should stick to what I know could be right. I could be taking a risky gamble on myself. This could be the worst idea I've ever had. I just don't know, and some nights I don't sleep very well because I think about it all the time."

"Me too. The therapists and psychologists keep throwing new ideas at me about how I should think about my life as a 'differently-abled' person now. I don't want to think. I just want to think about going to the eighth-grade dance and playing basketball. But I can't do that now. I have to think about the big things, and I don't know how to think about the big things anymore. When I start to plan for the big things, the little things start to bug me — like how do I button my pants, tie my shoelaces, or open a package of gum? I'm so tired of thinking, I could scream."

"Oh Hayden, I'm sorry cancer has turned your world into such a scary place. Being a teenager is frustrating enough without all the extra worry. So, how about this? We'll be each other's secret sounding boards. If you get overwhelmed, you can tell me and I'll listen. I'll keep you up-to-date with what's going on with me and maybe if I need some help to figure out the technology for college, you can help with that too."

Hayden smiles at me. "That sounds like a good idea. If what Jude said is true, you'll need all the help you can get. That drawing application I have is a great stress reliever. You can draw flowers and other stuff on it. It has a built-in coloring page. All you have to do is color between the lines if you want."

"I'd like to see what you made," I encourage.

"Okay, but just remember before this happened, I was much better with my right hand." Hayden is clearly stalling.

"Hello? You're talking to the girl who can't draw a stick figure."

Hayden grabs the tablet and swipes her finger across a few buttons. Suddenly, a picture of Jude pops up. She nailed his expression perfectly.

"Wow, this is pretty good. How did you do that?"

"I told you — my cousin sent me pictures from the concert in Nebraska. She stood in line to see you guys and got some good close-up snapshots."

"You did this all on this little tablet-y thing?" I examine the picture carefully.

Jude raises his eyebrow at Hayden. "Did I not tell you? Technology isn't her thing."

I roll my eyes at Jude. "Hey! I can tweet and take a selfie." I turn to Hayden. "Is there any way to make a copy of this? I'd like one because I think it's great."

"Seriously? It's not as good as what I used to be able to do."

"I love it because you made it. Did you draw one of me?"

Hayden takes the tablet back from me and flips it over to another picture.

It's a picture of me playing my guitar. "This one is cool, too. I'm glad your mom nagged you into showing me. I know it's not what you're used to doing, but they're still great. You haven't lost your artistic eye."

Hayden blushes. "Even though I think you're just being nice, I appreciate your vote of confidence. There's a printer in the office next to the play room. The staff lets us print out greeting cards and stuff. They probably wouldn't mind if we printed these out."

"This might be the coolest thing I've ever received from a fan. Thank you so much." I hug her carefully.

"I bet you won't forget me, huh?"

"I don't think there's any danger of that. Hayden, I'll remember you forever. I expect you to be in the front row when I graduate from nursing school."

"I don't know if I can do that, Tasha. What if it's at the same time as my high school graduation?"

"Well, that's a problem I would be happy to have."

"Here's to two girls figuring out a master plan to rule the world." Hayden gives me a high five.

Chapter Twelve

Jude

As I look around the room of the quaint house in Belle Meade, I can't believe how much my life has changed in just a couple of years. My mom would love this city. I wish she had the opportunity to travel as much as I do. There's so much to see here. The vibe is so much different in Nashville than anywhere else I've ever been. Every place you look there is a different motif.

A loud crash from the other room draws my attention. As I peek around the corner, I encounter Tasha sprawled flat on her butt with a suitcase handle in her hand. "Shoot! I should've listened to Mindy. She told me to get a new set of luggage before this trip. One of these days, I'll learn to take her advice seriously. She never seems to be wrong."

"What does Mindy have to do with your suitcase?" I ask as I try to figure out Aidan's honorary niece's place in the conversation.

Tasha gazes up at me with a puzzled expression.

"Oh, I thought you knew. Both Tara and Mindy seem to have some sort of psychic ability. At first, I was a skeptic — but now I have seen enough to pay attention." She sighs as she shows me the broken handle. "Or at least I should have. Maybe if I had, this would still be in one piece."

"Oh, poor *Sirena*," I say as I help her up and try to hide my smile. "I'm sorry, I know that was your favorite suitcase. What can I do to make you feel better?"

"I know it's stupid to be sentimental about luggage, but my grandpa gave me this suitcase before he died. He told me I would be going places in this world. I guess as long as I used this suitcase, I always felt like I was invincible and Papa could never be wrong."

"I'm sorry, Tasha. I believe you're going places whether you choose to stay on the stage or be by someone's bedside. I know you'll make your mark on this world. You were phenomenal with Hayden the other day."

"Do you think so?" Tasha raises an eyebrow. "I felt like the words were tumbling out of my mouth. I didn't always know what to say. Hayden's such a sweetheart to be going through so much pain."

"I agree, but Pennie was really grateful you handled it all so well."

"It kind of puts my broken suitcase handle in perspective, doesn't it?" Tasha remarks with a shrug. "Hey… do you want to get out of here? As nice as Stella's place is, I want you to see more of Nashville while we're here. It would be a shame if you didn't get to experience it all."

Grabbing my cowboy hat off the bed, I pick up Tasha's purse and hand it to her. "Do we need anything else?"

"No, this should do it. You just need to have an open mind, accepting heart and an adventurous spirit," Tasha says as she tosses her hair over her shoulder.

I suppose I should be worried about the challenging tone in her voice, but I'm too busy pinching myself that this beautiful woman who is walking out the door in front of me is my girlfriend and we're on vacation in Nashville with no one to please but ourselves.

By the time my good sense catches up to me, she's already out by our tricked-out rental car. The guy behind the reservation counter took one look at Tasha and "accidentally" upgraded us to a convertible. Tasha claims she has absolutely no idea how it happened and that it couldn't possibly be related to her legs which are a mile and a half long and gorgeous.

She looks at me. "You want to drive or do you want me to?"

I toss her the keys. "Since you know the city, you can play tour guide this time."

"Sounds good. Are you 'I want to look good in my jeans hungry' or 'Give me the best food on the planet that'll stick to my ribs hungry?'"

"You have met me, correct? Since when do I care about how I look in my jeans?" I smirk.

"I don't know. I just thought I'd ask. Logan's been showing me pictures of the amount of fan mail that's come in for you since you started joining Aidan on the stage. You might be getting ready for your own fashion shoot or something."

"Yeah … right … I've done like three little gigs with him. I don't know what's going on, but it doesn't make me a star. That first night was fun, but those were unusual circumstances. I don't know if we'll ever repeat the magic."

"All your fan mail can't be wrong. I think you have the makings of a huge star. There's no one like you, and you're an amazing artist. I think you're being a little hard on yourself. There are a lot of people who hang around Aidan — have you noticed him throwing anyone else up on stage?" Tasha asks me with a serious expression on her face.

"Well, there's Mindy —" I let my voice trail off.

"Uh hmm." Tasha nods her head. "and what have we established about Mindy?"

"That she is ridiculously talented at everything she ever tries to do." I concede.

"Exactly. If you weren't totally gifted at what you do, you wouldn't have caught Aidan's eye. I kid you not, he has tapes, DVDs YouTube videos and everything in-between being pitched at him, literally twenty-four/seven. He's listened to thousands of voices so far this year. If Aidan says you're good, you are good. You can't escape that. It doesn't matter if you're shy about it or don't want to make a big deal out of it. The fact remains, Aidan O'Brien and apparently several other people in your life have already come to the same conclusion: You are amazing."

I feel my face heat up as I blush. I've never blushed so much in my entire life. Before I met Tasha, I thought blushing was something mostly prepubescent girls did, but I do it on a fairly regular basis around her. I don't even know what to say in response to all her praise. All along, Tasha has been my biggest supporter. I couldn't have done it without her unyielding support and her constant cheerleading and sometimes poking and prodding my fragile male ego to goad me into believing better of myself than I ever have before.

"Okay, I accept that Aidan thinks I'm talented. It's weird — but I'm adjusting. The fan thing though, I'm not sure I'll ever get used to it. I've been virtually invisible for so long, the fact that people think I'm sexy when I'm just standing around is beyond strange."

Tasha grabs my hand and leads me into the restaurant. "Oh trust me, people thought you were sexy when you were merely standing around before. They just weren't bold enough to say anything."

I snicker. "All people, or just certain people? I'm not sure I'm exactly comfortable with everyone on our crew thinking I'm cute. I mean, I like Stella and all, but she's more like my *abuela*. I don't think I want to imagine her having a crush on me."

"Okay, maybe not all people, but I certainly noticed you a long time before we started dating."

As we enter the restaurant, I notice it's full of music memorabilia and art, and absolutely packed full of people. "What's so special about this place?"

"I can't really explain Puckett's to you. It's something you should experience firsthand — but trust me, you'll be happy you did. The food here is amazing." Tasha grins.

"I sort of guessed from the size of the crowd." I look around in dismay. "I wonder if we'll even be able to get a table."

Tasha smiles mysteriously. "Of course we will. I made reservations two weeks ago."

"Sneaky! You made this sound like it was a spur-of-the-moment adventure," I half-heartedly complain.

"It's an adventure for you, but somebody had to plan the vacation."

"Now, you sound like my mother. One time when we were little, she scraped up enough money to take Fernanda and me to Disney World, but she'd spent so much time planning the vacation that she couldn't relax enough to just enjoy it."

"Well, after you strike a deal with Aidan, you'll have to take your mom on an exotic vacation she doesn't plan. Where do you think she'd like to go?"

I pause to think about her question. "I don't really know. There are so many places my mom has never been. I think she'd like Nashville a lot because it's so pretty here and there are so many things to see. I think she'd like the scenery in Utah and Arizona. She'd love the trees we have in Oregon, but she'd also like to see the Lincoln Memorial in Washington, DC."

"That sounds like a great travel plan. It's totally different than traveling with my mom. We used to travel all the time when we were on the pageant circuit. For my mom, it was all about impressing other people with where she stayed. As a kid, I found hotel rooms to be universally boring no matter what name they had on the outside of the building. Sure, some of them had better bells and whistles than others — but they were all pretty much the same. I could never understand my mom's obsession with brand-name things. I'm not sure who she thought she was impressing with our travel plans. I can tell you, it wasn't me."

"So, I take it you wouldn't go on vacation with your mom if you had the opportunity?"

"No, not right now. She's too busy tearing down everything I try to do. Maybe someday, but the way our relationship is at the moment, I don't think it's possible."

"I'm sorry, *Sirena*. I wish things were better between you and your mom. I wish your *madre* was a better person and could see what an amazing person you are." I pull her closer to my side and wrap my arm around her waist.

Just then, the hostess calls us back to our table. Much to my surprise, there's a stage a few feet in front of me. "Are we expecting entertainment?"

"I don't know. I guess it depends on the schedule."

After we study our menus and place her orders, I turn to Tasha and ask, "What's it like for you to listen to other people sing?"

She gives me a puzzled look. "If they're not craptastically bad, I generally enjoy it. Why? Don't you?"

"I do, but since I've moved over to the performing side, my view has changed. I used to see songs from a songwriter's perspective, but now that I've been on stage, I see it differently. I just wondered what you see when you watch other performers."

Tasha nods and smiles. "Oh, that … It's why I prefer to listen to music on the radio. If I just listen, I'm not distracted by stuff and I can just listen to the music for the sake of the pure art of it. When I see someone perform live, I get distracted by the most benign things like 'Gee, I wonder if her shoes are comfortable' or 'That was a really long note to hold.'"

"That's exactly what I'm talking about. I was listening to Aidan perform one of his latest releases. The band was going at it. I noticed he was getting very winded. I thought, 'Man, the songwriter should've put a bridge in there somewhere to give the artist a chance to catch their breath.' Before I actually performed onstage, I never realized how much energy we expend running around and interacting with the audience. I would've never thought of how important that was when I was only looking at it as a songwriter."

"I understand what you're saying. The mechanics of singing are different than the art. It's hard for me to hear my own voice on tape. You'd think by now I'd be used to it — but I hate watching myself on tape or hearing my own voice. This makes the recording process difficult for me because sometimes we have to record several takes of the same track and Aidan will want me to pay attention to a certain inflection in my voice he wants me to repeat, but all I can focus on is how pitchy I sound that day or if I've got nasal congestion or some bizarre artifact in my voice."

"That's strange for me to hear because you seem so confident in all of your performances. It doesn't seem possible to me that you're ever insecure about how you sound."

Tasha gives me a grim smile. "That's years of pageant training ingrained in me. It's all about 'fake it till you make it' and never letting anyone see you break under pressure. I suppose I should call my mom and thank her for making me as tough as nails."

"Let's not do anything rash. We're supposed to be on vacation and having fun. Conversations with your *madre* are rarely fun."

Tasha wrinkles her nose. "You can say that again."

* * *

Tasha is right, the food here is delicious. The entertainment has also been phenomenal. Watching people perform music from every decade in every conceivable genre has been enlightening. Because this is Nashville, most of the performers have been related to country, but the wide variety of songs covered is astonishing.

An alarm goes off on Tasha's phone and she consults it briefly before grabbing my hand. "Come on, it's time for the adventure to begin."

"What adventure?" I ask with trepidation.

"You wanted quintessential Nashville, this is it. There's no time like the present to make your dreams come true."

"Do I even want to know what you mean?"

"Knowing you, you probably don't want to think about it too hard."

"What did you do, Tasha?" A feeling of dread grows in my stomach.

"Well, I may have done a little more than make reservations a couple weeks ago. Sometimes, being Aidan O'Brien's tour buddy comes with some cool perks. He knows the manager here personally. I was able to get us a gig here tonight, and it starts in twenty minutes."

"You have to be kidding me!" I exclaim as my panic level hits the stratosphere. "I don't even have my instruments with me, and I'm not even close to being ready to go on stage. Neither one of us has even warmed up."

"Jude, you know me better than that. I take care of you. Our gear is backstage, I had it delivered earlier while we were eating. We've got time to warm up there. You've got this. This isn't anything compared to what we've been doing with Aidan. This is a small group of people eating dinner. They may or may not even pay attention to us."

"I don't think you understand. I have to be prepared for this. I haven't made a play list or anything. I don't know if I can do this."

"Just pretend it's a jam session with the crew. You do great during those. You're an amazing musician. You've done so well with Aidan on stage, you can do this too. I'll be right up there with you. It's no big deal."

I try to breathe in and out slowly to calm my nerves. I know Tasha's trying to be helpful and understanding, but that's not how her words sound right now. Her words sound like a challenge. A challenge I'm destined to fail.

"How do you always talk me into *loco* stuff like this?" I respond after a few moments, but my voice is shaky. This is a bad sign. I'm not even on stage and I haven't started singing yet.

Tasha winks at me. "Just relax and have fun. That's what this is all about."

⸻ ◆ ⸻

As we're about to go on stage, the manager claps me on the back and says, "I've heard great things about the two of you. Go out and kill it."

I know he means it as encouragement, but for me it's like the last straw. My stomach tightens and the lump in my throat grows. Somehow I manage to choke out, "Thank you, it's an honor to be here."

I'm sure Tasha can feel my hands are sweaty as we walk hand-in-hand to our stools on the stage. Tasha straps on her guitar and then introduces us to the audience.

"Hello, Nashville! My name is Tasha Keeley. This is my friend, Jude Hernandez. We're pretty unlikely country music fans — I mean I'm from New York and Jude here looks like a hunky movie star. Nonetheless, we're here in Nashville and we'd like to sing you a few songs. I hope you enjoy what we've come up with."

With that, Tasha plays the introduction to *Islands in the Stream*. The campy duet is probably the perfect song to get the crowd on our side. For a few moments, I try to relax into the song — but I can't. The sound of the patrons dining roars in my ears. It's all I can hear. The tinkling of ice cubes in glasses and the scrape of utensils against plates is deafening. I dart a quick worried look at Tasha, but she doesn't seem to notice anything is amiss.

My nerves are getting the best of me and I miss a couple of chords. Tasha notices and tries to cover for me as she flashes me a quick concerned glance. I mentally curse myself. I haven't played guitar this poorly since I first started learning.

Tasha is quick to recognize my flub as a sign of my nerves. After we finish *Islands in the Stream*, she transitions into *Wichita Lineman* which is one of my favorite songs. I know it forward, backward, and inside out. I breathe a sigh of relief as I settle into my comfort song. I should be able to do it without any problems at all. I can do this one from rote memory, right? At least, that's what I'm telling myself as my heart races and sweat pours down my back. I don't understand this, I thought I had beaten this crap. I've been onstage with Aidan in front of an arena full of people and not had this much trouble. I can barely catch my breath. I can't get settled into the song. I can barely choke the words out to a song I can sing in my sleep. My vision goes grey around the edges and I sway a bit on the stool.

I shoot Tasha a look of panic as the song mercifully ends. She takes one look at me and places the card where we wrote our play list under her stool. That small motion has been our symbol one of us is going off script.

Tasha steps up to the microphone at the front of the stage and says, "I don't know how many of you remember me from what seems like forever ago, but I was actually the winner of a little TV show called *America's Next Star*. I'm going to perform my winning song and then I'll sing my current single, *These Jagged Wounds*."

I know what she's doing; I totally get why she felt like she had to do it. Even so, it makes me feel even worse that I'm not able to be present and available to support her like we planned.

I adjust my mic so the sound level is down in case I mess up again as I accompany her on my acoustic guitar. I want to disappear and fall through the floor at this moment. Not that I'm wishing for the apocalypse or anything, I just wish I could vanish. At this second, it feels like everything we've worked toward accomplishing is gone. I'm back to being the guy who can write songs but can't perform them. What if Tasha is wrong and I'm not destined to be anything other than an equipment monkey?

At the end of her songs, Tasha pauses and takes a drink of water. She glances over at me and whispers, "You ready to go get the song in a big way so we can finish on a high note?"

I nod mutely as I struggle not to pass out right in front of the audience. My face feels so numb it's as if I've been skiing the luge without protective gear. I'm frozen. The honest truth is I have no idea what's going to happen next. Breathing has become nearly impossible and I don't know if any words will come out of my mouth. If they do, I have no idea what they're going to sound like. It's almost as if my hands are paralyzed and I can't even play the guitar.

Tasha plays the introduction to *Imagine* by John Lennon. This has become a quintessential favorite of ours and the fans seem to love my country twist on it. This should make things easier. Inexplicably, it's not easier. After we play the introduction, Tasha waits for me to start to sing like I always do. When I miss my cue, she begins the introduction again.

I open my mouth to sing and nothing happens. I look to her with abject terror and mouth the words, "I'm sorry" as I lay my guitar across my knees. Gamely, Tasha finishes the song as if nothing was out of the ordinary. There's a large swell of applause when we finish our gig and leave the stage.

Tasha has her arm around my waist and is supporting nearly all of my body weight as she helps me to a beat-up leather couch. She picks up a napkin from a nearby table and wipes the sweat from my face. "What happened, Jude? I thought you had this. I intended this to be easy and fun. This wasn't meant to be the tough stuff. We're on vacation. It was supposed to be the stuff of fantasies and dreams, not your worst nightmare."

Chapter Thirteen

Tasha

As soon as I utter those words, I want to take them back. I know I can't. It's far too late. Jude looks like I punched him in the gut with brass knuckles. I want to kick myself. Sometimes my tendency to babble comes back to bite me in the ass. I'm not angry at Jude for freezing on stage. Honestly, I'm just frustrated — and ticked off at myself. I thought things were going so well, and then suddenly they weren't — but I don't know how to fix it.

It's clear that whatever I just did was the opposite of helpful. Jude won't even look at me. I flag down a waitress and order a Seven and Seven. Because of my height, most people don't even question my age, or perhaps she saw what happened on stage and took pity on me. I don't know or care at this point — but a few minutes later, she comes back with the drink.

I walk back over to where Jude is sitting, hand him the drink and quietly sit down.

He takes a sip and wrinkles his nose. "What is

this? If alcohol was going to solve my problems, don't you think I would've tried it a long time ago?"

I recoil from the viciousness in his voice. "Jude, I'm sorry. I was trying to be supportive. I didn't mean to sound like a jerk. I admit what I said sounded terrible, but that's not how I meant it. I've had bad nights on stage too."

Jude pins me with an angry glare with his jaw set. "It was a little more than a bad night, don't you think? I couldn't even sing or play. I warned you this might happen — but you didn't listen to me. You let me believe I could overcome it all. Well, I just showed you, didn't I?"

I am stunned into silence. I don't even know how to respond. Jude is right. What if I *did* push him into something he wasn't comfortable with? What if this is all my fault? I had to go and stretch his boundaries and dare him to do things outside his comfort zone. From the moment we met, I have done nothing but push, prod and cajole him into being someone else. *Oh my Gosh! When exactly did I turn into my mother?*

I turn back to him with tears in my eyes. "I can't argue. I won't. You're right. I shouldn't have pushed you so hard. I'm so sorry. I hope you don't hate me now. I'm going to catch a cab back to Stella's place and give you some space. I need you to know I never, ever meant to hurt you. Seeing you reach your dreams has given me courage to pursue my own. Please know I never meant to cause any damage, I swear."

Jude puts a hand on my arm as I stand up to leave. "*Sirena*, you don't have to do that. I'm mostly angry at myself, not you."

"I know, but you have every right to be angry at me. I put you in a bad situation. I shouldn't have done that. I'll talk to you later." I place my hand over his on my arm and squeeze.

As I slowly walk out of the crowded restaurant, I can't keep the tears from flowing down my face. I hope to God there aren't any members of the paparazzi here, but at this point even if there are, there's nothing I can do about it. How did an idea which was meant to help Jude reach his dreams go so epically wrong? I try to retrace every step we've taken together and determine whether it was really Jude's dream or mine. Have I done to Jude what my mom has been doing to me for all these years?

———— •◦• ————

As I'm sitting in the middle of the plush queen-size bed pretending to be absorbed in a book, drinking hot cocoa in July, my phone rings. I check the caller ID and notice it's Tara.

"Hello?" I answer, uncertain as to why my boss's wife would be calling me from their vacation while they're in Paris.

"Tasha? This is Tara, I'm calling to check in on you. Are you all right?"

I have learned from past experience that conversations with Tara go much easier if you just tell her the whole truth because somehow she always knows anyway. "I'm hanging in there, but things have been better."

"What happened? Can I help?"

"I can't help but feel that this is my fault. I was showing Jude around Nashville today and we stopped for dinner at Puckett's."

"We love Puckett's! There's a fun energy there, isn't there?"

"I thought Jude would think so too. When Aidan gave me his friend's number, I not only made dinner reservations, I asked to do a set onstage with Jude."

"It didn't go well?"

"I don't understand. I've been on stage with Jude in arenas with Aidan where we've had thousands of fans and he's been cool as a cucumber. Today, he completely fell apart on a tiny stage in the restaurant. I thought he was beyond all of his stage fright because he's been doing so well with the band."

Tara chuckles softly. "No, Tash, that's not the way it works. You haven't known me long enough to know this, but there was a time in my life I couldn't even leave my house because my anxiety was so high. I was date raped as a teenager and then my mother died. As a result of all the trauma, I turned inward and I became afraid of almost everything. This lasted for years. Some days, I felt strong and able to conquer the world. I became an expert in martial arts and self-defense. I felt like I should be able to handle life."

"Yeah, I can see why you would feel that way. You've really whipped Jude and me into shape in your self-defense class."

"There is a part of me you don't see. Something as

simple as someone's voice, or the smell of a cleaning product or a new car can send me right back to that dark place. I have no control over when it happens or how I feel about it when it does happen. My whole body freezes and my mind becomes numb. I can try to be logical and sensible and grown-up about it all I want to. Yet, when it happens, I am that teenage girl right back in the middle of the attack."

"Oh, wow! Even now — all this time later?" I ask in a hushed tone.

"Unfortunately, yes. Being married to Aidan and having his steady presence in my life has helped some as did the fact that I was able to face down my rapist and keep him in jail. Even so, some days it still sneaks up on me when I least expect it."

"So, what can I do? I seem to have done all the wrong things today," I ask, trying to keep it together.

"I've been in your shoes. It's so hard to help champion someone's dream without feeling like you're pushing them in all the wrong directions. There was a time when Aidan wanted to throw in the towel and never sing another note. I had to back off and let him rediscover music on his own terms. I have to tell you, it scared me to death to see him fall out of love with music — even for a brief amount of time. I've known Aidan since he was in elementary school, and there was never a time he wasn't completely enamored by music. It was heartbreaking when he felt like music gave up on him."

I can't contain my gasp of disbelief. "Tara, you've seen how talented Jude is. Are you saying I shouldn't say anything?" Even as I ask the question, my heart knows the answer.

Tara clicks her tongue. "You know better than most Jude will have to decide for himself what success means. You can't decide for him, no matter how much you believe in him."

"I know. What if by trying to help him, I've made things exponentially worse and thrown him off the path he's supposed to be on?"

"Unfortunately, you and I can't choose Jude's path. Only he can," she reminds me softly.

"What should I do in the meantime? I don't want to make things worse."

"I wish I had some wonderful sage advice which would fix everything, but I don't. This is just going to take some time for you guys to work through. You guys are on parallel journeys, even though it doesn't seem like it. If you don't start working at cross purposes, you can travel together — but you need to be patient."

"I hope you're right. I hope I have something left with Jude to save. He seems pretty devastated by my stupid comments."

"Oh, I don't have any doubt you and Jude have more than just a little 'something'. You guys remind me so much of Aidan and me," Tara says with a light laugh. "When you're not looking, Jude looks at you the same way Aidan looks at me. It'll be rough for a while, but you can't lose faith. This is a temporary setback — it's not the same as starting over."

Tara's kind words are enough to put me over the

edge. "Tara, I gotta go. I'm going to go take a shower and see if I can readjust my brain so the world makes sense and I can be a decent person to Jude. Today I came a little too close to channeling my mother, which is something I *never* wanted to do as long as I lived."

"I'm sure it wasn't that bad. I suspect it was a case of frayed nerves all the way around. Things will look better in the morning. I will talk to you later. If you need anything, give me a call," Tara says, and hangs up the phone.

It might have been minutes or perhaps hours later when I feel Jude get into bed with me.

"Hey," I whisper.

"Hey yourself." Jude kisses me tenderly on the lips. "I'm sorry I flipped out."

"No … don't apologize. I'm the one who should be groveling for forgiveness. I shouldn't have put you on the spot like that without talking to you first. I was wrong. I don't know what I was thinking."

"You were thinking I would have a good time in a cool restaurant on the little stage playing guitar and singing my songs." Jude moves my hair out of my face and cups my cheek. "We've been doing that together for months; it wasn't a stupid assumption. I don't know what happened. I wanted it to be so good for you — I wanted to showcase your talent and make it our best gig ever. The more I thought about it, the harder it became. Pretty soon, I couldn't breathe."

"I'm sorry I put so much pressure on you." I lean

into his hand. "I swear I feel like I was possessed by my mother. I don't know what came over me. Is this *really* what you want? Or have I been pushing you in a direction you never wanted to go?"

"Tasha, this *is* what I want to do. I've been working for Aidan for a long time. He's a super nice boss, but I'm a long way away from my family and if I didn't want a shot at the brass ring, I wouldn't be making these sacrifices. I could find another nice boss a whole lot closer to home."

"That's true. Still, I can't help but feel like I've been putting a lot of pressure on you to be somebody you're not comfortable being."

"I can't argue that you haven't pushed me beyond what I might've done on my own. I've worked for Aidan for years and never once told him I sing. On the other hand, I was one hundred percent willing to go in the direction you pushed me. I don't think you actually pushed me as much as encouraged me to do what I've always wanted to do. Maybe you've given me permission to go out on a limb when otherwise I would've played it safe. Either way, I'm glad you've been helping me. I'm sorry if I made it seem like I wasn't."

"So, now what happens? Have I pushed you so far you don't ever want to try again?"

Jude shrugs. "I wish I knew. I don't. If you would've told me a few months ago I'd be able to perform on the stage with Aidan O'Brien and Tasha Keeley I would've sworn you were certifiably nuts. To say we're in completely uncharted territory here is an understatement."

"Okay, how about if I promise not to spring any more surprises on you?" I offer.

Jude pulls my bathrobe down off my shoulder and kisses it. "I don't know… I kind of like some of your surprises. How about if you just talk to me before you throw me on a stage next time?"

<hr>

My phone rings as I'm trying to balance my phone on my shoulder and handle two cups of hot liquid from the quaint coffee shop at the same time. Jude said I couldn't surprise him with any more impromptu performances, he didn't say I couldn't get him his favorite coffee.

"Hello? This is Tasha," I answer, still distracted by the bustle around me.

"Hi, Tasha. I don't know if you remember me, but this is Pennie Rose, Hayden's mom."

I set the coffees down on the table and put the phone closer to my ear. "Of course I remember you. Did something happen with Hayden?"

Pennie lets a breath out that I can hear through the phone. "I could give you an answer to that question which would take about three days to explain or I could just tell you that we don't quite know what's going on. Hayden has an infection she can't seem to beat and she's feeling discouraged. I know this is a huge imposition, but is there any way you might be able to come visit Hayden on your way back through town? She was so happy when you came to see her. It's the perkiest I've seen her in months. It would be great if you guys could sing for her or something. I bet she would cheer right up."

Thinking of the promise I made Jude, I have to stifle my first instinct. Instead I play it safe and say, "Pennie, I'm so sorry to hear that. I'm not with Jude right now. As soon as I talk to him, I'll call you right back. He knows all about the logistics of this trip."

"Okay, I'll wait and I won't say anything to Hayden until I hear from you," Pennie replies. "Again, I'm sorry to bother you, but I don't know what else to do."

"Don't worry about it. I told Hayden to call me if she needed anything. Obviously, this is important."

Driving back to Stella's house, I stew over the situation. Memphis isn't far from Nashville, although I don't know how Jude is going to respond to the second part of Pennie's request.

As soon as I open the front door, Jude walks toward me with bare feet and his ever-present guitar. "I wondered where you went so early this morning, but I smell coffee, so I don't even have to ask." He has a wide grin on his face until he studies my expression.

"Are you still sad about yesterday? I'm sorry, I didn't mean to snap at you."

I shake my head as I stall to collect my thoughts by carefully taking a sip of the rocket-hot coffee. "No, it's not that. I got a call from Pennie."

"*¡Dios mío!*, is Hayden okay?"

Again, I shake my head. "Apparently, she has some sort of infection and they can't pin down the right antibiotics for her. Her mom says Hayden's really discouraged. Pennie wants to know if there would be any way we could stop by and see her."

"Let me get my shoes," Jude says as he sets his guitar down. "Memphis is only three hours away. It's not like we have anything more pressing to do on our vacation."

"Jude, wait … Pennie wanted to know if maybe we could put on a little concert for Hayden. Is that going to be a problem?" I ask in a halting voice. I hate not knowing the right thing to say.

"I don't know. I guess we'll see when we get there. If Hayden can face down cancer, I can put my big boy boxers on and sing her a few notes," Jude responds as he starts packing his duffel bag.

CHAPTER FOURTEEN

JUDE

IT'S CLEAR JUST FROM the way the nurses interact with us as Tasha and I walk toward Hayden's room that things are very different this time. The smiles are still there, but they seem a little less real and more forced. Voices are quieter and body language more subdued.

Tasha's grip on my arm is so tight it's almost painful. "It's going to be bad. I remember that look. I'll never forget it as long as I live. It means they know something and they can't say anything. My nurses always had that look on their face before I'd have to have something awful done. I learned to fear it almost more than a straight-out frown."

"I'm sorry, baby. Remember, we don't know the whole situation. It might not even be about Hayden. We have to have hope — if for no other reason than Hayden needs us to believe she'll be okay."

Tasha lets out the breath she's been holding. "You're right. Hayden can read every expression on our faces. We need to pull ourselves together. We're supposed to be her number one cheerleaders. I can't let my past color how I see this situation. It's not fair to Hayden."

"It's only human, Tasha. You have a history with this place. Unfortunately, you don't get to decide when your history comes up and slaps you in the face."

"You're right, I don't. I'll just have to deal."

As we turn the corner into Hayden's room, the reality of it all hits me. This is a very different girl than we saw a few days ago. Gone are the smiles and bright eyes. Her skin is paper-white and her cheeks are flushed with fever. She has an oxygen cannula in her nose and more IVs than I can count.

"Hey, I heard you like the food here so much you decided to stay a while," Tasha whispers as she walks up next to Hayden's bed.

Hayden opens her eyes and struggles to sit up as she whispers hoarsely, "Mom didn't say anything about you coming. I don't even have any makeup on."

Tasha winks at her. "Don't tell anyone, I was too lazy to put mine on this morning. My mother would totally freak out if she thought the paparazzi might catch me without any makeup."

Hayden smiles weakly. "I saw a picture in some gossip magazine of you all dressed up with makeup on when you were about eight. Was that Photoshopped or was it really you?"

Tasha rolls her eyes. "I don't know. I didn't see the picture. Chances are, it didn't need to be retouched any more than it already was. My mom used to have these studio pictures taken of me in all of my pageant gear, and they'd retouch them to make me look more pageant-like. Sometimes it was downright scary."

"Maybe that's why you don't like wearing makeup much now," I comment.

"You're probably right. Stage makeup can be entirely obnoxious," Tasha replies with a shrug.

Hayden sighs. "Maybe so, but I could use a little something. I look terrible. It's like the time my sister accidentally kicked a soccer ball into my face. These circles under my eyes are ugly."

I briefly look up at Pennie. "Aside from the masks, are there any other restrictions for Hayden?"

"As long as Hayden is careful and doesn't disturb her IVs, she's fine. Just wash your hands carefully. As a precaution, you might want to wear gloves."

I shoot Tasha what I hope is a silent message as I offer, "We never unloaded your stage makeup from the rental car. How about I take Pennie out for a cup of coffee while you two do whatever it is you do with those mysterious bottles, potions, and powders?"

Hayden seems to rebound a little as she grins at Tasha. "Really? You have the real stuff with you — like what you wear in your music videos?"

Tasha nods. "Yeah, I've got it all in a kit. When I was about your age, I had a fantastic makeup artist who taught me the ropes. I'm decked out like a professional, trust me."

Thinking of my overprotective mom and how she felt about my sister at that age, I ask Hayden, "How does your mom feel about you wearing makeup?"

"I have to wear it so it looks natural most of the time, but when we're playing dress-up, I can do whatever I want."

Tasha addresses Pennie. "Do you mind? It sounds fun. I promise to be careful."

Pennie shrugs as she responds, "Okay, but Hayden has some sort of infection. I would hate for her to ruin your makeup."

"I'm careful about that. I became a bit of a germaphobe after I spent so much time on the pageant circuit. I only use disposable applicators."

I step forward and kiss Tasha on the cheek. "Sounds like a plan. My sister would be so jealous if she knew she missed our party." I turn and wait for Pennie to walk in front of me. "We'll see you in a few minutes."

I have no idea whether I'm doing the right thing. I'm running on instinct here. I do know Tasha will take good care of Hayden. The two of them have been communicating via the computer for several days. Although Tasha was taken a bit off guard by the downturn in Hayden's condition, they've developed a close bond. I hope this is a positive thing for both of them.

⸻ ● ⸻

Pennie and I walk quietly side-by-side to a restaurant next to the hospital. She looks up at the sky and comments, "You know, I've been in Hayden's room for so long I forget what it's like to be outside. The weather is beautiful."

"The last time we were here, Hayden mentioned her dad. Is there a reason he's not here to give you a break?" I ask before I can censor my question.

"I wish we could afford to have him come with us — but when Hayden first got sick, we couldn't figure out what was wrong with her. I'm a teacher's aide at school. We had an influx of students and not enough staff. I couldn't take the time off to take her to her medical appointments, so my husband took time off from his job to do it. His company had recently been bought out and he had to find another job. He didn't have any leave and the medical bills were piling up. Finally, someone suggested St. Jude's and things have gotten better, but we have to be separated because there's no way we as a family can make it just on my salary. Our other daughter is in college, and she wanted to come home to help, but I didn't want to let her do that. She worked so hard to get into school and I didn't want to ask her to sacrifice her dreams. So, it's just me. It seems like it's always just me. We moved across the nation for Larry's job and I don't have any family —"

"*Lo siento mucho,*" I murmur.

"Listen to me spouting on and on. You probably didn't even want to hear half of that story."

"No, you misunderstood me. I said I was very sorry because I have seen my own family members struggle," I explain. "My uncle died of pancreatic cancer after a very long fight. Working to save his life just about killed my aunt too. She worried about him day and night until it consumed her existence. After my uncle passed away, my aunt didn't know what to do with herself because being a care provider had become her whole identity. She'd forgotten who she was and how to take care of herself while she was taking care of my uncle. So, if you ever need a shoulder to cry on away from Hayden, don't ever hesitate to call me. I've seen firsthand what it's like."

"Oh, I could never do that. You're on your way to be a very big star, you won't have time for the likes of me," Pennie insists as she wipes away her tears with a tissue.

After the waitress seats us, I study Pennie carefully. "You know, I'm not sure if that'll ever happen for me. Even if it does, I have one of the best role models in the business. You know how big Aidan O'Brien is, but he's as down to earth as they come. You would never guess he's at the top of the charts and can sell out tickets to an event in a few minutes. He still acts like a regular guy and cares about every single person in our crew. If I'm ever fortunate enough to make it big, I want to be just like Aidan." I sound like one of Aidan's gushing fans, but it's totally true. I have mad respect for the man over the way he treats his friends and family. "I promise I'll never get so big that I won't have time to listen to my friends like you. So, if you need to talk, you have my phone number. I expect you to call."

"Why are you being so nice to us?" Pennie asks suspiciously. "I've heard about stars meeting sick kids just so they can get their pictures in the paper for being charitable. You guys don't seem to be doing that though. In fact, you seem to do everything you can to avoid the cameras. So, what's in it for you?"

"I can't really speak for Tasha, but I've already told you a bit about my family and how alone my *tia* felt when my uncle was sick. Eventually, all of my aunt's friends and most of my family got sick of hearing how my uncle would eventually die, so they stopped hanging around because they didn't know what to say anymore. She was alone all the time with her thoughts and it was a scary place for her to be. I don't want you and Hayden to be alone. Knowing Tasha, I suspect she feels very much the same."

"I don't know how your aunt felt, but I have to be honest with you — most of the time I like to play make-believe games with myself. I like to pretend we're here in Memphis on some fancy vacation and my daughter doesn't have cancer and there isn't a chance she might die. I know that it sounds absolutely crazy, but it's what I have to do to survive."

"I understand. My *tia* would have me come over and play pinochle with my sister as if everything was normal and we were having a normal Friday night card game. Every week, we went like clockwork. It was hard to pretend everything was normal as he wasted away to almost nothing — especially at the end — but my *tia* wanted us to have some sort of normalcy because we'd held a family game night for as long as I can remember."

"Oh my goodness, that must've been hard on you." Pennie pats the back of my hand when I reach for sugar for my coffee. "That's one of the reasons I'm so glad Hayden's sister is away at college — at least she can imagine all of this isn't happening because it doesn't hit her in the face every day."

"As hard as it was, after he passed away, those were some of the best memories from my sister and me."

Pennie cries and I realize my comments could easily be taken two ways, so I hurry to explain. "But there's a difference — my uncle's health was terrible when he got cancer of the pancreas. He drank and smoked a pack a day. He was the poster child for bad health habits. He didn't have much reserve to fight with."

"That makes it hard. The doctors say it's a good thing Hayden is young and healthy. As frustrated as she is about not being able to play sports now, the fact that she was in them before finding out she had Ewing's sarcoma will make her recovery so much easier."

"Exactly! Hayden's going to recover from this, she'll figure out how to tie her shoes and go to the school dance and do all the things she wanted to do. She'll need to do them differently, but she will do them. She's bright and talented."

"I don't know what to do about the piano playing. She's absolutely devastated that she won't be able to continue playing."

"I don't know what the answer is. I sympathize with her because more than anything, I want to be on the stage like Tasha. I have been working for Aidan for years just to get up enough courage to approach him with a song or two I've written. I had overcome my stage fright enough to sing for a few nights with Aidan, but in the end it came roaring back without warning. Now, I don't know if my dreams of being able to sing on stage are just smoke and mirrors. What if I've been chasing the wrong dream all along? I don't know if I'll be able to overcome my issues either. They might not be as visible as Hayden's, but they make me just as scared."

"Wow, that's complicated. It must be scary for you not to know when you're going to be able to perform and when you're not. I know Hayden used to get so nervous before recitals. She was funny though, it was almost as if she fed on the excitement of it all. She loves being on stage and performing."

"Does she sing?" I ask.

Pennie nods and wipes away tears. "Mostly for fun — her focus was primarily the piano."

"I know Tasha's always telling me that my voice is an instrument. I suspect she might tell your daughter the same thing. Maybe now Hayden will gravitate toward singing as a way of expressing herself musically. Even though it's hard for me to do it in public, it was always something I did in private because there's just something inside of me that drives me to be creative."

"All of this has been so hard on Hayden. She used to love to draw and paint. She'd spend hours writing and illustrating poems, and now she fights so hard to try to learn to do this with her non-dominant hand. It seems everything is frustrating for her. I'd do anything to trade places with her, and it hurts my heart to see her so upset."

"Pennie, you have to cut yourself some slack. You need a break. You can't fix this. Hayden needs to learn those skills on her own. I think you guys are being far too hard on yourselves. You're still getting used to what happened to you."

"Nothing happened to me!" Pennie insists. "I stood helplessly by as cancer ravaged my daughter before she even had a chance to become a woman."

"No, I've been through this. Cancer happens to the whole family, whether you wanted it to or not. As Hayden's mom, you are the equivalent of a first responder. You can't keep blaming yourself for cells that went crazy in Hayden's body."

Pennie blows her nose and then responds, "I know, but I would've given anything to stop it."

"I know you would, but stuff just happens. There doesn't seem to be any rhyme or reason. Sure, there are cases with obvious causes like with my uncle, but there are cases like Hayden's where it happens because life isn't fair. It's wrong for you to think you're not also a victim of cancer too. Everything in your life has changed. All the dreams, hopes, and aspirations you had for your daughter have to be adjusted because she's been touched by cancer. Don't dismiss that about yourself. It's not fair to you, to your husband or to your daughters. When this is all over and Hayden beats this, in some strange way, you too are a cancer survivor. Don't forget that — it's important."

Pennie gives me a watery smile. "It's obvious why Tasha thinks you're the perfect man. Your heart is as big as Texas, and you're pretty darn smart too."

"I don't know about that, but Tasha means the world to me," I blurt as I fiddle with my food.

"Oh, I think it's clear — but what are you going to do when she starts school? How will you manage your career with Aidan? I can't imagine the two of you will want to be separated for long. If you don't mind me saying so, you two are like two peas in a pod. You seem so well suited. You play up each other's strengths well."

I take a moment to absorb the stark reality of her words. Tasha and I have talked about a lot of things, but I've never had it laid out in front of me like this. For us both to succeed, one of us will have to put our dreams on hold for a while. I suddenly realize, with Pennie sitting right in front of me, that person will probably be me.

I look up at Pennie and she's waiting for me to answer her. I shrug. "We still have some logistical details to work out. It depends on which school she gets into and if they accept her into the nursing program. It's been a little difficult for her because of the way she went to school. It wasn't always very consistent because of how much travel she and her mom did for the pageant stuff. "

"My goodness! You and Tasha have so many balls up in the air. It must be difficult to manage them all. The only thing I can say is when the times get tough — remember this moment when you were so in love with her that you couldn't imagine your life apart. Take a picture of that memory in your brain and burn it there. Sometimes life will come up and destroy what you thought you knew about the world. If the two of you can fight the battles together, rather than fight each other, it will be so much easier. If she's going to do something as complicated as a nursing program, it'll have to be the two of you against the world."

CHAPTER FIFTEEN

TASHA

"Am I gonna die?" Hayden whispers in a hoarse voice. "It's okay, my mom isn't here now. You can tell me the truth."

"I can't tell you that. I'm not God and I'm not your doctor. I'm just your friend. I wish I had some special skill where I could tell the future, but I don't. I know you feel lousy, but it doesn't mean you're going to die. Didn't you tell me the other day that your lab results came back and your margins were clean?"

"Yeah, that's what they say, but after they said all that I started feeling really sick again. It makes me super scared and I can't even tell my mom how frightened I am because she's afraid too."

"I know. There isn't any fun part of cancer. It's all scary and overwhelming. It's all about coping from one day to the next."

"For once, I think you're wrong," Hayden argues.

"Yeah? How's that?" I ask with a quizzical look.

"Well, if it wasn't for this stupid cancer, I would've never met you and Jude, and you are the coolest people I've ever met."

"Okay, you might have a point. I think it's pretty cool I got to meet you too. Still, I hate that cancer was the reason we got to meet."

I open my makeup case and set it at the end of the bed. I pull out a bunch of little white condiment containers and set them on the bedside table.

Hayden laughs out loud. "What are you going to do — put ketchup and mustard on my face?"

"No, although my friend who taught me how to do makeup used to put mayonnaise in my hair as a conditioning treatment. She was also very picky about keeping my makeup super clean, so she taught me to custom mix all my colors. Jude always laughs at me when I put makeup on because he says it looks like a science experiment run amok."

"That's weird, my friends just put on anything and everything."

"I probably would've learned that way too, except I was lucky. Charlize worked with a supermodel in Paris before she had her own kids and worked the pageant circuit. She really knew her stuff and didn't mind sharing it with a very curious soon-to-be teenager."

"No wonder you don't always wear makeup. It looks like a lot of work."

I grin. "I suppose it is. I guess I'm used to it. Why don't you tell me how you would like to look today? Do you want to look like a rock star or a fashion model, or would you like to try something you could wear to school?"

"If you're letting me choose, can we try something I might be able to show my best friend so she can help me do it for the school dance?"

"Sure," I reply as I wash my hands and put on a pair of gloves. "I'd love to. What color do you think your dress will be?"

"I don't know, I haven't chosen yet. I like red — but it makes my dad a little nervous. He thinks it's too mature for my age."

"I can see where he would be worried. You're very beautiful."

"What did your dad say about all the pageant stuff? I bet he about blew a gasket, didn't he?"

"No, my dad wasn't around. He left before I hit kindergarten. My grandparents were never big fans of makeup and grown-up hairdos, but I never had a dad to worry about those things."

"That's sad, I'm sorry," Hayden murmurs as she observes me removing things from my makeup kit.

"I was so little I didn't know any differently. It was all I ever knew. You know, it's just your normal when you're growing up."

"So, it was only your mom?" Hayden asks. She winces as she tries to shift in bed and sit up.

"Mostly. My grandparents were around a lot and after my Papa died my Nana moved in with us."

"If your grandma is anything like mine, she's probably super proud of you."

I can't hide my glowing grin. "Yeah, my Nana is probably my number one fan. She'd be my number one fan regardless of what I do."

"Does she know about your plan to go to school?"

"She knows it's a possibility, but I don't know if she knows how serious I am about it. I don't want to stick her in the middle of the controversy because I know my mom won't be supportive of my plans."

"That's tough. I hope it all works out." Hayden sounds glum.

Giving myself a mental and physical shake, I say, "Enough serious business. Let's get down to the fun girly stuff. That's what we're here for. After all, we don't want Jude and your mom to come back mid-makeover." I take my tray of lipsticks out of the case and carry them over to Hayden. "Which one is your favorite?"

"Are you serious? I've never seen so many colors of lipstick. It's like you own a whole store!"

"I used to have even more, but after I stopped doing the pageant stuff, I got rid of a bunch."

"That's totally insane." She carefully studies the tray and points to one. "I really like this one. What do you think?"

"I think it's an excellent choice." I dig to the bottom of my box and pull out a new tube of lipstick. "Would you believe it's my favorite? You can have this tube. I have a few extra."

"You're not just making that up?" Hayden asks skeptically.

I pull the used tube out of the tray and show her how much of it is gone compared to the other colors. "Nope, see? I'd say I use this color most days."

"We have good taste, don't we? We even think the same boy is cute."

"Absolutely, I can't even argue with that logic."

"You're so funny."

"What about you? Do you like any boys your age?" I ask as I pull her hair back into a ponytail.

Hayden blushes. "There is this one boy, Bryon Copell. I thought he might've liked me before I got sick, but I don't know how he feels now because he hasn't written me or anything while I've been in the hospital. I don't even know if he still likes me."

"Boys are funny about that kind of stuff. Sometimes they don't like to let us know how they feel. Is he nice to you? Does he treat you right? Is he smart?"

"Geez! You sound like my mom." Hayden laughs, then starts to cough. "Yes to all the above. He's chill, otherwise I wouldn't like him."

"Then I guess he either doesn't quite know what to say, he doesn't know how to reach you, or both. It doesn't sound like he's the kind of boy who'd purposefully blow you off. I say give him a chance when you get home and see what he has to say."

"That was kind of my plan. Before all this cancer stuff happened, I was hoping maybe he'd take me to the dance, but now I don't know."

"I say we better practice your makeup just in case," I state firmly.

———◆◆———

"Where did my little girl go, and who's this lovely young woman?" Pennie gasps as she walks into the room.

"Really? Mom, do you think I look okay? What do you think Dad will say? We tried not to overdo it. I don't want him to have a cow and not let me go to the dance. I want to look like the other girls though. I don't want to look sick — and I don't mean it like slang either — I mean I don't want to look like I have cancer."

Pennie tears up a bit. "I know what you meant, Sweetie. I can't guarantee you that your dad won't freak out. You look so much like your sister he will probably have a 'moment'. You know how he gets about his babies growing up. You look very much like the teenager you are and not the little girl he remembers."

Jude steps forward with his cell phone in hand and offers, "Why don't I take a picture of you lovely ladies so you can send it to him?"

Hayden's eyes lit up as she turns to me and asks, "Tasha, you don't have to go anywhere, right? So, you could do my mom's makeup and hair like you did mine, couldn't you?"

I look over at Jude and shrug. "If she'd like me to … sure. We're on vacation. We're not on anybody's clock except our own."

Pennie laughs self-consciously and pats her hair. "Oh good heavens! I don't know if you could do anything to help me. It's been so long since I've had anything done. Larry wouldn't even recognize me if I had my hair done and makeup on this face."

"Mom! That's exactly why you should do it. Dad would be so surprised. We should do it!" Hayden says.

Pennie sighs and looks at me. "Okay, I guess I'm game if you are."

"Oh my gosh! This will be so much fun. Wait until you see the way Tasha puts on makeup. She's like some sort of professional. My friends will be so impressed by all the things I've learned. I swear, I should record this like some sort of makeup tutorial on YouTube or something."

"Hayden! Don't you dare! It's bad enough you talked me into this but if you put it on social media, I would die of embarrassment," Pennie threatens.

Hayden giggles. "Don't worry, Mom. It's your lucky day. Tasha and Jude are off-duty. They're not onstage and I won't out them for being here. But consider yourself warned, if we were in our bathroom and it was just us, you'd be in deep danger. Makeup videos are all the rage and I could make some serious bank with all the makeup tips I've learned."

I grin at Hayden. "I appreciate you protecting our privacy. Not a lot of people would. I'll tell you what. Sometime down the road, when I have some free time, maybe you and I can put together a makeup video for teenagers and you can post it on your social media page."

"Serious?" Hayden gasps.

"Totally. It sounds like fun." I give her a high-five.

"You are like the nicest person ever." She pulls me into an awkward hug.

I glance at Jude from over Hayden's shoulder. "I try to be. But sometimes I completely miss the mark and then I have to say I'm sorry."

"*Está bien, Sirena. Te amo.*" Jude speaks so quietly, I'm not sure I heard it at first.

"Did you hear that, Tasha? OMG! Jude just said he loves you. You guys should go celebrate or something. That was like one of the most romantic things I've ever heard. Take pictures of the restaurant you go to and come back and tell me about it, okay? I'm sick of hospital food."

I hug Hayden again. "Okay, you have a deal. I might even bring you some dessert."

CHAPTER SIXTEEN

JUDE

I'VE BEEN THINKING THOSE words for quite a while. I don't know exactly how long — they just started floating around in my mind. I've just never found the right time to say them. This wasn't the right time either. Somehow I forgot to connect my brain to my mouth and they slipped out. Usually, my tendency to slip back into speaking Spanish disguises what I'm really thinking, but I don't get away with much around Tasha.

Tasha is wicked smart and knows a lot of Spanish. Some people just know a few cuss words or the words they learned from Sesame Street when they were young — not Tasha. Apparently one of her tutors from the pageant circuit, taught her a couple of academic years' worth. She's been practicing Spanish with me so she'll be better prepared when she meets my mom. Although my mom speaks English well enough to be easily understood, she prefers to speak Spanish. I am honored Tasha cares enough to make the gesture. I'm pretty sure it's going to make my mom and my sister cry.

My thoughts are interrupted when Tasha places her hand over mine to stop me from flipping the drink menu over and over in my hands. We're at some upscale barbecue place — because where else would you eat when you're in Memphis? Clearly, I am ruining the cozy atmosphere with all of my fidgeting.

"Are you upset you said the words? Are they a lie?" Tasha asks with a look of concern on her face. She's near tears. "I mean … after what I did to you, I don't blame you if you want to take it all back."

"*¡Dios Mio!* Of course not. That's not what this is about at all."

"Then why do you look like you're about to be sick to your stomach? Why are we not celebrating?" Tasha presses.

"This is so complicated. It'll take me a little time to unravel it all for you. It might not even make sense after I do, so please be patient with me. You know, when we met, I had a case of hero worship. I thought you were beautiful and sexy. You have one of the most amazing singing voices I've ever heard. But … honestly, when you turned down Aidan's offer to record, I wasn't sure I would actually like you. I thought maybe you were holding out for more money or a higher billing or something." I pull on the collar of my shirt and frown deeply as I spill all my misconceptions.

Tasha's eyes widen in surprise.

"I thought maybe you were one of those beautiful girls who thought you were better than the rest of us. I figured you were probably a straight up witch. I made a lot of snap judgments based on who I thought you might be. I didn't understand who you really were or the choices you had to make. I never expected we would end up as a couple, much less fall in love."

"Wow, that's honest," Tasha says as she sips her iced tea. "Okay, to be fair … I wasn't very nice to you in the beginning either, so I can't say I blame you."

"This is where it gets complicated," I warn with a grimace.

"More complicated than you starting a career in music when I am planning to leave show business?" Tasha asks with a sigh.

"In some ways, yeah. Although, at some point we'll have to deal with that too. We always seem to find reasons to put off the career discussion."

If you're not talking about our careers, what is this about?"

"This has to do with the way I grew up. You know my dad ditched me when I was a little boy?"

"I guess we have that in common."

"The whole time I was growing up, my mom would tell me these wonderful stories about how my dad came in and swept her off her feet. How wonderfully romantic he was and how he would change her life and make everything better for her. In her mind, my dad was the perfect man. It was something from a fairytale — or at least it was … until it wasn't. One day, my dad took off and he never came back. He stayed around long enough to father me and my sister. After that, he was gone. He never looked back, he never checked in on my mom. He never did anything. He broke every promise he ever made. How could a guy who convinced my mom he was so perfect be such a loser?"

"I don't know, some guys just are," Tasha remarks with an eye roll. "My dad was no prince."

"What if I'm like him? My *abuela* says my mom fell for him because he was a *gringo* and I don't fall far from the tree."

An angry expression crosses Tasha's face. "So, you think you fell for me just because I'm white? I've got news for you, I'm like a genetic potluck. I come from New York. I've got so many family trees in my background, it's like tracing a forest. Let me tell you, we didn't all come over on the Mayflower — that's for sure." Proverbial fire shoots from her eyes as she angrily tosses her hair over her shoulder.

I throw my napkin down on the table and almost knock over my water glass as I say, "No! I knew I would do a bad job explaining this. That's totally not what I meant."

She stares at me with a stubborn tilt of her chin. "Honestly, that's sure what it sounded like."

"It's not what I meant." My thoughts race wildly. "I wonder sometimes if I'll be a loser at relationships like my dad was. Will I fall in love and then bail out of your life when it gets hard? Honestly, when you told Hayden you probably won't be able to have kids I was relieved. I don't even know if I'm dad material. What if my *abuela* is right and I'm just like my dad?"

I watch Tasha carefully to see what her reaction is to my confession. I've been harboring my secret fear for as long as I can remember. I don't know what Tasha will make of what I've told her, but I feel better now that I've been honest.

Tasha is silent for what seems like forever. Initially, her posture is stiff and ungiving. I can sense that I've hurt her feelings which was the last thing I wanted to do. Finally, she shakes her head. "I don't know if I want to laugh or cry. Somehow I feel like doing both. I can't believe you're serious. Jude, you are the most stable person I know. Do you know how much everyone around you relies on your solid, calm, common sense?"

I shrug and glance down at the table.

"No, I'm serious. Jude, look at me."

When I meet her gaze, she continues. "You're starting to get a taste of it now, but when we're getting ready to go on stage, it's the most chaotic environment you can imagine. Somehow you constantly pull it all together and help make it make sense. You always have the equipment properly set up and the instruments ready. Everything is as it should be — right down to the tape marks on the floor. That might not seem like much to you, but to those of us who rely on it every day, it means everything. The fact that you respect and honor those small details tells me everything. You're not the type of person who would walk away from your responsibilities in a relationship — especially a personal relationship. If you ever decide to be a dad, you would be amazing."

"So I'm good at my job, but it doesn't mean I will make a good partner in life or a solid parent."

"Yeah, actually it does. You bring the same level of respect to our relationship. We've been together for months now. Whether we've called it dating or a really good friendship, you've been taking care of me in a million different ways — you make sure I've got food that makes me happy and you protect me from my mom. Heck, you even make sure I've got the contact lens solution which doesn't make my eyes turn red. I know how hard it is to find. I didn't ask you to, but you noticed I was running out of it and got me a bottle of it anyway. You might not make all sorts of grand gestures you see in the movies, but in all the ways that count, you are there for me."

"Any decent guy would do that. I'm not special."

"You'd be surprised how few decent guys there are in the world."

Tasha settles back and takes a long drink of her tea. "You're not the only one who is impacted by someone else's past. At least you heard good stories about your dad. I don't know if I've ever heard Ma say a nice word about my dad. She spews so much hate about him, sometimes I wonder how they ever got together to create me. To hear her talk, he's the lowest of the low," she adds after a few moments of silence stretch between us.

"Do you know what happened? Did he ever come back and explain?"

"No, I only have vague memories of him being part of our lives. He disappeared around the time I was diagnosed with cancer. My mom drops hints suggesting he couldn't handle me being sick. In a way, she blames me for him leaving."

I can't help myself. I reach over and gather Tasha

close to me. "Have I mentioned how horrible I think your mother is?"

Tasha grins up at me. "I think you've mentioned it a time or two. I once asked my Nana if she thought it was true and she said no — he did not run away because of me. She told me my dad was a decent guy and I probably got my musical talent from him. She talked as if she really liked him and thought he was a good influence on my mom for a while. My papa seemed to like him too. I guess they talked about the Yankees a lot. When you're from New York, it helps when you root for the same baseball team."

"Do you ever wish he was part of your life?"

"I don't know, my mom kept me so busy as a kid I almost didn't know what I was missing. My life was so bizarre that it didn't even resemble a normal kid's life. I didn't celebrate regular family events like Christmas, Easter, Thanksgiving, birthday parties or other traditional things kids usually do with their dads. I didn't have regular school events where I would need a father. It was just my mom and my nana. When my papa was alive, he'd sneak me away from my mom and do some really tomboyish things like take me fishing or out on his four-wheeler in the mud."

"He sounds a lot like my uncle who passed away from cancer. He was the one who'd let us use slingshots in the house and eat pizza for breakfast."

Tasha smiles at me. "People like that are fun, aren't they?"

I nod. "They are. I bet if your mom was the same as she is now, she wasn't much fun though, huh?"

Tasha shrugs. "As long as my mom's getting her way, she's not too bad. If she feels like she's being ignored, she becomes a bear. For a while there on the pageant circuit, I was on a pretty good winning streak, so my mom became quite popular with the pageant organizers. That was a good time."

"There's a reason I brought up my past. It's because my mom's attitude toward relationships in men has colored the way I see things too. I'm more likely to jump to negative conclusions about things and I'm more than a little touchy about trying to do things on my own without help. I don't always talk things through when I'm feeling cornered or stressed out. A lot of my attitude is because my mom taught me I couldn't trust anybody. Not men, and not other women. It was a very lonely existence. So, it would be silly of me to think that it doesn't impact the way we interact."

I have to clear my throat. "So where does that leave us? I barely trust myself to do the right thing and you don't trust me either. Can we handle all the things we're going to need to face together?"

"I don't know. I want to be able to tell you, 'Yes, of course we are stronger than our pasts. We can overcome anything together.'" Tasha answers with emotion breaking her voice.

"But?" I prompt. My heart drops to my stomach as I wait for her to explain.

"I've seen a lot of couples with a lot less odds against them split up. We're young and we don't have the best role models in our lives. We'll be going in totally different directions soon, and we have a lot of personal stuff to overcome. In some ways, we're as different as night and day. Sometimes, I wonder if we stand a chance."

"Does this mean you don't feel the same way about me?" I anxiously spit out the question that's been tormenting me since we started this conversation. I need to know once and for all if I've ruined our whole relationship by blurting out how I feel without understanding Tasha's point of view first.

Tasha swallows hard and takes a long drink before she answers, "No."

"No? No what?" I stammer, feeling like she punched me. "I should've seen this coming. You're a big star and I'm just the equipment guy. I don't know what I was thinking."

"Jude, stop. That's not what I'm saying at all. I'm saying I don't know where I am at in my life. I don't want to be the person who pushes you into something you don't want to do because you're trying to make me happy because we're a couple. I don't know how we'll make ourselves work as a couple if I'm in school and you're trying to make it with Aidan. I'm not even sure if I'm going to get into school. If I don't, I have no idea what I'll do, and you shouldn't have to wait around for me to figure out my life. I've got so many things I don't understand or know at this moment. It's not fair for me to weigh you down with all of my uncertainties — I'm bad for you right now."

"So, it's not because you don't love me?" I ask again.

"No! It's more like I love you so much that I don't

want to do this to you. I'm a mess. I haven't figured out anything about my life."

"*Sirena*, what makes you think I have? I'm a grown man who follows a guy around and picks up after him so I might have a chance to sing him a few songs. Before you came into my life, I wasn't even brave enough to open my mouth and tell the man I knew how to sing or write a song. I tried to work up the courage to do it on my own for years. Before you helped me, I couldn't even do it. You know what that tells me? We're better at figuring things out together than we are apart."

"True," Tasha concedes. "You helped me fill out all of those scholarships and financial aid forms — even though English is your second language. You were better at it than I was."

"I don't think our dreams are really going in totally different directions We can reach them traveling side-by-side on different paths. We just have to support each other."

For the first time during this conversation, Tasha looks hopeful. "Really? Do you think we can pull this off? I want so much to be like Tara and Aidan. They did it. They do it every day, and they are the most in love couple I've ever seen in my life. They have different dreams and different talents, but they're always supportive of each other. We could be like them, right?"

"That would be great, wouldn't it? I'm sure Aidan would help me work around your school schedule. He wants you to be as successful as possible. I think we can do this, I really do. I'm not willing to give up on us. If it means I need to stay home and just write songs that's what I'll do."

"I don't want you to do that for me or for us. If we're going to do this, I want us both to be successful," Tasha insists.

"Tasha, I like writing songs and managing Aidan's equipment. If I have to wait awhile to be a performer, it's not a big deal. I put it off for years by my own choice. Waiting my turn so you have a chance to go to school won't make any difference."

"As long as you're not changing who you are just to be with me, I'm okay with that. *Te amo*, Jude."

CHAPTER SEVENTEEN

TASHA

As we pull the rental car into the parking lot at the hospital, there's a throng of reporters waiting by the front door and a bunch of curious people standing around trying to figure out why they're there. There's an outside chance they have nothing to do with Jude or me, but I recognize some of them from the funeral.

Jude parks the car in a dark corner. "Why are those leeches here? Don't they realize this is a hospital?"

I shrug. "I don't know. Maybe it's a coincidence?" I grab a shopping bag from the backseat and grab a couple of baseball caps I purchased on a whim from a street vendor.

Jude smirks when he reads the saying on my hat. **Last I checked, Elvis has left the building.** "Somehow this seems fitting for the circumstances, doesn't it?"

I put my sunglasses on and try to hide my hair under the baseball cap. "I don't know if this will work, but it's worth a shot at least. Hayden and Pennie deserve to eat real food for a change, and the cheesecake is worth running the gauntlet."

Jude nods as he fishes a 'I heart Tennessee' T-shirt from the bag and sheds his usual plaid cotton shirt. "Okay, I'm game. Let's do this thing." Jude opens the glove box and grabs a neon orange camera on a florescent yellow lanyard and hangs it around his neck. At my questioning glance, he looks at me and says, "It's a force of habit, I keep it around in case my cell phone battery dies. My mom gave it to me for my high school graduation."

"Sometimes, you are way too adorable," I gush as I kiss him on the cheek. "I can't wait to meet your mom."

Jude and I try to stroll across the parking lot like any other visitors to the hospital, but it soon becomes evident it won't be possible. We're soon met with a chorus of voices as the reporters crowd around us and try to separate us. They shout questions at us as if they are miles away instead of inches from our ears.

"Tasha! Hey, Tasha!"

"Ms. Keeley? May we have a comment?"

"Hernandez, is it? Are you going to marry her for the rights to her music?"

"Our sources say you've been at this hospital several times. Are you sick again? Do you have a comment?"

"How long do you have to live?"

"Do you have anything to say to your fans?"

"Do you have cancer again? Is this the reason

you're retiring early?"

"There are reports that you are gravely ill and you've been forced from the music business — is this true?"

I've been traveling with Aidan long enough I should know how to deal with these people — but what I should do and what I actually do are often two different things. In this case, the absurdity of it all suddenly gets to me.

"First of all, back off. This is a *children's hospital*. Parents, grandparents, friends, and family members are trying to get in and out to see their kids. Y'all are being ridiculous. Yes, I know I'm from New York — but we're in Tennessee so I get to talk that way. Let's get away from the doors, shall we?"

I walk about fifty feet to a large open area and they follow me like little ducklings. I don't know if I'll ever get used to the idea that people are interested in my life off the stage. This is pure insanity to me. I climb up on a little brick wall and sit down on the edge. "I have to say I'm a little disappointed in all of you."

The members of the paparazzi look around at each other as if they're trying to figure out why I might say such a thing.

"No ... Really. I guess there are probably more than a dozen of you here today, right? I have no idea why you're here — but the other day when Aidan and I held an event to highlight the need for donations to St. Jude's, six of you showed up to our event to cover it. That's it. Only six. Now, I don't have to tell you St. Jude's means the world to me. The medical staff at this hospital saved my life and they didn't charge my family a dime for the care. In the grand scheme of things, it was a lot more important for you to cover what we said the other day than for you to camp out here and ask me about why I'm visiting a friend in the hospital. Although it's none of your business, I'll answer your questions. No, my cancer is not back, thank goodness. I'm visiting another friend who is fighting cancer. There's no story here. Go home. If you want to write a story, write a story about how phenomenal the doctors and nurses who help fight pediatric cancer are. That's the story."

"Are you gonna tell us about your friend who's fighting cancer? Are they near the end?"

"That's enough! Your question is so far out of bounds, you should be ashamed to ask it," Jude bellows. "Ms. Keeley is finished responding to questions. Have a good night."

Jude places his arm around my waist and starts to escort me toward the front door. We are just a couple of feet from the door when Howard, one of the more persistent paparazzi, places his hand on my arm. "Tasha, some guy told me to give this to you."

Jude narrows his gaze and asks, "What guy?"

Howard shrugs. "I don't really know. I didn't recognize him, but I figured he was one of your road crew. He had an Aidan O'Brien jacket on. I thought he was just in a hurry to get somewhere. He seemed to know we're friends and felt comfortable using me as a go-between — at least that's what I thought. Did I do something wrong?"

I take off my baseball cap and let my hair down,

pulling it off my neck with a sigh. "No, Howie, it's all right. It's been a freakishly long week. Things are a little topsy-turvy in my world. Thanks for passing it on."

Howard grins at me. "No problem, Tasha, but if you have news of anything, please give me a call. It's been a lean month, if you know what I mean."

Jude takes the envelope from me and tucks it into his back pocket. "We'll deal with this later. We have some cheesecake to deliver. It'll go bad in this heat."

Howard perks up. "Can I quote you guys on that?"

I shake my head. "Howie, you and I go back a really long way. You know I love you, but I'd really rather you didn't. This family means a lot to me and I wish you wouldn't expose them to all of this. They need to save their strength to fight cancer. After they win their battle, if we do something together, I promise I'll introduce you."

Howie steps aside gallantly and lets us through the door. "Ms. Keeley, you might be young, but you're one classy broad."

I curtsy as I grin. "Why thank you, Howard. Despite your profession, I think you're a pretty all right guy yourself."

Jude shakes his head with a bemused expression. "Have you guys ever noticed you're the same kind of weird? I think you've been friends for too long."

I glance back at Howie as we walk away, "I don't know, I guess so. I can't remember a time he wasn't around. He's kind of a fixture. Usually, his questions are relatively tame and he at least tries to print decent pictures of me. I don't mind him much. There are others who are much worse."

Jude hugs me to his side as we make our way up the elevator. "That was pretty smooth, *Sirena*. You handled the paps like the star you are. You didn't even bat an eyelash. If I didn't know better, I'd think you handle that stuff every day of your life."

"You think so? I was so nervous, I thought I would throw up. I guess all the time I spent on stage as a kid paid off, huh? Maybe I should call my mom and say thanks. I don't know what I'm thinking. This is the second time recently I've been grateful for all the weird stuff I went through as a kid."

"I still don't know if I would recommend something so drastic — a call to your mom might be more traumatic than talking to the paparazzi."

I involuntarily shudder. "I know you meant it as a joke, but sadly it's true."

When we walk into Hayden's room she's hunched over her iPad. She looks up at me and squeals, "Oh my Gosh! You were epic!"

"I just had barbecue chicken for dinner. I'm not sure that was so epic," I comment, looking around the room as I try to figure out what she's talking about.

"No! Just now with the paparazzi I was watching you on TMZ's Internet channel. You handle the media so much better than lots of stars. You had them eating out of your hand. I bet you lots of them go back and do a story on St. Jude's now because you made them feel so bad about skipping your presser the other day."

I raise an eyebrow. "Presser? Look at you and all your showbiz lingo —"

"Hey, I work on the yearbook. I'm not only a band geek. I think being a journalist would be really fun."

"I agree, it does sound fun. The paparazzi can be annoying, but the truth is most of those guys — at least the ones with manners — are nice. They have a job to do — as unpleasant as it is."

"How did they even know you were at the hospital?" Pennie asks. "Did you tell anybody you were coming here?"

I look over at Jude. "I didn't tell anybody, did you?"

"I left a message with the receptionist at Silent Beats to give to Stella to let her know we would be away from her house for a couple of days."

"Why didn't you just call Stella?"

"Stella told us not to call her directly because she's in recording sessions this week."

"Oh, you're right. I forgot."

"She probably didn't even pick up her messages, so I have no idea how anybody would've found out we were here. The whole situation is strange. Even if they'd figured out we were here, how would they have known you're thinking about retiring?"

Hayden's eyes widen. "I swear Mom and I didn't tell anybody. I didn't even tell Juliann. She's my cousin and one of your biggest fans — but I never said a word, even to her."

"Relax, Hayden, I know you didn't squeal on me. I trust you guys. The information could've come from anywhere. I've got scholarship applications plastered from coast-to-coast and I've applied to half a dozen nursing programs in the Pacific Northwest. I've got three in Portland alone. Lots of people see those, and not everybody follows the same rules of confidentiality."

Hayden looks glum for a moment. "I was hoping you might go to school somewhere close to me."

I smile as I set out the boxes of food on Hayden's bedside table. "I know you were, Hayden. I appreciate your support. I wish it were possible — unfortunately, I can't be at two places at once. I want to stay close to where Aidan's company is located so Jude doesn't have to relocate."

"So, when are you going to tell everybody about your plans? You can't keep it a secret forever."

I sigh as I respond, "Yeah, I know. I guess I'm waiting until I get accepted into a program and get some scholarship dollars behind me. I don't want them to award money based on who I am."

"That makes sense, but I still don't understand why you have to apply for scholarships. Aren't your songs doing amazeballs now? I thought you guys get paid for that kinda stuff."

"We are — but I'm just one of several musicians on the hits with Aidan. He's a really great boss, but nursing school is righteously expensive."

"Speaking as a parent of a college kid, I think you should use every single word of any sob story you can come up with. Make it a darn Hallmark movie with your own soundtrack if you must. College is far more expensive than we ever dreamed. We thought we were prepared, but every time we turn around there's a new fee, charge or class Jayne needs to take."

"Don't you think I would be taking advantage of my status?" I point out with a shrug. "I'm worried my fans might think I'm abusing their trust. Even worse, what if they think I'm just riding on Aidan's coattails after he was so good to me? In a way, I would be doing that. I'd hate to take advantage of the situation Aidan's put me in."

"So what?" Pennie asks me as she waves away my questions. "How many times over the past few years have you had to sacrifice your privacy and your chance at a normal life so you can entertain fans?"

I look down at the floor and roll my shoulder. "More times than I'd like to admit. It was especially difficult after *America's Next Star*. I felt like I didn't have any life at all. The paparazzi followed me everywhere. It was especially embarrassing after I won but then nothing spectacular happened in my career because Five-Star never followed through with all of their promises to promote me."

"See? My mom is right. You've already paid the price in advance, so you might as well take advantage of your notoriety now and let people know what you're up to. I bet they'd be excited about the fact that you want to be a nurse and give back to the profession which helped save your life when you were a little girl. I know I'm a fan and I think it's super cool you want to be a nurse who helps kids like me with cancer. I think tons of other people will think it's great too — especially girls who think pop stars are supposed to be vacant and stupid. You can prove them all wrong."

"You know, I think Hayden's right," Jude remarks quietly. "There should be more to being a star than what you wear and who you date. If you give people an opportunity to follow your journey in college, you never know who you might inspire."

"You're right. When I was being tutored, one tutor told me girls like me should just forget about math because we would never be any good at it. I was able to give him examples of stars like Danica McKellar, Mayim Bialik, and Pauley Perrette. Not only did it shut him right up, those women showed me what was possible," I say with a conspiratorial grin.

"I love *NCIS*, but Mom says I have to wait before I can get tattoos like Abby. I think it's cool Pauley has a degree like her character," Hayden adds.

Jude grins at Hayden. "I watch that show all the time. You have great taste." Turning back to me he says, "I think Hayden's on to something. I'm sure Aidan and Tara would be supportive of you sharing your story. Both of them are big advocates of overcoming obstacles and following your dreams. Your story fits right into their approach to life."

I chew on my fingernail as I think about what Jude suggested. "I don't know. Aidan's sad about losing me — even if it is for a really good cause."

Jude puts his arm around my shoulder. "*Sirena*, I understand that you can't go on tour with Aidan, but do you have to give up *everything* music related? Can't you still sing on his albums and work around your school schedule?"

I'm silent for a few moments as I think about his proposal. "I don't really know. I probably could. I don't know how much time I'll have to spend studying. Aidan's flexible so I suppose it's theoretically possible. I guess I built it up in my mind as an all-or-nothing proposition. I didn't really think about doing both things."

"It sounds like you guys are will figure it all out. I won't lie, college is a tough adjustment for some people. Be sure to let Aidan know if it's too much for you," Pennie advises. "If it's not working, don't try to be everything for everyone."

"I'll try to find some balance, Pennie. I've spent far too much of my life trying to make everyone else's dreams come true," I pledge.

Jude walks up behind me and embraces me. "I'll do my best to make sure she keeps that promise."

Hayden giggles. "Jude, don't forget to take care of yourself, too. Becoming a mega-superstar is hard work."

I salute Hayden. "Okay, we have our marching orders. We want you guys to keep fighting to get well. We'd like to see you at a concert the next time we come to town."

Hayden's eyes twinkle with mischief. "Can I have front row seats and back stage passes?"

"It's a deal!" I vow, hoping I get to keep my promise.

Abruptly, Pennie hops up from her favorite recliner chair and places her arm around my shoulder as she escorts Jude and me out the door. Once we're in the hallway, she hugs me and declares, "Tasha, if the nursing school thing doesn't work out and you decide not to be an extremely gifted musician, you might want to think about being a cosmetologist."

I bite back a grin. "Okay, whatever you say — but it was just a little makeup. It was the least I could do."

Pennie shakes her head. "To you it was a bit of makeup, but to me, it completely changed my mood today and made me happy. I went on a virtual date with my husband and felt glamorous for the first time in a long time. It was like our problems fell away for a few minutes and it was like old times. I know it seems silly, but it took Hayden's mind off of things too. Thanks for giving us a few minutes of normal."

I blink away tears. "You're so welcome. I'm honored to play a tiny role in whatever brings you joy, Pennie. I wish nothing but happiness and love to your family."

CHAPTER EIGHTEEN

JUDE

THUNDERSTORMS ARE TYPICALLY NOT my favorite thing in the world, but I've never been so grateful to see one as I am at this moment. The deluge of rain has encouraged the paparazzi to abandon their posts at the front door of the hospital, and Tasha and I return to the rental car without any more issues.

I pull my sopping wet T-shirt away from my chest and remark, "I never thought I'd say this in July, but I'm sure glad there's a great shower and a big, fluffy down comforter in our hotel room."

Tasha smirks at me. "Just one of the perks of being a superstar, babe."

I let out a bark of laughter because the remark is so atypical for Tasha. "Are you sure you're ready to go back to being a regular civilian? Maybe you've gotten spoiled over the last few years hanging out with Aidan."

Tasha shrugs. "I probably have. Then again, I have this amazing boyfriend who'll soon hit the charts like a tropical storm. He'll soon reach the pop stratosphere

"

and I won't have to worry about my status as a lowly college student. I'll just be an industrial-strength groupie. He'll get me all the rock 'n' roll perks I'll ever need."

I want to laugh at Tasha's joke. I know she means it to be funny, but there's a growing knot in my stomach. I might not be able to go through with all my grand plans. What if my stage paralysis is a permanent thing and I can't ever sing again? Tasha thinks that if we go back to the beginning and start our process over, we can erase the bad experience at Puckett's. I don't know if it's so simple. I wish it was. I keep turning it over and over in my head. The words from my family echo in my brain. I don't want to go home unless I can figure this out. I left everyone behind with the goal to either make it or throw in the towel. I'm not ready to give up. I guess I need to come to grips with what will happen if the worst happens.

Tasha glances over at me. "I thought you might be a little more excited about the prospect of lounging around at the Peabody with me. It's been a rough day. I'm ready to unplug and not think about anything. These visits with Hayden have been an interesting two-way street."

"How so?" I ask

"When I first agreed to help Aidan with this, I thought we would be the ones providing all the help and fun presents. I guess I never stopped to think about the impact Hayden and her family would have on my life. Pennie's daughter, Jayne, is the same age as me. When Pennie was proudly showing us pictures of all the stuff

Jayne designed as part of her classes and bragging about her grades, all I could think about was how great it would be to have a mom like hers."

I nod in agreement. "Yeah, it was really sweet, wasn't it? You can tell there's a whole lot of love in their family. It's a great thing because the environment will help Hayden adjust to her new life."

"Pennie gave us some great advice, didn't she? You can tell she and Larry have been through some tough times."

"Been through … and still going through tough times. But even though they're apart, they seem to be a team. They remind me of my aunt and uncle and my grandparents. It makes me homesick."

"I know we said all the right things in front of Hayden, but do you really think everything will be all right?" Tasha frets. "It's so weird. A couple weeks ago I didn't even know Hayden, and now she feels like a kid sister or something. I would be devastated if something happened to her. I'm so angry! Cancer sucks. Why does it have to strike somebody like her? Why not the sick deranged people on the planet? Why does it have to happen to good families like theirs? It's not fair!"

I reach across the car and grab her hand. "*Sirena,* there are no great answers about why bad things happen to good people. People has been trying to figure that out forever."

"Aren't you angry, Jude?" Tasha demands as she pulls her hand away from mine. "How can you look at Hayden's beautiful face and not get pissed off? She looked so much worse this time. It was beyond scary. I wanted to collapse to the floor and cry for her, but I knew tears wouldn't be helpful."

As we pull into the hotel parking lot, I scrub my hands over my face and take a deep breath. "Of course I'm scared, furious as hell, and tired of cancer taking people I love away from me. I look at all the crazy things we're able to do now. We can send space vehicles to another planet or store millions of files of data on a single chip the size of a grain of rice, but we can't stop cells from going crazy and killing little kids? It makes no sense. A teenager shouldn't have to learn to tie her shoes again at thirteen. The only thing Hayden should have to worry about at a junior high school dance is whether another girl is wearing the same dress and if her shoes hurt her feet. She shouldn't have to be anxious about whether her friends will hate her because she can't play basketball on the varsity team anymore."

"I know. It's so sad." Tasha wipes away tears.

"When she asked me if I could change the settings on her iPad to make it easier for her to use with one hand, she reminded me so much of Fernanda. It was enough to break my heart. I know my little sister always trusts me to fix everything in her world. She never has any doubt about my ability to make everything okay. I saw the same kind of trust in Hayden's eyes today. I'll be darned if I didn't want to wave a magic wand and fix every cell of her body."

"Exactly! I feel helpless. It's silly of us to think this way because Hayden would never put this kind of pressure on us. Even so, I still feel like I should be able to do more. I'm scared for her future."

"I know, but the best we can do is hope the doctors at St. Jude's can get to the bottom of what's going on and get Hayden back on the right path."

"I feel like we're spinning our wheels here. Thinking about it won't change anything, but I can't stop trying to solve everything."

"I know what you mean. I feel that way about a lot of things. Right now I feel like I have a whole gang of hamsters running around in my head. I just go from one problem to another and drive myself nuts trying to figure everything out. I think we need a break from thinking. What do you say we actually go on vacation like we're supposed to be doing? I suggest we go pretend to be rich and famous in this swanky hotel. I took a look at the room service menu and it's pretty killer. I'm thinking we should lock ourselves in the room at the Peabody and not leave for a couple days."

"It sounds like a great idea. I'm tired of thinking so hard. Hanging out with you in the lap of luxury sounds like the perfect plan. It might cure me of my dislike of hotel rooms."

I chuckle as I open the door for her and place my arm around her waist and walk with her into the hotel lobby. As the elevator closes I whisper into her ear, "I'll do my best to make sure you're not bored."

"That's what I'm counting on," she replies with a wink.

⸻ ● ⸻

"I can't believe this — my goosebumps have goosebumps. Who knew a little rainstorm could cause so much damage? It was weird. It's kinda like walking through a very warm wet sauna."

I reach around the shower door and test the water. "I've never had such a luxurious shower before, so I didn't realize it would take so long for the water in those fancy pipes to heat up. My teeth are chattering so hard I feel like they might crack. We're in Tennessee and we're talking about how cold we are in the middle of July. There's something wrong with this picture."

"I agree, usually it's hot as blazes out there," Tasha says as she starts to peel off her jeans. "I think we should've thought twice before cranking up the air conditioner in the car while we were drenched."

As I stand up and do the same, struggling to shimmy out of my wet, sticky jeans, something hits the floor.

"Oh crap, I totally forgot about that," Tasha says as she sees the envelope the paparazzi handed us earlier.

Finally, I'm able to untangle the wet jeans from my ankles and kick them aside. I bend down to pick up the letter. "What do you think this is?"

Tasha shrugs. "I don't know. It's hard to say what arrangements Aidan and Tara made to cover Silent Beats when they were gone. It might be something from their law office dealing with all the crap from Five-Star."

"I don't think so. It's too girly to be a business letter — but it could be something from Stella. She promised to stay in touch over the break and she's pretty old school. She doesn't use email much. She prefers letters. Maybe she had someone from the crew deliver it."

Tasha smiles at me as she grabs the letter from my hands, "I bet you're right. Stella is a big-time letter writer. I bet she just wants to check in on us to see how we liked her house. Look how frilly this is. It seems like it has Stella written all over it."

I smirk at Tasha as I observe, "Geez, anxious much? You're like a kid waiting for a letter from Santa Claus —"

"What can I say?" Tasha replies with a self-deprecating laugh. "I don't have much family and I didn't get a lot of mail when I was a kid. When I did get something, even if it was junk mail, it was a big deal."

"Whatever you say," I tease. "I think you just like presents."

Tasha gives me a sideways glance and raises an eyebrow. "Are you done making fun of me? Because I'd like to open my mail. I don't get awesome stuff like this often and I'd like to enjoy my experience."

"Thanks for giving me the key to your heart. I'll just send you love letters in fancy cards," I joke as I watch Tasha's excitement grow.

"That'd do it," Tasha quips as she leans on the edge of the vanity and examines the envelope. "This is so beautiful; I hate to tear it all to pieces."

I bend down, scoop my pants off the floor, and retrieve a small pocket knife from the pocket. I take a second to dry it off on a nearby towel before I hand it to Tasha. "This should help."

She flicks open the blade and cuts a slit in the top of the envelope. She squeezes the envelope so the sides bulge, but as soon as she looks at the contents, she shrieks, "Oh, hell no! How did he find us here?" Instinctively, she drops the envelope on the floor as she sinks down to sit on the toilet.

Taking a towel off the rack, I cover up my hand and pick up the letter. I gingerly peek inside and immediately understand why she's so upset. "You've got to be kidding me! How in the world did they get a picture of us while we were in the hospital?" I exclaim as I study the gruesome pictures.

"I don't know, but it's from the other day when we were waiting out in the hall for them to change Hayden's IV. I was wearing a red shirt because it's Hayden's favorite color."

"That's sick," I growl. "I wonder how close he was. I hope the jerk was using a telephoto lens. I don't want him anywhere near you. It's time to call Logan." I walk over to the dresser where my cell phone is.

With my free hand, I grab a paper towel from the minibar and set it down on the dresser. I lay the letter on it before I start to search through my contacts for Logan.

"Stop!" Tasha directs. I freeze as I look over at her. "Did you even get a look at the picture? There was a target on your head. *A target!* The man was close enough to take a picture of us a few days ago. He handed this envelope to Howie. He wasn't even strange enough to set off any alarm bells. As a reporter, Howard studies people for a living. Doesn't that scare the crap out of you?"

"Of course it does! I'm supposed to be protecting

you. I should've noticed someone strange taking pictures of you. Instead, I was focused on kissing you. I should've kept my head in the game. I let you down. You know how Tara's always telling us to be aware of our surroundings. Obviously, I wasn't — I was off in la-la land."

"That's not what this is about!" Tara yells, then softens her voice. "I obviously was in la-la land with you. I didn't notice anybody taking pictures of me either. We were distracted by Hayden's condition and how upset Pennie was that day — it's not surprising we weren't focused on the other people in the hallway. It could've been anybody. To be honest, I don't even notice people's cell phones anymore unless people start being obnoxious about it — everybody and their dog takes pictures of me these days. If I got upset about everybody who takes pictures of me on the sly, I'd get nothing else done. I don't let it bother me anymore. To be fair, I've never had anybody take pictures and be like this. This is beyond Fifty Shades of Crazy."

She angrily wipes away tears. "Jude! The guy Photoshopped bullet holes in your head with a target. That's a death threat. We have to call the police."

"I agree, we need to call somebody. I just think we should call Logan first. I have a hunch Aidan will want him to coordinate your protection."

Tasha raises an eyebrow. "Actually, first I think we need to get dressed. I don't think we're going to get our nice warm shower right now. Later, I'll get all pissed off at the missed opportunity because I was looking forward to taking a shower with you and warming myself up in all those cushy down blankets after the thunderstorm — but we have bigger things to worry about right now."

For the first time in a while, I take note of how I'm dressed. Tasha has a point. The police would probably take me more seriously if I had clothes on. "Well, the letter accomplished one thing for sure. I'm not cold anymore. How about you?"

Tasha slowly shakes her head. "No, I'm not cold anymore. I'm scared out of my mind. It's a totally different sensation. I feel like my stomach is on fire. This is worse than stage fright."

"I don't know. I might argue with that sentiment. It doesn't feel good; I'll grant you. I feel like every nerve ending on my skin is on high alert," A shudder travels throughout my body.

"Should I take the time to take a quick shower?" Tasha asks as she looks down at herself in dismay. "I feel dirty simply because I touched the letter. It won't take long. Can you ask Logan what he wants us to do? I'll do whatever he recommends. As he so politely says, I think this will 'escalate things.'"

"That's a no-brainer. I think we should consider them officially escalated — like to Defcon one million thirty-seven. I'm going to call Pennie and let her know. The hospital staff might want to up the security on Hayden. Those pictures weren't taken too far from her room."

"Oh Gosh! What a horrifying thought. What if I put Hayden in danger? I'd never forgive myself," Tasha says in a broken whisper.

"We don't know if anything like that will happen. It's a precaution to keep Hayden and Pennie safe. I'll call Logan and see what else he wants us to do." I gesture toward the steaming shower. "There's no sense in wasting this. You're cold and feel nasty. You might as well take a shower while I get dressed and make some calls."

"Gah! This is so annoying! How can someone I've never met ruin my first real vacation with my boyfriend? That's just too insane. How does Creepy Stalker Dude even know we were here? What if this isn't the same guy? What if this is a totally different obsessed crazy person?"

"I don't know, *Sirena.*" Those are all great questions for Logan. Maybe he'll have some answers for us. I'll let you know what he says after I call."

"I hope so because none of this is making any sense," Tasha answers as she wipes away her tears again. "I'm just somebody who sings songs for a living — who could hate me so much?"

"I don't know the answer either. I can't imagine anybody hating you."

———•———

"You know what this feels like?" I ask as I pull Tasha tighter toward my body and tuck the blankets around her again.

Tasha shakes her head. "No, I don't know what this feels like. I'm petrified."

"Did you ever tell ghost stories around the campfire when you were young?" I ask, trying to distract her for a few moments. She's been shaking uncontrollably for hours.

Tasha laughs out loud. "I was going to ask you if you've met my mom, but then I remembered you actually haven't had the pleasure yet. Ghost stories are not her thing. Actually, campfires aren't her thing either. I wanted to join the Girl Scouts, but she said they would interfere with the pageants she'd scheduled for me, so I didn't get to do that either. I haven't really had the chance to do the whole campfire-ghost story schtick." She trails off with a hitch in her voice.

"I can see what we'll be doing on our next vacation. You have to go through the ritual at least once in your life. It's a rite of passage. I'm surprised you haven't had the opportunity to do it with Aidan and Tara at the Creative Arts Center they run. Sometimes they have a bunch of deaf kids there. Let me tell you, you haven't heard a ghost story until you've seen it acted out by deaf teenagers who are high on chocolate, marshmallows, and Mountain Dew."

"Tara didn't interpret for the kids? She loves to do that."

"I've only been to one overnight session," I explain. "I usually go on the rock climbing trips. The time I was there I guess she was planning to, but she wasn't feeling well that weekend so one of her former classmates filled in for her."

Tasha interrupts, "Hey, you never told me why tonight reminds you of ghost stories. I don't think this is like summer camp at all. I'm so scared that I can hear my own heartbeat."

"Well, if you didn't do this as a kid, this story probably won't make much sense to you — but my sister and I used to build blanket forts all the time. Whenever things got scary or intense, we'd always hide in the most obscure blanket fort we could build. We'd carry all our books and puzzles into the fort with as many flashlights as we could scrounge up in the house, and then we'd hide there as long as we could without being discovered. Sometimes it would take all the grown-ups in my house an ungodly amount of time to find us if our hiding place was any good. The entire time Fernanda and I were hiding out, we would hold our breath, sometimes literally — sure we'd be discovered at any second."

Tasha shifts her position so she's looking at me and wraps the blanket so it covers both of us again. "Actually, that sounds like so much fun. I always wished I had a sibling growing up. It was always just Ma and me after my dad exited the picture. Loneliness was my constant companion. Brothers and sisters would've been awesome. I think it's cool you played with your little sister. I've heard big brothers don't like to play with their siblings."

"Don't give me too much credit. I entertained myself by making it like a big game of cat and mouse — sometimes at Fernanda's expense. We'd try everything we could to conceal our location from our parents because we didn't want them to know we were hiding from them. We thought we were so clever — but we had our weaknesses. Fernanda would get so nervous she'd want to cry, so I'd try to keep her calm by reading her favorite books in a very quiet whisper until she fell asleep."

"What was your weakness?" Tasha asks with a quizzical glance.

I chuckle softly as I admit, "I had a couple. First, I was always hungry. You have no idea how much noise food wrappers make. I would give us away. Even worse, I was always impatient. I always wanted to know what my parents were up to. I'd frequently get us busted when I was peeking around corners or sticking my head over barrier walls because I wanted to see what was going on."

Tasha snickers at me. "That cracks me up because you give the appearance of being so mellow and laid-back. Are you telling me it's all one big carefully well-crafted lie?"

"Pretty much. I'm okay as long as I know what's going on and I'm not left in the dark. I need to feel like I've got a say in the decision-making process — even if I'm not the one in charge."

"Okay, that I'll buy. You are like the radiator of our organization," Tasha remarks.

"What?" I ask with a startled cough.

Tasha gathers up her hair and pulls it out of her face as she explains, "You know, on a car everybody talks about the fuel injection system in the engine and even the transmission. People sweat over the color of the car and whether it has leather seats. They brag about how fast it can go, zero to sixty in such-and-such a time. They brag about the model and the brand name and the year. You know what? If your radiator isn't working right, your car isn't going anywhere."

I chuckle. "True enough."

"That's what you are to Silent Beats. You're the invisible heart of the organization, everything has to go through you for it to work smoothly. Without you, everything would blow apart."

I've never considered my job in those terms, but she does have a point. Even though I think of my job as just moving junk around and cleaning up messes, I do coordinate a lot of stuff on many levels of the organization.

"Blow apart. I guess that could apply to a lot of things in my life right now."

I cringe as I watch Tasha recoil from my words.

"Sorry to have completely ruined your life," she mutters angrily.

"Wait, I didn't mean it like it sounded. I don't mean us. I mean everything around us," I try to clarify. "I never expected to find you — or anyone like you. I've been following bands around since I was fifteen, trying to break into the music business and soak up everything I could. A few years ago, a buddy of mine decided to go to college and told me about the gig with Aidan."

"Thank God for small favors," Tasha mumbles under her breath. "If he hadn't, there would be no us."

I nod. "I know. I risked everything I had to move to Oregon. It could've been a complete disaster. I didn't know anything about Aidan. Frankly, I didn't even know what kind of music he played. It could've been opera for all I knew — but my friend said Aidan was a nice guy, and I gambled my future on his opinion. As you know, it turns out Javier was right."

"So far, so good; it doesn't sound too blown apart to me," Tasha challenges skeptically.

"This is where it gets tricky. I went to Oregon with a plan. My plan was to make a name for myself as a singer-songwriter. I've been practicing since I can remember. There isn't a time music didn't play a role in my life. After my mom got ahold of my videotapes and ran them by that music producer, she started dreaming my dream with me. It wasn't anything she could do publicly because my grandparents were so adamantly against the whole plan, but privately, I could tell my mom wanted me to pursue singing. It may have had something to do with my father. I know he liked to sing — at least as a hobby if not more. Maybe in some way, I remind her of him when I sing."

"Trust me, I totally know what it's like to have a parent who wants you to pursue a dream," Tasha remarks dryly. "They tend to lose sight of reality sometimes."

"The difference is, becoming a successful performer has always been my dream for as long as I can remember. My grandparents are dead set against my choices and I don't want to face them again until I've actually made it. I don't want them to be right. The fact that I'm still struggling makes me doubt everything in my life. What if they're right? That's what I mean by blowing up in my face. There's the whole stage fright issue, and then —"

"So we tackle this one issue at a time. It's not as if you going one step back undoes all the progress you made. It's just a bump in the road," Tasha says as she leans forward to hug me.

"Maybe this isn't a bump in the road. What if the stage fright is permanent? Now that I've had a taste of what's out there, it's going to be hard to settle for what I once had. It may not be enough for me anymore."

Tasha looks like she's about ready to shake me. "So don't settle for less than you deserve. You can't give up so easily. There are lots of things we can try that we haven't done yet. You know, there are psychologists who are like sports psychologists for performers; we haven't even gone down that road yet. It's too early to think it's all over. It's just not. I have faith in you. I won't let you give up. You haven't invested this many years of your life to reach your dream just to give it up over one bad performance. I know you're too stubborn to do that."

I hang my head and rest it against her forehead as I admit, "You're right. I am."

"Okay, so, that's one thing off your list, what else is blowing apart?" Tasha probes as she pulls away and studies my expression.

I heave out a deep breath. "Are you sure you want to hear this? I'm not even sure it's important enough to dump in your lap. It's not like you don't have enough on your plate."

"Okay, that's a stupid comment if I've ever heard one," Tasha replies. "How much random stuff have I shoved off on you, including my phone?"

"I feel dumb even bringing this up, but the situation with Hayden is stressing me out. I'm about as helpless as I was when my uncle died. I know she's probably not going to die, but it's hard to watch her go through so much pain and not be able to do anything about it. I want to fix everything and I can't."

Tasha leans forward and hugs me tightly as she whispers in my ear, "Jude, we're singing the same song. Some nights I dream about Hayden and her family. Sometimes they're happy dreams and other times they're nightmares. I love that you care about them enough to worry. It shows me you have a huge heart."

"I don't think I'll be able to check this one off my list until we know she's going to be okay — and I don't know what to do about that."

Tasha gives me a crooked grin. "Sometimes there's a downside to being both cute and smart. You'll have to take your methodical brain and put it in the wait-and-see mode for a few years. I should be through with nursing school about the time she gets her clean bill of health and graduates from high school."

I groan. "I know you meant that as good news, but it seems like forever from now."

Tasha shrugs. "I'm sorry, Cowboy, it's the best I've got." She kisses me tenderly. "Got anything else on your mental checklist?"

"Are you really going to make me talk about this?" I ask.

Tasha nods. "Obviously. Not talking about it is keeping you awake at night."

I flinch. "I was hoping you couldn't tell."

"Judas Vicente Hernández, you are a heck of a musician and your songwriting skills put mine to shame, but you're a terrible actor. Your fake sleeping wouldn't fool a toddler."

I sigh and roll my eyes. "I swear, you and my sister will be the best of friends. She started telling me the same thing when she was about six."

"I would love to meet your sister — but, don't think that will get you out of this conversation. Start talking," Tasha says with an intense glare.

"Why do I have this feeling you're going to use all the skills we've learned in Tara's class to kick my butt?" I ask.

"I might — if you don't stop procrastinating," Tasha threatens. "I'm already on edge. You're starting to make me think you're about to break up with me or something."

My mouth drops open in shock. "Shut up! Why would you think something like that?"

Tasha pushes on my chest. "Because you're being super weird and I'm scared to death. This has been an amazingly crappy day. In case you've forgotten, somebody sent us pictures of you with bullet holes and a target on your head."

"No, I haven't forgotten. I haven't forgotten the picture, and I will never forget the picture of you being blown up," I snap. I drag my hand through my hair and clench my jaw in frustration.

"You know that really wasn't me, right?" Tasha asks gently.

"No, it wasn't you *this time*, but what if those threats are real? What if the letter sitting over there on the dresser is from the same person? You know what that means? The person who threatened to blow you up was close enough to take pictures. That kind of crap keeps me awake."

"I'm sorry," Tasha whispers.

"It's not your fault. If anything, the responsibility for this might fall squarely into my lap. I watch people file in to see you in concert every night. Young, old, male, female, country music fans, rock 'n' rollers, jazz fans and everything in between — but I have no idea what this person looks like. I've known you for years. It's possible I've helped this person find their seat at a concert or even given you something for you to sign directly from their hands — heck, maybe I even introduced them to you backstage. How would I even know? I don't know who this person is and neither do you. The scary thing is even with all of Logan's military experience, he doesn't know either. We're all in the dark. All I can think of when I close my eyes before I go to bed at night is every fan who struck me the wrong way. Should I have done more? Should I have said something? Should I have noticed something about someone else I missed? Those questions tumble around in my brain like pebbles in a fast-moving spring."

Tasha captures my face in her hands. "Jude! Stop. You *cannot* do this to yourself. We have professional bodyguards who didn't see anything either and that's their job."

"You know how this works, *Sirena*. Aidan has said it a million times: The team is only as strong as its weakest link. What if I'm the weakest link? We were in the hallway and I saw no one — even though you and I have been taking those classes from Tara. She's been drilling it in our heads to stay alert to our surroundings. I knew you were in danger, I read those messages and saw those pictures, but I was still more interested in making out with you in the hallway than protecting you from danger."

Tasha raises an eyebrow. "Are you done yet? As I recall, there were two of us in the hallway, and I was as involved in the kiss as you were. I've heard those same instructions in Tara's classes. Since the death threats were about me, don't you think I should've been paying attention? Don't you think the responsibility should've also been on my shoulders? Isn't it a tiny bit chauvinistic to think because you're the guy, somehow you have some elevated sense of responsibility to protect me?"

I grind my teeth in frustration. This whole situation is screwed up beyond belief. "Okay, fine, whatever. The bottom line is there's a death threat sitting over on the dresser, and we missed it. I carried it around in my pocket for an entire day. Who knows where this lunatic is right now? He could be in this hotel, for all we know."

Tasha springs to her feet, throwing the blanket off her shoulders. "Don't you think I've thought of that? Why do you think I've been shaking like a leaf all night? You are so *not* helping."

I slump back against the headboard. "Yeah, I know. I suck at this when I don't know what to do. I knew I shouldn't talk about it because once I get started, all sorts of crap just flies out of my mouth. Do you want to go to the police department now? We could do that instead of waiting for Logan, if it makes you feel more comfortable."

Tasha throws her hands up in the air. "I don't know what to do. When Logan said he wouldn't be able to be here for a few hours, it didn't seem like such a big deal — but the longer we wait, the harder it becomes. Maybe we should just go."

I can see the indecision tearing at Tasha. My stomach tightens and I feel like I want to hurl as I admit, "I want to be the hero here and tell you exactly what to do — but, I don't know the right answer. Logan said to sit tight until he got here. Still, something in my gut says we should go to the police right now — but what do I know? My gut's been wrong this whole time. I'm not sure you should listen to anything I have to say."

"I think you're carrying way too much blame on your shoulders. First of all, it's not our job to figure all this stuff out. I guess it's time to go tell someone whose job it is to fix it. Logan can help them sort it out later. This is probably more my fault than yours because I let it escalate by not calling in help sooner. You don't need to fix this for me — you can stop trying to be the hero here."

I know Tasha's trying to relieve the pressure, but there is a big part of me that's beyond pissed off that I dropped the ball. If there's anything I've learned from my mom, it's that every woman deserves a hero in her life. I just don't feel like much of one right now.

CHAPTER NINETEEN

TASHA

THE ATMOSPHERE IN THE car on the way over to the police station was ice cold. The conversation between us was better way back when we were perfect strangers. It's hard not to take all of this personally. I know Jude's stress level is through the roof and all of this probably isn't directed at me. Even knowing that, his stony demeanor is disconcerting. Now, as we wait in the interview room, the distance between us is obvious and palpable. I wonder how the officer will interpret it — but then again, I'm a TV junkie. I watch way too many crime shows. Maybe none of this means anything and I'm letting my imagination get away from me.

Just before I gnaw my fingernails down to the quick, the door swings open and a police officer in a rumpled suit enters. "Sorry to keep you folks waiting, what can I do for you?"

"We'd like to report a threat," Jude answers before I can even form a sentence.

The officer's eyebrows furrow. "What kind of

threat?"

"Umm," I begin.

"You're not comin' in to report that somebody unliked you on Facebook or something, are you? I had one of those this mornin'," he interjects in a tired voice.

I straighten up in the hard, wooden chair as I respond, "No. Not exactly."

He pins me with a sharp glance. "What do you mean, 'not exactly'?"

"Well, I received one really serious threat over my phone messaging app, but the latest threat was delivered in person," I try to clarify.

The officer's eyes travel over me in a slow perusal. "Usually in cases like this we look at the ex-boyfriends — or … ex-girlfriends."

Jude abruptly leans forward in his chair so he is in the officer's personal space. "That might be what you usually do, but that's not Tasha's story. We think the creep is after her because of her job."

"Uh-huh, I've heard it all before," the officer responds dryly.

Jude visibly bristles and frowns fiercely. "Disrespectful much?"

The officer shifts in his chair and takes a long sip of his coffee. He grimaces and sets his coffee down, nearly tipping it over. "I apologize. You're right. Let's start over. My name is Officer Browning. I was out of line. It's been a stupidly long day. It seems like half our force is out with Norovirus and the rest of us are stuck working doubles and triples."

As I study him closer, I can see clear signs of fatigue. "I'm sorry, that sucks. I'm Tasha. Tasha Keeley."

"You don't sound like you're from around here, Tasha," he comments.

"That's because I'm not. I'm from New York, but we live in Oregon now."

"What brings you to Tennessee?"

"We're on tour with Aidan O'Brien," I answer.

"So, you travel from state to state like tailgaters?" Officer Browning asks.

I can see the tips of Jude's ears grow red, and I know his temper is about to erupt. I jump in to smooth things over before it happens. "Actually we're a little more official than that. We're both part of the band."

The officer's eyebrows climb in surprise as he says, "No kidding? It sucks for my daughter that today isn't 'Take Your Daughter to Work Day.' She tried hard to get tickets for your concert in Nashville, but it sold out in minutes."

"Gee, I'm so sorry. I hate it when we have to disappoint fans."

"So, what brings you into the 201?"

Jude carefully lays out the note on the table in front of the officer. He left it on the paper towel where he placed it last night before I took my shower. It looks deceptively benign just setting there — yet, for us, it's anything but harmless.

Officer Browning glances back and forth between us as he tries to decide which one of us will give the most coherent explanation. Apparently, he decides I must be the most levelheaded because he turns to me. "What is this?"

"There are threatening pictures and a note in the card. I opened it because I thought it was from a friend. It was hand delivered to a reporter who's a longtime acquaintance of mine. I can't guarantee that it's from the same sender as before, but I guess it's the latest threat in an ongoing campaign against me. It has the same sinister undertones as the letters before it."

"So, you have a stalker? Do you have the local authorities in Oregon involved?"

Jude whips out his phone and pulls up his copy of the first group of messages I received. "We tried. We showed them these graphic, disturbing messages, but they didn't seem overly concerned. I can't imagine why not. The threats seem pretty real to me. I guess it didn't rise to the standard you all need to take action. Maybe Tasha isn't a big enough star, I don't know — but in any event, nothing happened. Then the band had to go on tour ... and here we are."

After studying Jude's phone for a few moments, Officer Browning looks up at us and asks, "So it's your contention that whoever sent you the emails has followed you to Tennessee?"

I shrug. "I don't know. We don't know what to think. We were visiting a fan at St. Jude's Hospital and apparently, whoever wrote the card handed it to one of the members of the press I deal with pretty routinely and told him to give it to us."

"Okay, so maybe this was a publicity stunt to get you more press coverage? Why involve us?"

"No, that's not what this was. Aidan and I did a public service announcement about St. Jude's Children's Hospital, but I never mentioned that I was visiting a child through the Dreaming While Awake Foundation. I merely talked about St. Jude's mission and how they helped me when I was a child. Aidan and I had a press junket related to raising funds for St. Jude's. It had nothing to do with anything else. The rest of it's extremely private and confidential."

"I'm not saying I don't believe your story, Ms. Keeley, but you wouldn't be the first 'star' to invent a controversy to get media coverage. A lot of stars do stuff to boost their ticket sales or to command bigger fees on the speaking circuit."

"I can promise you I'm not that kind of star. I wouldn't waste law enforcement's time with a hoax. I can't tell you for sure if this stuff is related to my problem fan, but I can tell you that both of them are creepy as heck and keep me up at night. Do you know how hard it is to get up on stage and act like nothing's wrong when I get stuff like this?" I ask the officer bluntly. "I'll just tell you. It's darn near impossible. I have to watch my back all the time and I can't trust anyone. I don't know what they want from me, I just sing songs for a living. I mind my own business and try not to throw flames on social media. I'm not even edgy. This time they came after Jude too. It's incredibly bizarre. He has done nothing to these people. Until a few months ago, he was completely in the background."

Jude grabs my hand. "Tasha, you haven't done anything either — except work your butt off to become one of the best singers out there. I'm not sure why anyone would have anything against you. I don't know if we can make sense of this. Clearly somebody has mental health issues they need to take care of. We need help from the police to figure out who it is."

"Sadly the Internet seems to make some of the more unsavory folks among us even more brazen. What makes you think this person is anywhere near you?" Officer Browning asks. "They could be in another country for all you know."

"They were close enough to get a picture of Jude and me standing in the middle of the hallway in St. Jude's Hospital. As far as I can tell, aside from the bullet wounds and the target over Jude's head, the rest of it isn't doctored."

"Well, that certainly would make you sit up and take notice," Officer Browning mutters.

"Exactly. That's why we're here. Tasha didn't sleep a wink last night. She was shaking like a leaf. I can't ask her to live like this. We have to figure out who is doing this to her — I mean us." Jude can barely hide his agitation.

"Are you sure it's not some misguided ad executive somewhere within your record label trying to drum up publicity? In this age of reality TV shows where sick and twisted is the name of the game, you never know what some upstart trying to make a name for themselves might come up with."

I nod as I say, "I'm sure. I've known Aidan O'Brien since I was thirteen years old, and I know everyone in his company. There isn't anyone who would do this to me. Everyone treats me like family — actually, they treat me better than family. When Aidan found out about the threats against me, he doubled his security force. He doesn't want anything to happen to any members of the band or crew, or anyone else associated with this company."

"I imagine not. America is a very litigious country, the risk to his company could be huge," the officer comments.

"No, that's not it at all. Aidan doesn't want us to get hurt because he's that kind of person," I insist. "Look, you don't even have to take my word for it. Logan Anthony will be here in a couple hours. He'll have all the nitty-gritty details about what's already been done and what they're planning to do for security. They've been trying to solve this for months. You can rehash it all with him."

Officer Browning sighs. "I know it seems as if I'm being confrontational. I'm not trying to be. I don't want to give you false hope. My hands are probably tied. There's a limit to what I can do. Agency resources are stretched, and without witnesses to a direct threat, I don't know how much we'll be able to track down. I can have my forensics folks look this over and see if anything stands out to them, but beyond that — it's a crap shoot."

The sense of hopefulness I had coming into this meeting drains out of me in an instant. I start to collapse abruptly as if someone unplugged me from the wall. Jude notices my change in demeanor and shoots me a look of concern. He starts to say something and I just shake my head sharply.

Alert to my cue, Jude clears his throat and says, "It's been a long day for all of us. We're going to go back to the hotel and wait for Mr. Anthony to arrive. We'll be back later if you need more information from us. We're staying at the Peabody if you need us for anything. Our cell phone numbers are on the statements we filled out with our incident reports. Thank you for your help."

I don't know if it was his fatigue or mine, but I could swear Officer Browning looks more than just a little relieved as he stands to escort us out the door.

⸻ ● ⸻

"They probably won't do anything, will they?" I ask as I crack the hard sugar shell on my crème brûlée.

"It's too early to tell," Jude responds. "By all appearances, we caught the cop on a really bad day. After he's had some sleep, he'll look at it all again. I mean, think about how tired we are and we've been on vacation. I suspect once he's got backup from Logan and Nick, he might come around."

I snicker. "Yeah, once those two get their military mission faces on, they can be intimidating. It could be a motivating factor, for sure."

Jude snakes his spoon over and helps himself to a bite of crème brûlée before I can bat his spoon away with mine. "Hey! I was eating that," I protest.

"Really? It didn't seem like you were eating it quite fast enough. It'd be a darn shame to let it go bad," Jude teases.

"Yeah right!" I answer as I crack the crunchy

toffee topping. "The sugar is still warm on the top. I want to write a memo to myself to remind us to have crème brûlée for breakfast more often. This is amazing."

Jude shrugs. "I don't see why we couldn't. It's full of all sorts of healthy, wholesome things like eggs, milk and vanilla —"

I take another big bite and lick the spoon as I finish his sentence. "… and sugar. Lots of sugar. Yet somehow today I can't bring myself to care."

"You're on vacation, you're not supposed to care about that stuff," Jude reasons. "On the other hand, if you really don't want to finish it, I would be happy to take care of any leftovers for you —"

"Not so fast there, Hernandez. You weren't kidding when you said you're always hungry."

"I did try to warn you, right?" Jude says with a cheesy grin as he tries to take another bite. "It's not my fault I have a ferocious appetite for all things amazing."

CHAPTER TWENTY

JUDE

TWO MONTHS. WE'VE BEEN sitting on pins and needles for two months. I don't know why I thought this process would go any faster in Memphis. I knew Logan and Nick were working Tasha's case for months before we got the card outside of St. Jude's Hospital. Even so, I thought once we had the attention of real-life police authorities, things might speed up a little. I guess I was wrong. Maybe it's what I get for watching police dramas on television. In real-life, things aren't wrapped up in twenty-two minutes.

I watch as Aidan and Tasha finish playing a duet on the piano. "See? I told you I have no business singing in that key," Tasha says to Aidan.

"I don't know, Tash, I think you should go for it. It would shock your fans for sure."

"I can't help but wonder if you're saying that because you can't really hear how bad I sound," Tasha teases.

"Okay now, don't forget who signs your very

generous paycheck." When Aidan looks down into the pit and sees me he asks, "Which version do you prefer?"

"If I give you an honest answer, is it going to affect my paycheck too?" I counter with a smile.

"Nah, you know me. I'm all about artistic integrity, yada, yada, yada —"

"In that case, I vote for keeping it in the key of C. Tasha sounds better in her lower register. It's where she's most comfortable. Otherwise, her nerves can get to her and it shows in her voice."

Aidan looks at Tasha. "Ouch, your boyfriend pulls no punches." He glances down at me. "What brings you by, Jude?"

"Logan wants to talk to Tasha and me."

"Why didn't you say something? Tasha and I were just goofing off. Go! Take care of business." He holds his hand out to help Tasha off the stage.

On the way to Logan's office, Tasha asks me, "Do you know what this is about? Is one of us getting fired? Aidan doesn't have a policy about employees dating each other, does he?"

I smirk. "If he does, he should've said something long before now. It's been almost a year."

"Yeah, your sister said something about having a special dinner to mark the occasion."

"I talked to Fernanda. I told her it sort of defeats the purpose of a romantic date if my sister tags along like a third wheel."

Tasha lifts her eyebrow at me. "I don't know … your sister cooks like a five-star chef. There is an upside to her plan."

"You're just a sucker for homemade tortillas and enchiladas. Fernanda definitely found your soft spot."

"I know. If I keep hanging around her, I won't fit into any of my costumes."

Right before we step into Logan's office, I stop to quickly kiss Tasha. "I don't know why he needs to talk to us, but you know I always have your back. I love you. You are the best thing to ever happen to me. Singing on stage with Aidan is a dream come true — but it's nothing compared to being with you."

"Jude Hernandez, why do you always have to do this? Now I'm an emotional mess. Logan has to wonder why I seem to always be on the verge of tears when he is around. You don't make things easier when you go around saying sweet stuff. Just for the record, I have your back too. *Te amo.*"

When I knock on the door frame, Logan holds up his finger to indicate he's on the telephone. He waves us in anyway. Tasha and I quietly tiptoe into the room and sit down as he wraps up his phone call.

"That was Officer Browning from the 201 in Memphis. They've located your stalker."

Tasha slumps against me briefly before she straightens with resolve and asks, "Okay, so hit me with the bad news — who is it?"

Logan consults his notepad. "Does the name Frankie Carlino mean anything to you?"

Tasha bites her lip as she concentrates. Finally, she blurts, "No. *No!* Why? Should it? I don't even know what to think about this. I didn't expect it to be a stranger. I didn't want it to be someone I knew either. How crazy stupid is that? It has to be one or the other," she adds, panic coloring her voice.

My brain is spinning. I need some more details. "How did they find him? It's been weeks — we've been back in Oregon a solid month and a half. I would've expected them to nab him the same day it happened."

"He showed up on some hospital surveillance tape they thought had been lost in a system upgrade. Apparently, he took a taxi to meet the reporters at the hospital. He was good. He fit right in with the paparazzi. He stood there for hours before making his move toward the journalist who knows you."

"Howie said he had a tour jacket from our bus. We recently got those, so I don't know how he could've gotten his hands on one. There weren't very many of them issued. He must've paid a pretty penny to get his hands on one."

I can't help myself; I shudder. "What did he do? Pay with a credit card?"

The corner of Logan's mouth hitches up. "I'm sure you'll appreciate the irony of this. He was careful enough to wear gloves, pay with cash, and register under an alias at the hotel."

"So ... what was his '*America's Dumbest Criminals*' moment?" Tasha asks as she grabs my hand. "I'm assuming he had one."

"Oh yeah, he sure did — and you won't believe what it was." Logan picks up a printout off the printer and grins broadly. "Creepy Stalker Dude dropped his

Starbucks card in the taxi. It just so happens the taxi driver has been robbed at knifepoint several times. He had his own little surveillance set up in his rig. It took a while for word to filter down to him we were looking for someone who had taken a ride that day. When it did, the driver happily handed over both the footage and the Starbucks card. That's how we found out about Frankie Carlino and his strangely compelling addiction to Starbucks coffee."

"What the — ?" I start to say with a healthy amount of righteous indignation, but I'm interrupted by Tasha's softly uttered question.

"*Why?* All I want to know is why? Why of all the people in the world did he come after me? Does he hate women in general or am I something special?"

Logan hands Tasha a tissue. "I want more than anything to be able to give you those answers — but I don't have them. Carlino — formally known as Creepy Stalker Dude — hasn't said much. He lawyered up pretty quick once he realized what the cops had on him."

"Who is this dude? What do the cops have on him? What's his problem with Tasha?"

"Jude, you're going to have to take it down a notch or two — or a hundred." Logan comes around and sits on the edge of his desk. "I understand you're concerned. We all are. Unfortunately, this isn't my investigation. I'm only playing a consultant role on this case. Browning is working on it, but it's the early days."

"Okay, I get it. I need to be patient, but that's not my strong suit. You've worked with me long enough to understand." I stand up and pace the room. "So, what do they have so far? This guy terrorized the woman I love for months. I think I have the right to know anything and everything about him — including what he eats for breakfast, don't you think?"

"Personally, I think you deserve that and more. Professionally? The rules become a little murkier. The local law enforcement folks have to follow the rules, and you know, that pesky thing called the Constitution."

Tasha's sighs and rolls her eyes. "It's always something."

Logan snickers and shuffles the papers in his files.

"So, that's it then?" Tasha asks. "We're back to square one with no real leads or answers? All we really know that we didn't know before is what he looks like."

"Not exactly true," Logan clarifies. "He did spill a bit before he decided to clam up. Apparently, this isn't personal. Somebody paid him to do this."

"Excuse me? Did you say what I thought you said? He was a hit man? I have a freakin' hit man! At what point did I wake up in the middle of some spy movie? I'm a singer. You know, like Donnie and Marie. Neil Diamond, Judy Garland, Britney Spears —" Tasha's voice shakes with shock as she tries to make sense of it all. "I sing songs. Why would somebody want to hurt me?" She turns to me and asks, "Jude, is this some sort of weird nightmare? Please tell me he didn't say somebody paid Creepy Stalker Dude to kill me. That's just too screwed up to be believed."

Logan answers her before I get a chance to do anything other than gather her into my arms for a hug.

"I think you hit it right in the head, T," Logan replies in answer to Tasha's string of questions. "It's all about what we can believe and then ultimately prove. We don't even know if we can trust this guy. He's just saying he was paid to do this. We don't know anything about his story or whether it's true. We know he's some insurance guy from New York. His business dealings seem to be shady, but beyond that, he doesn't seem to be a criminal mastermind — much less a hit man."

"So who does this so-called hit man claim hired him?" I press, still trying to wrap my brain around the whole scenario as Tasha clings to my side.

"Interestingly enough, he's not saying. That's when he clammed up and insisted we contact his lawyer."

Tasha abruptly stands up to her full height and faces Logan. "I am so tired of people threatening me. First, it was Five-Star, then it was the tabloids after I won *America's Next Star*. Now, like a bad penny, Five-Star is back to try to take credit for something Aidan and I created together. To top it off, I've got crazy people hiring other crazy people to take me out. It's like a bad movie. I hope it's not like one of those Hollywood blockbusters where the person who hired the hit man hires another hit man to deliver justice because he didn't get the job done. I'm sick of this whole thing." Tasha flops back on the plastic chair and rests her head against the wall.

Logan nods sympathetically. "I know where you're coming from, Tash, I really do. We're not without leads now. Since we've had one arrest in this case, it will lead us to more evidence. If he's right and someone did hire him, there will be phone records and probably evidence on social media or another digital footprint. People don't live in caves and isolation anymore. They nearly always leave a bit of themselves behind. We just have to untangle it all now that we've figured out who one of the players is. I'd venture to guess there are probably a few more."

"Just to be clear, we are going to act as if nothing is changed and Tasha still isn't safe?"

Logan nods. "Don't forget, Jude. One of those letters prominently featured a threat to your life too. So, yeah until they figure out the who, why, where, and what, I'm changing nothing about your protection. As far as I'm concerned, we're still on high alert."

Logan's blunt assessment causes Tasha to flinch in my arms. I place my arms around her waist and give a gentle squeeze of reassurance. "Trust me, I haven't forgotten a single second of this incident. It haunts me whether I'm asleep or awake."

"Me too, Hernandez, me too," Logan answers as he scrubs his hand down his face.

"Nobody ever prepares you for this side of it, do they?" Tasha rubs her temples. "When I was little, I used to think becoming a singer meant being on stage all the time or being a guest on TV shows while I wore pretty clothes and makeup. I never in a million years thought I would be trying to outwit and outsmart a deranged hit man. I'm still trying to figure out how this became my reality."

"I don't know," Logan answers with a shrug. "I do know it's spun way out of control. This seems far more than an obsessive fan. To me, this feels almost personal."

"Personal how? I don't even have a life. Jude is my first serious boyfriend because I never even went to high school. I was home-schooled. I don't have ex-boyfriend drama. If you go back to my pageant days, you might find a rival — but I didn't have very many. I stopped competing a long time ago."

Tasha runs her fingers through her long hair and starts to twist the ends. "Even when I did compete, the only person who thought I was in the elite class of competitors was my mom. Sure, I frequently scored top ten, but I was rarely on the podium with the winners. My stellar winning record was mainly a figment of my mom's active imagination. The pageants I did manage to win were mainly small, inconsequential ones. I can't imagine someone being jealous enough of those to want to kill me over them — but then again, I can't imagine anybody being upset enough over any of this to bother with me. I'm only in the top two hundred on the Billboard charts, not even near the top. This has never made any sense."

"As frustrating as it is, I think we need to stop trying to make it make sense. I think it just is our new reality," I say as I pull her into my arms and rest my chin on her head.

"Are you suggesting we just give up? I don't want this to be my 'new reality.' I'm sick of looking over my shoulder and trying to evaluate every fan who hands me a piece of paper to sign. I'm tired of not being able to trust anything or anyone. I just want this to be over. If I had my way, I would start school tomorrow and walk away from all of this. I'm done."

Tasha pulls out of my arms and spins around on Logan. "I'm sorry, Logan, I can't deal with this right now. I thought once we caught the creep, we would have all the answers. Instead, it seems we have more questions."

She yanks off the earpiece that is hanging around her neck and throws it on Logan's desk. "I never wanted to do any of this. This was all my mother's idea. Just send me to school to be a nurse where I can deal with people one at a time. I hate to say it — but let some other unsuspecting fool with stars in her eyes become the next pop star. Maybe she'll have better luck than I've had."

Tasha exits the room and slams Logan's door behind her.

I stare at the closed door in complete shock for a couple of minutes. "Got any advice for me?"

Logan pauses as he regards me seriously and replies with a soft chuckle, "Hunker down. This one's gonna be a rough one."

CHAPTER TWENTY-ONE

TASHA

As I study the lyric sheet to Aidan's new song, I see something move from the corner of my eye. When I look up, I realize it's Jude sneaking into our bedroom. It's obvious he's hiding something behind his back, but I don't know what it could be. He already surprised me earlier this week with a birthday party for my twentieth birthday.

"What are you doing?" I ask as he slinks up to the edge of the bed.

"I have a surprise for you." He smiles smugly.

"Yeah? Is it something good?" I try to peek around his torso to see if I can guess.

"I really hope so. We could use some good news around here," Jude comments as he produces two long, ivory envelopes and deposits them in my hand.

It's all I can do to not drop the letters. My instinctual reaction is to burn them without opening them. Out of self-preservation, I throw them down on the bed. My history with letters has not been positive. "Why are you handing these to me to open? That plan hasn't gone well recently. The last one I opened was from Five-Star and it was a letter informing me they intended to sue me for breach of contract. My day has been crappy enough, I don't need to make it any worse."

"I know, that one was scary — but Aidan's lawyers took care of it. The lawsuit was dismissed on summary judgment. It was like Stella said, they didn't have a leg to stand on. It was just the Clover chick trying to make a name for herself in the organization. I knew you and Aidan didn't cheat. There are only so many notes in existence, they get repeated sometimes, but it doesn't mean a song isn't an original."

I grin at Jude. "You know what the funny thing is? All the publicity around the lawsuit has made our single shoot up the charts again. A bunch of people who had been promised record deals from Five-Star are looking at Silent Beats. Rather than go through another bruising publicity battle with Aidan O'Brien, Five-Star is quietly letting people out of their contracts. Even some big-name stars who were downsized from bigger labels during the conglomeration deals are coming on board."

Jude looks at me and shakes his head slightly. "I've been with Aidan for a while, and sometimes times were pretty lean. I can't say I'm sorry to see that sometimes karma bites back hard."

"Even though that one turned out okay, you can see why I'm afraid to open the mail. They still haven't found out who was funding Creepy Stalker Dude. Maybe this is from Creepy Stalker Dude version 2.0.

Maybe his private benefactor moved to another person?"

Jude leans over the bed and kisses me soundly. After he breaks away, he says, "Tasha, you are working on an important project with Aidan. I would not interrupt you to deliver a letter from a stalker. I love you. I wouldn't do anything to hurt you. I thought these two letters might make your day go a little better. Take a look at who they're from."

I pull back and pick up the letters from the bed. As I examine the return addresses, I exclaim, "Seriously? I've been waiting months for these and now these two arrive on the same day? How weird."

"Hopefully, it's a sign our luck is turning around," Jude sits down on the bed next to me. "Hurry up! Open them."

"Now who's anxious to open the mail? I thought I was the only one. Which one should I open first?" I ask as I gingerly handle the envelopes.

"I don't know. Do you have a stronger feeling about one over the other?"

"I wish. It'd be nice if I was like Tara and I had some sort of premonition about the future — but unfortunately, I'm totally clueless."

"Is there one school you'd like to get into over the other?"

"Both have their pluses and minuses, they're about equal." I lift one letter and then the other, trying to gauge the weight.

Jude takes the ink pen I was using to mark up my

lyric sheet from behind my ear. "Well, that settles it. You'll have to resort to the tried-and-true method I always used in high school to determine what order I did my homework in."

The expression on Jude's face is filled with mischief, so I have to ask, "Don't keep me in suspense … what is this tried-and-true method?"

Jude takes the envelopes from my hands and places them face down on the bed as he mixes them around a bit. "It's easy. You just place your choices on the bed and then you throw your pen at them. Whichever one is closest to your pen is the one you start with. It works every time."

"Is that how you decide which bus to clean first when we come back from a long tour too?" I ask with a snicker, remembering a scene in front of the studio when I saw him throwing a windshield cleaning sponge near the buses.

Jude shrugs. "Sometimes." When he sees my expression, he grins ruefully. "Why should I mess with the system which works for me?"

I take a drink from my water bottle. "I guess it's as good a method as any — knock yourself out."

I'm trying to stay calm and act like this is no big deal, but somewhere in those envelopes is the key to my future. Part of me is ready to face it, but the other part of me wants to put it off as long as possible. What if the admissions committees decided I'm not a good candidate to be a nurse? What if all the time I've spent in the public eye works against me?

Jude makes great ceremony out of throwing the

pen. Much to my surprise, it lands right in the middle of one of the envelopes. As I turn it over, it's the one from the University of Washington. Of the two envelopes I received today, this is the farthest away from Jude.

Jude sees my shaking hands. "Do you need me to open it?"

I nod. "I don't know why this is so scary. It's what I've wanted to do for as long as I can remember. Why is it so traumatic to trade one dream for another?"

"Any time we take a new journey, it's scary," Jude assures me gently as he opens the letter.

He starts to hand it to me, but I freeze up and push it back toward him. "You read it. I'm afraid it's bad news."

As I impatiently wait, Jude studies the letter for what seems like forever before he says, "They loved your application and your personal story. Your test scores were really solid."

His words hit me like blows to my chest as I ask hollowly, "What are you not telling me?"

"*Sirena*, I'm so sorry. The timing was just wrong for this year," he replies gently. But the look on his face tells me he would rather be doing something else, anything else — even going to the dentist for a root canal. He looks positively miserable. This was not how it was supposed to happen. I search his face to see if I can figure out more clues, but he looks almost as hurt and confused as I feel.

"What does that even mean? What am I going to do now?" I sob.

Jude gathers me into a hug and holds me quietly for a few minutes. When my breathing evens out he says, "It's only one letter. You have others pending. Even this letter isn't all bad news. They were so impressed with your application they'd like you to apply again next year. It was a timing issue. You got a late start that's all."

"I don't even want to read the letter from OHSU. It's the school closest to us, and I was hoping I'd be able to stay close to home."

"Tasha, before I open this, I need to know if you understand that whether you get into school or you don't, you're still amazing. If we have to wait a year or two until we have everything organized in our lives, then we'll do it. If I have to go somewhere and pump gas or pick strawberries to make it possible for you to succeed, I can do that too. It's nothing I haven't done before. The point is I love you for who you are, not for what you do. We'll figure this out."

I study Jude's intense expression and realize how often our roles have changed. When we first met, I was the cheerleader, the instigator, and the coach. Yet more often than not, Jude plays those same roles in my life now as he helps provide balance and stability when things are uncertain.

I take a deep breath and let it out as I choke back tears. "I have to tell you — I am one of the most blessed people I know. Most people don't get the chance to live one dream, and I'm on the cusp of living two. It means the world to know you'll support me whatever path I choose. I guess maybe it's a good thing Aidan wouldn't accept my resignation from the tour. If the first letter is any indication, I might not be needing to use that option for a while," I add with a watery smile.

"Something tells me Aidan will not be entirely sad about your decision."

I shrug as I respond, "The upside is we can still do that *Live Tour Album*. I might need the money for school."

———•———

"Why is my iPad ringing?" I mutter to myself as I struggle to sit up in bed and grab the tablet Jude got me for my birthday. He's right, the songwriting applications are cool. Yet, most of the time, I still use my pen and paper.

I haphazardly stick my headphones on as I answer the FaceTime call.

Hayden laughs at me when she sees my face pop up on her screen.

"Are those *Little Mermaid* pajamas? I thought you were a grown-up. This is not your most glamorous look," she chastises. "Maybe next time, I'll have to do a makeover on you."

"Very funny. Of course I'm not at my most glamorous, it's not even ten o'clock in the morning. What do you expect?" I answer as I yawn.

"Ten o'clock in the morning is late. What planet do you live on?"

"I live on the planet where I was performing until two o'clock this morning and we had three encores," I explain as I try to run my fingers through my hair. *Darn it*, I forgot to wash the hairspray out of my hair last night before I collapsed into bed. This is going to be a nightmare.

"Oh, sorry. I forgot you guys had a gig last night."

"Speaking of that, why aren't you in school?" I ask when my brain engages.

Hayden shrugs. "Some district in-service day."

"Lucky you," I murmur, rubbing my eyes.

"You won't be performing much longer, right? What school are you going to go to? Have you decided yet? I want to come visit you at college."

I sigh as I respond, "Well, you'll have to wait a while longer. I guess I won't be going to school this year."

"Why? You showed me your application stuff, and I thought it looked great. Are they making a big deal of the fact that you are a performer? If they are, it's not fair," Hayden huffs indignantly.

"Thank you for saying that — but I don't have anyone to blame for this except me. I was so afraid of making the people around me upset, I sat on my applications for a long time before I was brave enough to fill them out and send them in. As a result, I was too late for this school year. One school liked me so much they'll give me priority consideration for next year, and two schools wait-listed me for this year if I want to enroll starting winter term, but I'd be out of sync with the rest of my classmates. I talked to a couple of the advisors, and they said it would probably be best if I waited to start next fall."

"I know I should be sad for you, but in a weird way I'm not," Hayden says.

I wrinkle my nose as I reply sarcastically, "Gee, thanks … I think."

"No, I didn't mean it like that. I just think Jude isn't quite ready to fly on his own yet, so it's a good thing you'll be around for a little while longer. Don't tell him I said that — I don't want him to get his feelings hurt. I think he's amazing, but I think he's a little too shy."

I chuckle at Hayden's assessment of my boyfriend. "Hayden, it's all right. I think Jude would be the first person to agree with you. He's gotten much better, but he still isn't super comfortable performing in front of people and he's even less at ease meeting fans one on one. He hasn't ever gotten used to the fact that most everyone thinks he's sexy and handsome."

"Do you think he would be okay with meeting my cousin Juliann again? Because guess what?" she quizzes me enthusiastically. "For my birthday I get to come see you in concert wherever you are. Isn't it cool? My immune system has built back up to the point where I can go in public again, so my mom said I can choose a concert and take Juliann with me. I decided I wanted to see you and Jude."

I laugh out loud as I say, "You do realize that Jude and I aren't headlining this concert tour, right? It's actually Aidan's tour. We just help him out."

"Okay, so that might be technically true, but Juliann and I still think you guys are the best part of the act. I like Aidan O'Brien okay, but he's not you."

"In case I haven't mentioned it today, can I tell you that you are quite possibly my favorite fan?" I blow her a kiss over the computer.

Hayden giggles. "I'm not supposed to be your favorite fan, Jude's supposed to be your favorite fan, so I'll be your second-favorite fan."

"I can make that deal. We'll be playing in Boulder, Colorado over Thanksgiving break. Is that close enough to your birthday?"

"Yeah, it's only nine days away from Thanksgiving."

"Well, consider that your birthday present. I'll fly you and your family and your sister — if she's home from college — to the concert. Tell your mom not to worry about it."

"Oh wow, that's a lot of money," Hayden says. "Are you sure it's okay?"

"I'm sure. A certain production company accidentally gave us tons of free publicity and Aidan and I were able to push three songs up the charts. Sometimes, someone else's bad karma is your good karma. I'm just paying it forward. I'm looking forward to seeing you guys at the concert. It'll be a blast."

Chapter Twenty-Two

Jude

Tasha is in beast mode tonight. I haven't seen her this happy in a while. It's almost as if having the decision about nursing school behind her has freed her to fully enjoy music again.

I join her as we sing harmony on the last chord of the song. I wink at her as she gives me a high five before moving over to her next mark. I always feel a buzz when I sing with Tasha.

She literally gave the musician in me a voice. It was an incredible gift I'll never be able to repay.

The stage will never be my second home like it is for Tasha, but I'm gradually finding my bearings. I walk up next to Jerome as he plays the bass. He flashes me a bright smile as Aidan and Tasha play a complicated guitar riff. I lean into the mic next to him and we play our own embellishment. It's great fun to be part of this group even if I am still on the fringes. Every day, I live in fear of having another incident like I had in Nashville. I even went to talk to the psychologist Tasha found. Although she usually works with actors, she was happy to work with me. We've talked a lot about what happened during my worst-case scenario and how I survived it and I'm still alive, so if I can make a plan to get through my nerves, I can survive anything. So far, knowing I have an exit strategy and I'm prepared for whatever comes up has helped me just relax and enjoy what's happening on stage. Because after all, it is really all about the music.

Speaking of the music, my girlfriend is amazing.

Tasha is strong and completely sexy as she leads a guitar solo. She is shredding the guitar with complete confidence. The guys in the band are struggling to keep up with her tonight. She is totally in the pocket. She looks and sounds amazing. Her dark hair is falling around her shoulders like satin. I have to give myself a mental pinch when I realize despite all of her beauty, fans and fame, when we go home, she's all mine. My life is unbelievably good.

Tasha and Aidan start to jam on his new song, an anthem for soldiers who serve overseas and their families. I've met a couple of the guys who inspired this song because they're good friends of Aidan's, and they're stand up guys. Tyler works for a sheriff's office near where we live and he had to talk me down after it seemed like the Memphis force had put Tasha's case on the back burner. Tyler's about as solid as they come. If he tells me things are progressing like they're supposed to, I guess I need to take it at face value.

Aidan and Tara's whole group of friends is in the audience tonight, so this whole concert has been like one huge party. Mindy's parents are even here, and Mindy is waiting in the wings backstage to come onstage. Tasha and Mindy have been working on a brand-new song that's absolutely killer. Both of them are excited about it. I am not psychic like Mindy, but I have a feeling this one could do well on the charts.

Mindy and Tasha's duet is next on the play list. Even though I do more than manage the equipment now, old habits die hard. I quickly scan the stage to make sure both of their guitars are on their marks for the scene change. Tasha catches me looking and gives me a thumbs up as she goes to the edge of the stage to do a guitar riff. She's grinning from ear-to-ear as Aidan dances around her, effectively highlighting her playing skills.

Suddenly, every light in the arena goes out and I hear Tasha shriek my name. Through my ear piece I hear Logan tersely command, "Sit-rep. Now!

I hear Stella say, "Green!"

Jerome follows. "Green for me and all the band on the dais."

I hear Aidan breathe heavily. "I'm green but Tasha is red. She's down."

At that moment, my brain shuts down and I struggle to follow protocol as I check in, "I'm green. What do you mean she's red? What the heck do you mean, Aidan?"

Just then, Tasha's voice comes over my earpiece. "For gosh sakes, chill out. I am not red! At most, I am yellow. I fell off the stupid stage in the dark. I may have broken my ankle, but who knows. I fell over the monitor, so I didn't even fall far. I'm yellow. I'm *not* red — repeat, I'm yellow. Jude, did you hear that I'm yellow? Do not freak out, okay? There's a whole audience here."

As usual, Tasha has a point. Although I cannot see the audience because it's still dark, they're still there and they're as scared as I am. Only they have no idea what happened to the people on the stage.

Using a skill I learned from my grandfather, I whistle through my teeth. It's piercing and loud.

The audience quiets some, but it's still noisy. I try again and more people settle down.

Jerome makes his way over and taps me on the shoulder. He's lucky I didn't punch him; I was not expecting him to be anywhere close. "Brother, you're a good songwriter, but I doubt anybody here can talk as loud as me."

I step aside and say, "By all means, I was just going to tell them what's going on."

"Do we know what's going on?" Jerome asks barely loud enough for me to hear.

"Not precisely, but I was planning to tell them we're all fine and the power should be restored shortly. Ask them to sit tight."

"Good plan," he responds quietly. Turning back toward the audience he yells, "Yo Eugene! Never let it be said Aidan O'Brien concerts aren't exciting. Everything's good though — everything's good except for our resident rocker who danced her way off the stage in the dark. If you all could make the way clear for the paramedics, we'd appreciate that. Otherwise, just sit tight. By the way, if you've got a glow stick, now would be a good time to use it."

———•———

Tasha probably would not be pleased if she knew she was snoring. Honestly, I'm happy to hear the sound. It's been a grueling night. I can tell from the light coming through the blinds it's morning now, but Tasha just got to sleep. We've been waiting for an orthopedic radiologist to come look at her x-rays. They're not certain if she has a fracture or not. She had some extremely painful muscle spasms in her ankle and foot, so they hooked her up to some IV pain medication — which makes her sleepy.

The scene at the concert venue was completely chaotic. At first, I was afraid the power outage had something to do with the threat on our lives, but it turned out to be caused by a sixteen-year-old learning how to drive. He had a very painful run-in with a power transformer. It took out the grid serving the arena. For reasons no one can explain, the generators didn't kick on as they were supposed to. By the time Tasha was transported to the hospital, she was in tears. I'm glad to see the medication seems to control her pain for the moment.

I stand up to stretch my legs. I need to get out of here. The smells in this place remind me too much of when *mi tío* was passing on. I know Tasha won't die, but the memories are there all the same. As I enter the hallway, I can't help but look over my shoulder to see if anyone is taking pictures. It's become second nature to me.

I'm surprised to see Howard Manis sitting quietly in the vibrantly colored chairs in the little waiting room off the hallway clutching a bedraggled bouquet of spring flowers.

With his head propped against the wall, he appears to be half-asleep. As I approach, I announce myself quietly. "Howie … It's Jude. What are you doing here?"

He startles for half a second before he straightens his glasses and focuses his eyes. When he sees me, he asks immediately, "How's my Tasha?"

His phrasing is odd, but then again, he and Tasha go back a long way. Perhaps, I don't know the whole story. I rake my fingers through my hair as I explain, "We're still waiting for a definitive diagnosis on her foot and ankle. She landed funny on the monitor when she fell, so there could still be some damage."

"Oh, my poor baby. Is she in any pain?"

The hairs on the back of my neck stand up. "Mr. Manis, I have to ask you, are you asking this as a reporter?"

Howard appears embarrassed as he looks around the hallway. He lowers his voice to a whisper. "No, right now I couldn't care less about my job. This is about Natasha. I don't want anything bad to happen to her."

I crowd into his personal space. "If you know anything about who is stalking her, you better talk. This crap is getting serious."

"Somebody's trying to hurt Tash?" Howard asks with a look of genuine surprise. "No, no I don't know anything about that."

"Then what are you talking about?"

"I was talking about Nadine," Howard confesses. "That woman is horrible. She'll make Tasha feel responsible for this even though she had nothing to do with the accident." Howard leans down to pick up the flowers he dropped and hands them to me. "I just want to make sure she gets these. Maybe they'll make things a little easier."

"Thank you, I'm sure she'll appreciate them, but can we go back to the fact that you know about Nadine? I know Tasha doesn't share that part of her life with very many people. How do you know about her relationship with her mother?"

"You're right, I don't really know about how things are currently, but I know what kind of person Nadine is," Howard clarifies.

"Howard, you still haven't explained how you know this? It doesn't seem like the kind of thing Tasha would voluntarily share, especially with reporters."

"I already told you this has nothing to do with my job as a reporter — although most people wouldn't call me an honest reporter. This is more personal than that. I know how Nadine acts because she used to be my sister-in-law."

My brain is going into overdrive as I try to process all the things he just told me. "Wait? So… you're Tasha's *uncle?*"

He nods as tears gather at the corners of his eyes. "Natasha Leslie Keeley was 7 pounds, 8 ounces when she was born with the brightest eyes you've ever seen. She was the apple of my brother's eye. I've never seen anybody so proud. He was on cloud nine."

"If he was so happy to have her in his life, where is he now?" I challenge.

"Shortly after Natasha won her battle with leukemia, Lester lost his. I buried him in his favorite Yankees jersey. He and Tasha used to watch the baseball games in the hospital, and he taught her all the songs about baseball."

"Tasha never said a word about her dad having cancer. Did she even know?"

Howard shakes his head. "No, Lester refused to tell them. Nadine was busy trying to make sure Tasha made it. Lester didn't want to make it any more complicated than it had to be. He went to visit Tasha one day in the hospital, kissed her goodbye, and never came back. He went to go visit a friend of a friend who had a cottage in the Caribbean. After he said goodbye to Tasha, it was just a matter of time."

I'm still trying to get this straight in my head, so I ask again, "He knew he was dying and he didn't bother to tell his wife?"

"That about sums it up. He didn't tell any of us until after it was too late. He figured Nadine's efforts needed to be focused on Tasha and not split between the two of them. Nadine was so tired and they fought all the time. It was easy for everyone to believe they'd gone their separate ways. Even as his oldest brother, I didn't know the truth until I had to get his affairs into order."

"That's a mind-blowing story. I don't know how Tasha will react to this. I think she believes the only family she has left is her mom and her Nana. Even though she'll be psyched to find out you are her uncle, I'm not looking forward to being the one who tells her that her father is dead. After all these years of not having any word one way or the other, I believe she still harbors the hope that one day he'll pop back into her life and apologize for all the years he's been missing."

"I never planned to tell her who I was. I've been watching her grow up for years. I was so glad when Mr. O'Brien took her under his wing. It's been a pleasure to watch the two of you fall in love. I have beautiful pictures of your relationship on stage if you'd like them. I didn't set out to upset my dear Natasha. Lester would've done anything to prevent that. We can keep this conversation between us. I want you to know — if she's in danger, I'll be helping to watch out for her too."

I reach out to shake his hand. "For now, that might be the best approach. When Tasha's feeling stronger, we might have a different conversation. I am grateful Tasha has one more person in her life who cares about her though."

Tasha's phone rings in my coat pocket. I hold up my finger and whisper to Howard, "I'm sorry, I have to take this."

He nods and walks toward the nurses' station with his bouquet in his hand.

I turn and head toward the exit of the hospital as I greet the caller tersely, "Hello."

I don't know why, given what I've just been talking about with Howard, but I am surprised to hear Nadine's voice.

"Oh no, it's you again. What are you doing with my daughter's phone?"

"I have it so it doesn't wake her up," I explain simply.

"It's nine o'clock in the morning, why wouldn't my daughter be up?" Nadine demands.

I roll my eyes so hard I'm sure that Nadine can hear the motion through the cell phone. "Ms. Keeley, it's nine o'clock in New York, but it's six o'clock in the morning in Oregon. We've had a very rough night. Tasha has a good reason to be sleeping."

"Yes, I know. They called here to check the status of Tasha's health insurance. I had to verify her phone number with the hospital. It's just disgraceful that my daughter won't even give me her cell phone number. You'd think she'd care more about her mother since I'm her only family. It was downright embarrassing that I didn't know my daughter's phone number. I had to pretend to have Alzheimer's in order to get it. I'm sure glad I live in New York and not out there in the wilderness. I'd be so embarrassed to show my face," she rambles on.

I bite my tongue to stop myself from revealing what I know about Tasha's whole family. I'll probably regret this later, but something about her tone sets me off. I walk out the front door of the hospital and down the sidewalk a way before I state sardonically, "In case you were wondering, when Tasha fell off a stage several feet above ground, she wasn't horribly injured."

"If she isn't so injured then why is she racking up a hospital bill? Shouldn't Aidan be picking that up because she was injured on the job?"

"I'm beginning to understand why your daughter has a difficult time talking to you. I think you missed the headline here. Your daughter could have been seriously injured, and she wasn't. That's the good news. The bad news is, she hurt her ankle. If I thought you cared at all about Tash, I'd let you talk to her, but obviously, you don't. You only care about the dollars and cents of your daughter's career, and her artistry and skill are so far above the dollars and cents that you'll never get it."

"Well, you don't get what she's about, either. You're just hanging on because she can teach you how to sing on stage. I've been watching the tabloids about the two of you. You're nothing but a pretty-boy gold-digger. She has you fooled. She doesn't even plan to stay in show business — even though that's what God designed her to do. She's been singing since before she could talk, but she plans to turn her back on all of it so she can go be Florence Nightingale and dump bed pans. Have you ever heard of anything so ridiculous?"

"I don't think it's so ridiculous. I'll admit I didn't understand Tasha's decision at first, but now I do. I support whatever dream she has because it's her life."

"You know what kind of skill my daughter has. You've heard her sing and you admitted she's one of the most talented people you've ever heard. How can you let her throw it all away? I've been planning her career for years, and she just throws it back in my face like it's nothing. All the hard work and sacrifices I've made for her?"

"I don't know what to tell you to make you feel

better about that, but I know Tasha's dreams are important too. This is Tasha's life and not yours. If you wanted a career in show business so badly, perhaps you should've pursued it yourself. Now, if you'll excuse me, I need to go back and check on Tasha and make sure she's okay."

"Well, I don't know where you think you get off, young man. You don't have the right to talk that way."

"Perhaps not. But I know I love Tasha very much and it's my job to protect her from things that cause her pain. It seems you're one of the chief causes of her pain, so while she's unable to protect herself, I'll speak for her."

"Why, I never! I have lots of influence with Mr. O'Brien. I can make sure you're fired and can't work in the industry anymore. No one speaks to me that way. Do you understand? No one!"

"I apologize, Ms. Keeley. However, if you don't want people to be rude to you, you shouldn't be rude to them or to the people they love."

I push the end button on my phone and hope I haven't pushed the end button on my relationship with Tasha.

Chapter Twenty-Three

Tasha

I'VE GOT MY FOOT propped up on a couple of guitar cases on a chair and I'm trying to write a snippet of notes and lyrics before they slide out of my brain. They were there this morning when I was in the shower, but now that I'm attempting to put them down on paper, they seem to have vanished into thin air. I wish I had Jude's ability to see a song all the way through from start to finish in living color. Unfortunately, my songwriting brain doesn't work the same way his does. I need to go note by note and phrase by phrase. It's much slower and more methodical. I can't see the finished song until it's done.

Mindy peeks her head into the break room. "Please don't kill the messenger. This is not my fault. I swear."

Mindy is usually full of exuberance and confidence, so the pensive look on her face is disconcerting.

"What's up?" I try not to smile at her petrified

expression.

"Your mom's here."

"Like physically here or like spiritually here?" I retort with a feeling of dread growing in my stomach.

Mindy rubs the bridge of her nose. "Unfortunately, I mean really here — like in Uncle Aidan's office here. Tara's running interference by showing her pictures of all the famous people they know. I don't know how much longer it'll last. Your mom and Jude are shooting evil looks at each other like laser beams."

"I thought you were supposed to warn me when stuff like that is going to happen," I complain.

Mindy looks surprised. "I did warn you! You didn't listen."

"When did you warn me?" I ask. "The only thing you said was 'old pain would resurface'. My foot's currently in an air cast, anything could be old pain. How was I supposed to know you meant my mother?"

Mindy shrugs. "It's part of the rules of my gift, I can't tell you anything which will affect the outcome unless it's life or death. I'm sorry I couldn't say anything more. It's like a riddle. You have to figure it out on your own."

"Okay, I can sort of respect that — but you were more specific about my broken luggage," I reply with a frown. "In the grand scheme of things, I think it would've been more helpful to know about this."

I struggle to get up on my crutches and find my mother. It's not difficult; I just have to follow Jude's glowering stare.

"Ma, what are you doing here? Oregon is a long way from New York although I can't help but notice you had no trouble finding this place."

My mom spins around in a grand gesture. Her long flowing fur coat and high heels are decidedly out of place in the casual environment of the recording studio where the typical uniform consists of jeans or yoga pants and sweatshirts. As usual, my mother's makeup is impeccably done and finished off with bright red lipstick and perfectly arched eyebrows.

She purses her lips at me in triumph as she responds, "Those Air B-n-B folks are so helpful. I told him I was writing a blog on all the independently owned businesses in the area, and he told me all about Aidan and his company. I guess he's pretty big stuff around here."

"Ma, Aidan is pretty big stuff everywhere. I've been trying to tell you. But I'm sure you didn't come here all the way from New York to talk about Aidan. Why are you here?" I ask as I hobble over to give her a hug.

She gives me an air hug, trying to avoid touching me. "You wouldn't return my calls when I wanted to check on you. Are you doing enough physical therapy? If you had been doing your dance training like you're supposed to be doing, you wouldn't have hurt your ankle to begin with. Dancers have very strong ankles."

Tara steps up and interjects, "With all due respect, Ms. Keeley, I was a professional dancer for years. It wouldn't have mattered if Tasha danced for hours every single day. She would've still been hurt when she fell off the stage. That's how it works."

My mom puffs up with indignation as she turns to me and asks, "Are you going to take the advice of a has-been ballerina? I am your mother and I know what's best for you."

"Actually Ma, I'll take Tara's advice — in addition to being an exceptional athlete, she studies martial arts and kinesiology. She knows more about body mechanics than anyone I know."

My mom whirls around on me and hisses, "I am so sick of these people! It's always Aidan this and Tara that. Do you think they're somehow special? They're like the rest of us. They still put their pants on one leg at a time. They've just managed to get a few more breaks in life."

Mortified, I close my eyes and harshly whisper, "Mother, stop it. You are embarrassing me where I work. These people are my bosses! Knock it off."

"What kind of bosses are these people? They're willing to let you throw away a lifetime of singing and dancing lessons so you can go be a college student and get drunk and high with all the rest of the stupid young people in America."

"They're the kind of bosses who want me to succeed," I answer in a brittle voice. "They care more about me as a human being than a dollar sign. They want me to be happy."

"You could've been somebody and been happy. I don't get this New Age mumbo-jumbo. If you would've stuck with me, you would've been in the middle of your

Miss America reign and you could've written any ticket for any career you wanted. Instead, you're following these guys around like they're related to some Woodstock band. For the life of me, I'll never know why you wanted to throw everything we have built together away to sing for these grifters."

"Ma! Listen to yourself. You don't even know what you're talking about. I'm happy here."

"How could you be happy here with all those death threats? Someone is threatening to blow you up. Being a pageant girl would be so much safer."

I have never been so grateful to be on crutches in my life as my knees buckle and I sway. Jude catches the movement out of the corner of his eye, and he swoops in to catch me and escort me over to a chair.

After I sit down, I look up at my mother and ask, "I'm sorry, Ma, can you repeat what you just said?"

Jude meets Logan's gaze above my head and nods tightly. Logan's features are grim as he observes the conversation.

Aidan signs, "I'm sorry."

Everyone except my mother seems to understand that something monumental is about to occur. My heart is beating so fast and hard I can barely hear over the sound of my racing pulse.

My mom smirks at me. "What's wrong, Tasha? Have all those years of playing on stage damaged your hearing?"

"In a way, I hope they did," I reply quietly.

"I said, I wonder how you can be happy with all

those death threats hanging over your head," my mom repeats.

And there it is. Right there, out in the open for everyone to hear. All the members of the crew look at each other in disbelief.

"Ma, what have you done?" I ask in a voice I hardly recognize. My shock is palpable.

My mom is finally becoming alert to everyone's shift in mood. "What do you mean?"

Aidan steps forward and faces my mom down. "What she means, Mrs. Keeley, is that the contents of those notes were kept strictly confidential on the advice of law enforcement. The only way you could have known what was in those notes was if you wrote them yourself."

My mom flushes bright red and then blanches to a pale shade of white as Aidan continues to wait for an answer.

"Well, uh..." My mom starts to tremble and fans herself.

Stella steps forward and offers my mom a bottle of water. I hold up my hand to stop her. "Don't worry about it; this is just part of her deal. She used to do this all the time when we were on the pageant circuit to get sympathy from the judges. She'll be fine as soon as the attention is off her."

"Why you little cow —" my mom sputters.

"Careful now, Ms. Keeley," Jude says. "You and I have talked about respect before. Your daughter's name is Tasha. She asked you a question. In case you missed it, I'll ask it again. What did you have to do with the threats against us?"

My mom glares at Jude as she leans forward in her chair, trying to get in my space. "She made me do this. I told her to stay with the pageants and do it my way — but she had to go and follow Aidan around like he was her dad or something. It was sick. I tried asking politely, and it didn't work. Then I tried convincing Dottie's doctors she needed to stay in the hospital so Tasha would come home, but even that wasn't enough. The last straw was when she wouldn't even take my phone calls. I knew I needed to do something to get her attention. I figured if she was too scared to stay on the tour, she'd have no option but to come home and be with me."

Tara is the first to regain her power of speech. "What good would it do to have your daughter back home with you if she is so sad and angry she doesn't even want to talk to you?"

"I figured once I had her home, I could convince her she loved the pageant life. It worked once. Why wouldn't it work again?"

My jaw is completely slack as I'm listening to my mom essentially rationalize her whole terrorism campaign against me. "Mom, I was never really happy doing pageants, you know that. I only did them to make you happy. I am an artist who loves to create music. I'm not the type of girl who fits well into the pageant system. I've never been the type they look for. If I wasn't happy the first time, I would be miserable if you made me do it again."

"Why do you hate it so much?" my mom asks with a look of bewilderment. "Why do you hate *me* so much? I only tried to provide what was best for you."

"Ma, this was never about you. I love you, but I don't love when you try to turn me into something I'm not. I've never been very good about fitting into cookie-cutter molds and pretending to be somebody else. That's just not what I'm about. I've never been."

"Then why are you onstage every day?" my mom snaps bitterly.

"I'm on stage every day because I perform songs which matter to me. The lyrics have a message, or they make my audience happy. It's about my talents as an artist and a songwriter. It's not about how beautiful I am or how I walk. It is about who I am as a human being — and I'm proud of that."

"If you're so proud of it, why are you leaving your singing career behind too?" she argues as if she's discovered some huge hole in my logic.

"You're right. I struggled with my choice for a long time — almost too long. It cost me a whole year of progress because I was afraid of letting someone down."

"See? I'm right," my mom declares. "You don't know what you're doing with your career. That's why you should've left it in my hands, if you would've done what I ask you to do, you might've even had some huge career like Gretchen Carlson or one of the other huge newscasters. Beauty contestants do quite well on network news. Haven't you noticed?"

I shake my head in disbelief. "Ma! I've never even

expressed an interest in doing news, network or otherwise. There are only two things I've ever wanted to do in my life. One is to be a pediatric oncology nurse, and the other is to be a musician. Aidan and Tara have gone above and beyond the call of duty to make sure my second dream has come true. Next year, I will start working on the dream I've had for as long as I can remember to become a nurse."

"So, that's it? I'm excluded from your life because you're better friends with Mr. and Mrs. Perfect over here?" my mom blusters.

I look her dead in the eye. "No, Ma. That's not the reason. I'm excluding you from my life because you thought so little of me you felt you could scare me into doing what you wanted me to do. You caused everyone in my workplace a huge amount of stress, not to mention causing police agencies in several cities a huge headache. I'm not okay with that. I'll never be okay with it."

My mom's voice gets very small. "What do you mean, Princess? What are you saying?"

"Ma, I love you, but I'm done dealing with you," I respond with a determined voice. "I've given you several chances to respect my boundaries, and you refused. So I'm going to set the final boundary. I'm not going to have any more contact with you."

"Well, you can kiss access to your Nana goodbye. She lives with me now and I pay for her Internet access and cable TV. So, if I say she doesn't contact you, she doesn't contact you. Two can play this game."

Aidan, Jude, and Logan simultaneously stand up.

"You may think you can compete in the game, but I will win any game you start. Are you sure you want to go there?" Aidan asks with deadly calm.

My mom picks up her purse with a flourish. "You guys want her, you're more than welcome to her. All I ever tried to do was make her happy. I could never figure out how to do that. Maybe you'll have better luck."

Somehow, even though my mom just admitted to a room full of people that she ran a systematic campaign to terrorize me and the people I worked with, she manages to storm out of the room as if I'm the one in the wrong.

Jude steps behind me and hugs me from behind. It's almost as if he can read my thoughts because he whispers in my ear, "Her bad decisions don't make it your fault."

Jerome closes and locks the door behind her, brushing his hands together. "Nothing personal, Tash, but there's nothing I like better than when the trash takes itself out. Your mama is a piece-and-a-half of work. Whenever the good Lord catches up with her, she'll have a lot of explaining to do."

I chuckle. "Knowing my mom, she's probably already got her outfit and makeup ready and her speech rehearsed. St. Peter won't know what hit him."

EPILOGUE

JUDE

"Is this everything we need?" I ask as I place the big bowl of salad in the middle of the table.

Mindy looks up at me with a puzzled expression on her face. "What?"

"I asked if there was anything else we need for lunch," I answer. "What's with you today? You've been off your game all day. Izzy even beat you through the crossword puzzle and that *never* happens."

A look of pain crosses Mindy's face. "I can't really explain. I guess I've been distracted. I'm thinking about something."

"You want to talk about it? Are you having problems at school? Do I need to have a conversation with somebody?"

Mindy gives me a weak smile. "You're as bad as my uncles who aren't really my uncles. No, Jude, this time it's not about me — but I shouldn't say anything."

Tasha walks into the kitchen with her headphones

on and she almost hits the counter because she's carrying a book. I take off her headphones and kiss her. "You're just in time; we're about to eat lunch."

Tasha lifts the lid and peeks into the pot of spaghetti. "Yum. Have I missed anything? I didn't mean to be gone so long — I got caught up in this book. I love being on vacation. I can't wait until Hayden and Pennie get here."

"You haven't missed anything yet. Mindy's just about to tell me why she's been acting like a space cadet all day."

Tasha immediately focuses on Mindy. "Is it happening again?"

Mindy wipes away a tear as she nods silently.

"Oh no!" Tasha exclaims. "I've been around long enough to know the rules by now. I can't ask you any specifics, so I'll simply ask you on a scale of one to ten, how bad is this?"

"Is there a number beyond infinity?" Mindy asks sadly.

"*Crap!* Is there anything we can do to stop it?" Tasha exclaims as she draws in a sharp breath.

"What? What is she talking about?" I try to follow the conversation and figure out why Tasha is so upset.

"Remember what I said about the luggage?" Tasha explains. "Mindy has the same kind of gift as Tara. Somehow they know when things are coming. I've been hanging around Mindy long enough to know when she's not completely with us, she's having an episode."

"My *tia* is like that," I comment. "So, I take it this

is bad?"

"The worst," Mindy confirms.

"We can't change it?" I ask, but I can tell from the look on Mindy's face what the answer will be.

"We can't. It's already done."

"What can we do?" I ask.

Mindy looks at me with haunted eyes. "It's your turn to step up. Aidan doesn't have time for you to be scared."

"What do you mean?"

"I'm so sorry, I can't say more —" Mindy starts to answer as I hear Aidan bellow from upstairs.

"Someone get Logan. He's outside with Nick on the snowmobiles. We need to go to the hospital."

When we first had the security scare with Tasha, Logan replaced all our cell phones with upgraded models which can be used as walkie-talkies. I push Logan's code in and yell, "AJ is down. Code Red! A.J. is down."

I look up at the stairwell which drops down into the open plan kitchen in the log cabin and see Aidan carrying Tara down the stairs. I push the button on the phone again and correct my message using their code names. "Code Red victim is Gracie, not AJ."

"This is bad," Logan mutters. "Ask Aidan if he wants to go lights and sirens."

Aidan reaches the bottom of the staircase with Tara in his arms. Now that she's closer, I can see her yoga pants have a large trickle of blood going down the leg.

Aidan heard Logan's question and answers, "Yes, dammit. I want it all."

Mindy walks up to Aidan and lays a hand on his shoulder as she solemnly shakes her head. "Uncle Aidan, you don't. It's too late. They can't help her. If you do that, the whole story will be all over the news and Howie won't be able to lead them off the trail. I think you should have Jerome drive. The media already knows that Logan is your security. They already watch for him."

Aidan looks at Mindy with wide pleading eyes. "Mindy, please tell me this is only something you think and not something you *know*."

Mindy grabs his hand and does some sort of sign language gesture as she responds, "I'm so sorry, Band-Aidan. I know."

———•———

"Jude, I don't think pacing will help the call come any sooner," Tasha says.

"I know, but they've been gone a long time." I look at my cell phone for about the hundred thousandth time.

"It'll go as fast as it goes. Remember how long I was in the hospital with my ankle, and I wasn't even bleeding."

I sit back down on the bed and remove my boots. "I suppose you're right, but I'm worried about Mindy too. I've never seen her so broken up about anything."

Tasha shakes her head. "I can't imagine having to live with the things she and Tara know. It has to be horrifying."

"What do you think is going on?"

As I ask the question, my phone rings in my hand. When I pick it up, it's Aidan. "We lost the baby," he announces somberly.

"Tara was pregnant?" I ask numbly, and then immediately kick myself for the stupid question.

"Yeah, we weren't going to say anything this time until she was in the safety zone. She had three days to go until she would've been through her first trimester."

"That sucks, man. I'm so sorry. Is there anything I can do?"

"I don't know. I don't know how to go on from this. My wife is shattered into a million pieces. Right now, my career, the show, and everything else mean absolutely nothing to me. I want to fix things and make them right — but, I can't. Tell me, what can I do?"

"Go take care of your wife and tell her we all love her. The rest of us will come up with a plan. We'll deal with Hayden and Pennie. I trust them not to tell the press."

"I totally forgot they were coming. Geez, life has the world's worst timing," Aidan says with frustration pinching his voice.

"Like I said, don't worry about it. We'll figure something out. It's our job now. Let us handle it. Your job is to love your wife like you always do. Aidan, I'm sorry. You would've made a heckuva dad."

"I know, and Tara would've been an amazing mom. That's what makes this so hard. Jude, I hate to put this all in your lap, but I've got to go. Tara needs me."

When I hang up the phone, I turn back toward the bed and see Tasha has dissolved into tears.

She looks up at me. "The baby?"

"How did you even know?" I ask as I climb in bed and cuddle her close to me. "I had no idea."

Tasha grabs some tissue from the bedside table and blows her nose. She swallows hard. "I didn't know officially, but I knew Tara and Aidan have been trying for years. I tried to figure out what would upset Mindy so much and I put two and two together. You know, Mindy rescued her baby sister, Becca, when she was a baby. Knowing she couldn't save this one is probably heartbreaking for her."

I rake my hand through my hair as I admit to Tasha, "I may have promised the impossible. I told Aidan we would take care of the concert arrangements for the day after tomorrow. I have no idea how."

"It won't be easy, but we can do it. We'll just have to call in reinforcements. I learned some valuable lessons working with the Girlfriend Posse. We've got this."

"Seriously? You're not worried?" I ask, incredulous at her lack of panic.

"Oh, I'm plenty worried, but we don't have time for fear. All I can say is it's a really good thing Hayden's a freakin' genius on social media. We'll need every one of her skills." Tasha pulls out her iPad and starts to take notes.

———•———

Hayden taps me on the shoulder and hands me a bottle of water. "Tasha says you need to drink this."

I salute her. "Yes ma'am. How do the crowds look? Did we get massive cancellations?"

"Not many. Most people were happy when Aidan offered to refund the tickets and still hold a concert."

"We'll see how many people still feel the same way after they hear me sing my whole play list," I joke.

"You are so full of it!" Hayden sticks her tongue out at me. "I told you that you and Tasha are strong enough to do your own show. The new guy, Declan, is funny. He could MC the whole show and not miss a beat. He's super smart. Did you see his wife? Jade has the coolest tattoos ever. When I grow up, I want to go to her shop. Can you believe they came all the way from Florida to sing for Aidan?"

I pretend to wipe sweat off my forehead. "Yeah, he picked some good people for his label. I can't tell you how grateful I am that they're here. Even with as many songs as Tasha and I cover, it would not be enough to fill the play list. I'm worried we'll sound disjointed though. I wish we had more practice time."

"Are you kidding?" Hayden exclaims. "You all sound like you've been playing together as a band for years."

"*La canción fue muy buena*," Juliana adds shyly.

"*Gracias*. I'm glad you liked it. Do you think I

should sing some music in *español*?"

Julianna nods her head vigorously. "*¿Por favor?*"

"We had to throw our play list together at the last minute and I have nothing in Spanish prepared with the band. How about I plan to do it for the next concert?"

"Okay by me," Julianna answers with a grin. "I like all the new stuff — I'm sad for Mr. O'Brien."

Hayden nods. "Yeah, that's super sad, but the song Mindy's singing with Joe Summers gives me goosebumps. Your acoustic guitar solos are haunting, and to put three of them together is amazing. It's the perfect tribute song."

"I'm worried about it. Mindy insists we're ready to do it, but it's so brand-new I'm not even sure I know all the words. She says we'll do just fine. She says Tara and Aidan need to hear the message from us. *Gone Too Soon* is killer on the emotions. I hope everyone can get through it when we're in front of a live audience. I don't know how it'll go over. What if people aren't in the mood to be emotional and reflective? What if they wanted to come for a good old-fashioned country music party? I just don't know. Putting together a whole play list is hard. I don't know how Aidan does it all the time. I knew he worked hard, but there are so many moving parts. I'm sure I'm going to miss something important."

"Hey, Jude, here's what my vocal teacher teaches me at school. You need to be able to breathe to sing. Stop second-guessing yourself and asking all these questions, and just breathe through it. Everybody at this concert is going to know it's a last-minute emergency thing. So go out and have fun. Besides, Declan does street concerts all the time. If something goes wrong, he's gonna know how to fix it. The man has full concerts on the bus — a moving bus. I think he can probably deal with whatever comes up."

I raise my eyebrow at Hayden. "You're pretty good at this. You sound like my performance psychologist. Maybe you should think about doing it for a living."

"I'll admit, it's cool to be on this side of putting together a concert. I like doing the pep talks because I know what it's like to be in your shoes. I've done many shows since I was a little kid, so I know exactly what it feels like to be on the stage. Being a psychologist to help people through stage fright and other anxiety issues would be a good career choice for me. Did Tasha tell you I was picked for the All-Star Academic team based on my science score on the state-wide tests?"

"No, she didn't, but that's very cool." I look around the backstage area and don't see Tasha anywhere. "Speaking of Tasha, do you have any idea where she's at? Usually she's fussing all over me to make sure my costume is clean and my hat is on straight."

Hayden gives me an ear-to-ear grin. "You'll never guess what she's doing! This is even better than when I was in the hospital. My dad's company gave him time off to come on vacation with us so he's here with my sister! Jayne is going to babysit me tonight — like I need a babysitter ... but Mom and Dad are worried because of the cancer. I guess they think I'll get locked out of my hotel room or something. Mom and Dad are going to go out on a real-life date and not just a virtual date. Tasha is helping your sister give my mom a makeover.

This nice lady named Stella is giving my mom a bunch of clothes. Now, my mom has all these glamorous clothes to wear on the date. Tasha's doing her makeup and your sister's doing her hair. My dad will be so surprised. Jayne is keeping him busy looking around the arena and stuff."

"Whoa! That's a lot of information. What you're telling me is you've recruited all of my coworkers and family to help send your parents on a date?"

Hayden looks crestfallen at my question. "Well, yeah. I guess it seemed like a good idea at the time, and then it mushroomed into something bigger and bigger and bigger. I'm sorry. I didn't mean to cause a problem."

"Slow down Hayden, I never said it was a problem. If everybody is prepared for tonight, I think it's a righteous idea."

"Really? You're not mad at me?" Hayden asks.

I shake my head.

She grins at me. "In that case, can you sing *I Love the Way You Love Me* by John Michael Montgomery for my mom and dad? I guess they sang it at their wedding and they think it's all kinds of romantic. I bet they would like it."

"I'll see what I can do. I don't know what it is about the two of you — you and Tasha can seem to talk me into almost anything even if it's way outside my comfort zone. It's a little scary."

"It's like Tasha always says, never underestimate a smart woman who's willing to be adventurous," Hayden replies with a laugh.

As we're waiting for the warm up band from the local community to finish playing, Tasha has me backed up against the wall in a loose embrace as she squeezes my hands. "What do you think, Cowboy? Did you ever think way back when I first asked you how adventurous you were feeling that you would be the headlining act?"

"Tasha, you're not helping my stage fright, you know."

"See, I know that's not quite true. I saw you taking pictures of the marquee earlier, so I know you're aware of what's going on. It isn't sneaking up on you this time. This time you've done the work. You've worked with Dr. Powell to desensitize yourself to all your triggers. So, between your prep and the fact that you got Joe and Declan to sing with, we're good."

"I hope you're right. I'm worried about Mindy's number because I barely know the words. You know me, I like to practice stuff a lot."

"Lucky for you, Joe Summers is a huge Chris Daughtry fan and knows *Gone Too Soon* like the back of his hand. He already told us if we get lost just lean on him. How do you think I feel? I'm playing the piano on that number. I haven't consistently played piano since … I don't know … the eighth grade."

"I'm sure it's not that bad, I hear you and Aidan messing around on the piano all the time." I give her a reassuring hug.

"Exactly. That's what I'm trying to tell you. You're not the same person you were before. You've taken your fear and turned it into your own song. It's your version of Jude's Song — so let's go show everyone how it's done."

As the applause dies down and the MC introduces us, Tasha and I walk hand-in-hand out to the center of the stage. We take a bow and go to our stools. We pick up our guitars and start to play *Imagine*. I can't help but think how symbolic the John Lennon classic is for the journey I've taken with Tasha. Never in a million years did I ever imagine I would match the woman I love note for note on a stage in front of an auditorium full of people — completely enjoying myself and secure in the thought that this is the first day of the rest of the song of my life.

There's definitely something to be said for being adventurous and open to new experiences.

Note from the Author

Dear Reader:

Thank you for reading *Jude's Song*. It was great fun to write about characters seeking out new paths. I hope you found it exciting and insightful.

The next book in the series, *Paths Not Taken* is about making choices not everyone understands.

It's bad enough when Jordan makes a fool out of herself at work. It's worse when she does it in front of a customer.

To make matters worse, after she walked away from her job, Jordan Shepherd has to go home and face her friends and family.

Jordan is not even sure anyone will want her around after what happened the last time she was around her brother, Jaxson.

While she's busy trying to figure out creative ways to eat crow. The customer who witnessed her last day at work wants to hire her to design clothes.

It's what she's always wanted to do. Is Jordan brave enough to throw caution to the wind and follow a new path?

If you like to root for unlikely heroes, this is the book for you.

Get *Paths Not Taken* in paperback, e-book, or read for free with Kindle Unlimited now.

~Mary

Because love matters, differences don't.

ACKNOWLEDGEMENTS

Originally, this book started out as an idea for an anthology. Unfortunately, that anthology never came together so I decided to write Tasha's story anyway so that I could honor the medical personnel at St. Jude's Hospital and other hospitals like it.

As an author when you write a book, the characters which speak to you the loudest often surprise you. Such is the case with Jude's Song. I expected my shy, somewhat awkward male lead to play a bit of a background role in this book. But, that's not the way things turned out.

This is one of the most fascinating aspects of writing. I can go into a project with one plan and come out with something entirely different. That's what makes it so exciting.

I would like to acknowledge some people who have helped me along the way. First, I would like to thank Lys Aguirre for her beautiful custom artwork.

Kathern Watts does an amazing job of keeping me motivated and on task in the face of seemingly insurmountable odds. Thank you for your research skills and your ability to come up with story ideas to get me out of a jam.

To my beta readers and my fellow authors online, you are an invaluable resource. Following your advice has made me a better, stronger author and I appreciate the fact that you have taken the time out of your busy lives to give me feedback.

I'd like to thank my son, Brandon Crawford, who although he is mere months away from graduating from medical school, takes the time to pretend to diagnose and treat my characters to ensure that my stories are plausible. I know you're busy, so thank you from the bottom of my heart.

Kudos to Justin Crawford who makes the best scrambled eggs ever and who knows I have a weakness for deviled eggs. Somehow, he can tell when I need to put down the caffeinated sugar and eat some protein to be able to make it through my day. I love you more than words can say. Thank you so much for taking such good care of me.

My husband, Leonard Crawford, deserves a shout out too. Your steadfast belief in my ability to do anything I want makes it easier for me to believe in myself. I love you. Because of you, I persist.

To my fans, I cannot fully express how grateful I am for you and I can't adequately thank you for supporting my vision of inclusiveness and diversity in fiction. Diversity matters and every time you choose to support an author who highlights diversity and inclusiveness, we change the world one book at a time.

About the Author

I have been lucky enough to live my own version of a romance novel. I married the guy who kissed me at summer camp. He told me on the night we met that he was going to marry me and be the father of my children.

Eventually, I stopped giggling when he said it, and we've been married for over thirty years. We have two children. The oldest is a Doctor of Osteopathy. He is across the United States completing his residency, but when he's done, he is going to come back to Oregon and practice Family Medicine. Our youngest son is now tackling high school, where he is an honor student. He is interested in becoming an EMT.

I write full time now. I have published more than thirty books and have several more underway. I volunteer my time to a variety of causes. I have worked as a Civil Rights Attorney and diversity advocate. I spent several years working for various social service agencies before becoming an attorney.

In my spare time, I love to cook, decorate cakes and, of course, I obsessively, compulsively read.

I would be honored if you would take a few moments out of your busy day to check out my website, MaryCrawfordAuthor.com. While you're there, you can sign up for my newsletter and get a free book. I will be announcing my upcoming books and giving sneak peeks as well as sponsoring giveaways and giving you information about other interesting events.

If you have questions or comments, please E-mail me at Mary@MaryCrawfordAuthor.com or find me on the following social networks:

Facebook: www.facebook.com/authormarycrawford

Website: MaryCrawfordAuthor.com

Twitter: www.twitter.com/MaryCrawfordAut